Mémoires Intérieurs

François Mauriac

MEMOIRES
INTERIEURS

Translated from the French
by GERARD HOPKINS

FARRAR, STRAUS & CUDAHY
New York

Manufactured in the United States of America

TO CLAUDE MAURIAC

I give you this picture of myself,
reflected in the reading of a lifetime.
It bears witness to my confidence
in your destiny as a writer, and to an
affection which will never end.

F.M.

I

FRIENDS HAVE sometimes said to me: 'Why not write the story of your life?' Yes, indeed, why not? Is it humility that has held me back? Indeed, no: pride is quite enough to explain my unwillingness. What should a man have to tell about himself who has touched but the fringe of great events, and has seen nothing of them at first hand? But that, alas! is just what these well-meaning counsellors are after! – the story of a writer who, from inclination and the necessities of his craft, has, for much of his life, been more intent upon himself than upon the confused battlefield of politics. No doubt they think that wars will never lack generals and politicians to prove in many volumes that others, and not they, were responsible for the losing of them; whereas the secret struggles of a man's own destiny, what the author of the *Imitation* calls the 'divers movements of nature and of grace', is a worthy subject for an author's declining years.

But I am not going to let myself be tempted. What is nowadays demanded of us is no longer self-knowledge and self-description in the manner of Benjamin Constant or of Stendhal. Modern readers demand something very different, even if they do not put their requirements into words. For the past half-century Freud, no matter what we think of him, has compelled us to see everything, beginning with ourselves, through spectacles which we shall never, now, be able to lay aside. Since the ending of the First War, his has been the dominating influence on everybody. I can still see clearly the patch of gleaming pavement at the corner of the Avenue Victor-Hugo, where Drieu told me in confidence – or, maybe, it was Crevel – that he was going to write a book, to be called *The History of my Body*. One of them, for all I know, may have. (It suddenly comes back to me that their poor bodies had, both of

9

them, the same end, and were found frozen stiff in a bath-tub.)

The history of their bodies would have been the history, like-wise, of their passions, their thoughts and their dreams, for no one, since the Freudian revelation, can any longer classify his destiny under those three headings which were so neatly arranged in the philosophy textbooks of my youth – intelligence, sensation and will. Today, the writer of an autobiography is condemned to tell all or nothing. If he cannot reveal everything, then he should abandon all attempts at revelation. The monologue should be the expression of a magma.

*   *   *   *   *

So I, then, shall tell nothing. My main reason for making this decision is that, were I mad enough to try to tell all, that madness would not involve myself alone. At the source of a man's own being there lies not himself but the swarming life of a whole race. I see my childhood as a nebula with, as its centre, the shining figure of a loving mother. My personal story would, from the very first chapter, lay violent hands upon that merciful oblivion which it is in the province of death to give to every creature who has lived with decency and devotion, as have those from whom I am sprung.

Already, and in spite of myself, too much of the dead has passed into my invented fictions. I used, when I was young, to resent the wall which the *bourgeoisie* of those days erected against prying eyes, and, in certain cases, the so carefully muddied waters intended to conceal what should not be known. Today, I take a more just and a kindlier view when I try to imagine what the story of my life, told by myself, might be, what permanent risk of outrage must exist in that monstrous monument of the written word, the substance of which is drawn from a class and from a family.

Childhood is the whole of a life, since it is childhood that holds the key to a man's future. But the little creature whom I question, even at the age of reason, has not yet quite finished being born, but still lies, as it were, coiled in the womb of a beloved family. He is the outcome of all those obscure destinies with which he is still intermingled, which in him will be accomplished. Each of them, should I undertake to write my life, would have to be detached and made the subject of a separate study, not from the outside only, as is the case with most writers of memoirs, who describe their oddities, and present them as quaint characters. That is to take the easy way of satisfying the demands made by autobiography: the disjointing of those anatomies, so humble, so pathetic, any one of which might provide an answer to the enigma posed by the writer who is flesh of their flesh.

Sleep in peace. I shall not speak of myself that I may not be condemned to speak of you. Oh! I know, only too well, that, maybe, my silence will not save you, and that even when I am joined with you in death, I shall still remain, in your eyes, someone to be feared according to whether I am accepted or rejected by the oblivion in which you lie at rest. If, for a little while, I float upon the surface, if the inquisitive still pore over unpublished texts, letters and all the wrack that drifts above the spot where I have been engulfed (which goes by the name of survival), then all that touches me will touch you, too.

*　　*　　*　　*　　*

I shall remain that part of yourselves always exposed to the eyes of the world. So long as a man's work lives on it is an open wound through which the members of a particular race of mortals can never cease to bleed.

The refusal to write the story of one's life does not imply a determination to let nothing of it be known. Renounce, though we may, any direct approach to what we were, some reflection of it is still to be found in the books we loved. Our reading brings about a change in us, but we have also left our imprint so clearly on what, in it, has mattered most to us, that to speak of it is enough to give ourselves away. In my written criticisms I follow, from book to book, the shadowy figure of what once I was, from those early children's tales which first impressed, first influenced, first wrought a change in me.

Therein, perhaps, lies the justification of the quest on which I am embarking, somewhat at random: not to discover and formulate a body of critical thought, but to see whether I can find what remains of my own story in the books which have supported and consoled me ever since I became a conscious being. It is as though each of those streams of living water had kept a reflected image, first of the child, then of the tormented youth, lastly of the mask imposed by life, for each, in turn, has leaned above that limpid surface.

Not death, nor the sun can we gaze upon directly – nor yet, upon ourselves. But we can, at least, confront the reflection of what once we were, which shimmers still upon the pages of the books we used to read, with the person we have since become. That is the clue I follow on this journey of mine through all that, so long ago, did first enchant me.

But it is only from the moment when we first look for our own image in books we loved, the moment, that is, of puberty, that the prose and poetry of those days can be said to have retained the imprint of him who, half a century ago, began to read so passionately. The trace can still be found of what it was that we, ourselves, contributed to make those books conform to the desires we felt, and to our dreams. They are wedded to what is most secret in us, so that to speak of them is, indirectly, to speak of ourselves – of ourselves as we were then, and remember that we were.

Nevertheless, such comments as I shall make, perhaps too often, in these pages, will not be wholly devoid of the critical spirit. The function of criticism is to disengage from any work what still remains of value to us once the magic of mere youth has been dissipated. This residue we contemplate and judge in terms of life, not as we dreamed and imagined it to be when we were twenty, but as we have come to know that it is, having learned to take its precise and horrible measure.

All that in literature partakes of the romantic continues to exercise its influence so long as something of youth still mutters deep within us. Then, as the storm withdraws from the now ravaged forest which will never be green again, so are those passages of prose and verse in their turn ravaged, stripped of the sense of the infinite which was our gift to them. But a trace of it remains in them, and we find there the signs, visible to us alone, of that life which, as I have said, words cannot capture. And so it is that, almost without my realizing it, vague memories join hands with the notes I scribbled in the margins of the books I read so long ago.

*   *   *   *   *

The childhood which I see so dimly luminous behind me – all that separates me from it belongs already to dark night – my nebula of childhood, is ordered round one single point of an especial brilliance, like one of the bright stars of winter: Christmas, the enchanted season, made magical by a little boy, for from him it drew its power to enthrall. If genius is the ability to secrete one's own universe, how great must have been the genius of the seven-year-old poet of whom I am thinking.

Of pretext for so extravagant a happiness I can find but little. The midnight Mass was forbidden ground to him. Little boys do not stay up late. That, with us, was an inexorable rule. For sudden joy and tenderness to leap up in my heart, enveloping all living creatures, men and beasts and the inanimate objects of my humble existence, no more was needed than my slipper on the hearth and, at my grandmother's house, on the 24th December, a not very elaborate crèche lit by a few pink and blue candles which burned just long enough to let me sing 'Come, Blessed Saviour' through to the end.... At the hour when a child drops like a stone into the great depths of sleep, the sudden booming of the Cathedral bell, close at hand, would fill my room with a voice that was at once sanctified and terrible.

But that was not all. No matter how devout that little boy might be, his ecstasy of happiness extended far beyond the Christmas mystery, passed through it but was not identified with it. Its source lay somewhere deep within me, and had begun to bubble even before that clanging bell had torn the night to shreds. It had needed no carillon, no chants, to spread about me. For many days, alone and unassisted, I had been setting the scene of this enchanted world.

*   *   *   *   *

No more was needed than for me to see, on my way home from school, the light spilled across the pavement from the windows of those humble shops in the Cours Victor Hugo (in my family it was

13

still known by its ancient name of Cours des Fossées). How contemptible to schoolboys of today, especially to those who live in
Paris, would seem those windows all a-glitter with toys for the
very poor, and sickly, unwholesome-looking sweets. But I ran like
a young lunatic, far outdistancing Octavie who had been sent to
fetch me, and flattened my nose against the glass which separated
me from all those many marvels. Not that I really wanted them. It
was a sign I saw in them and adored. What sign?

Yes, what? The smell of damp asphalt was in my nostrils. It is
all I can remember as accompanying my joy, though it cannot have
been its cause. The poets of seven-years-old (that is the title of one
of Rimbaud's pieces) have in themselves a transfiguring power
which makes hay of mere appearances. Reality provides them with
just enough substance to stir into life that secret world through
which they move alone.

Today, I pretend not to see, not to hear the little grandson playing close beside me. I will not allow myself to break into that dream
where he walks, all wide awake, but never seeing me. He has his
secret treasures, and the mother-of-pearl button which he has
picked up somewhere, concentrates in itself, for him alone, all the
coloured blaze of an aurora borealis. He does not know that, all his
life long, it will shine beneath his spread of sky, and that when, as
an old man, he turns his face to the wall for the last time, he will see
it glittering still.

It matters not that this nebula of childhood holds in abeyance all
the sorrows of the puny schoolboy still to be, all his terrors, all his
secret tears – and God knows I had enough of them! Not for that
reason does he hoard the less that mystery of a happiness so sharp
that through the thickening barrier of the years its point can reach
me still – that happiness for which Christmas was but a pretext. The
damp, mild winter of Bordeaux wrapped him in a fog which did
not, then, stink of petrol fumes. It was the very breath of the pure
night and the dark river, at the precise moment, at the precise point
when it is about to be mingled with the ocean and be whelmed in
its depths with all its load of reflected hillsides, houses and men's
faces.

A line comes back into my mind from one of the poets of my youth, Henry Bataille, I think:

Mon enfance, adieu mon enfance! Je vais vivre!

He did not know that the childhood to which he was bidding farewell stays with us till the end, till that day, that evening when we say to it: *'Adieu, mon enfance, je vais mourir.'* But even then the farewell is not final. The mad joy which made me run, and then pause for breath with my nose pressed to the scantily lit window of a toyshop, will be with me on the frontier of the world of shadows. I shall find it there again, and step aboard old Charon's boat clasping in my arms a seven-year-old poet.

Together we shall set out to find the fountain-head. We shall reach it on the farther side of humble shops, of the smell of wet pavements, of the wide estuary and the great ocean which nibbles at the dunes: and we shall move upstream until we reach the very source of all that joy of other days. Eternal childhood of God! And then I shall know why, sixty years ago, in the fog of ancient streets, I ran till I was out of breath, and leaped like a wild goat.

★   ★   ★   ★   ★

Happiness. . . . When, as the shadows gather, we try to track it down from the days of childhood, we fix our thoughts on a few boyish triumphs which, we remember, made us drunk with joy, on certain meetings. But the memories have grown cold, and there is nothing now to make them warm again. I remember having been happy, and suppose that the circumstances must have been such and such. But the sensation of happiness is, for me, connected less with facts than with atmosphere, and, most of all, with that of a special season of the year when the summer holidays were not yet come, but were approaching.

God knows that, at an age so commonly called happy, nothing was less like happiness than the sense of deep distress within myself, the consciousness of, as it were, a subterranean tide already lapping round my boyhood days. And yet, no sooner were the solemn ceremonies of prize-day discernible on the horizon, and the last turning of the academic year was about to be rounded, than I was

15

in the grip of an inexplicable feeling of joy which far exceeded the pleasure of knowing that I should soon be freed from school.

To have the sense of it in every nerve and fibre I need no Proustian *madeleine,* no Proustian tea. It is there, deep down in me, without the reviving agency of taste or smell. I am conscious of the savage intensity of the July heat, all mixed up with the terror of end-of-term essays, of the examination which is to decide whether or no I am to be promoted into a higher form. And there, behind the railings of the 'yard' I watch the workmen whistling at their task of putting up the flimsy platform underneath the trees, which is to serve for the presentation of the prizes.

The sight of those planks as pale as crusts of bread, the smell of the fresh wood-shavings, laid me under a spell which was already, happiness. On the morning before the great day, awnings of red-striped canvas were brought out, and golden fringes, which had shielded from the sun the participants in many similar occasions long ago. On the thick grass, where careless hands had dropped it, the gleaming treasure lay which was to throw wide open the gates of an unknown paradise.

I pretended to forget the pain – part and parcel of all holidays – which, from the very first week of them, would lay hold on me. No sooner were they started than, with each hour that passed, the crumbling process would begin. I had lived the allegory of *La Peau de Chagrin* long before Balzac was even a name to me. The holidays shrank under my very eyes. The days of happiness were numbered. They were far from resembling those I had imagined when, through the railings of the yard, I had watched the platform taking shape, or, on the triumphant morning when, under the eyes of doting parents and of Monsignor Toureau, the Vicar-General, our arms loaded with gilt-edged and unreadable books, our heads crowned with wreaths of green paper, we, the prize-winners had heard a diminutive band playing in our honour the overture to *If I were King* and *Le Voyage en Chine.*

Only the two or three days immediately following the prize-giving were not disappointing. Over them I spilled the joy which

I had accumulated in anticipation. But that joy was not born of the days themselves, which held within them the seeds of inescapable destruction.

The miseries of school gave place to others born of empty, torrid hours. I had received nothing at their hands, and now, already, they were gone beyond recall.

As summer moved towards its end, a sadness came to me mingled with the love I felt for the park and the heath which hedged it in behind innumerable pines. My love for all that arid, gloomy countryside grew ever fiercer as it began to take on the look which it would wear on the October morning when, between us two, the last word would have to be said. That would be a moment of heartrending beauty: the coming of the first wood-pigeons, the cow-bells sounding in the mist, a wind from the west smelling of the sea. Those portents were not with me yet, but I sought them in advance, as, on a much-loved face, one looks for the tell-tale signs of sagging flesh and the first wrinkles.

Each season carries in itself the season to come after. In the hottest days of summer the birds fall silent and get ready for the great migration.

Summer had already received its death-wound in the eyes of the child who looked so closely at it from the secret lair he had constructed for his pleasure. But what, then, could these days mean, the expeditions in the forest, the picnics at the mill, the hours spent in hunting for crayfish, the dragonflies skimming the surface of the stream – what, if not happiness? Happiness. . . .

*   *   *   *   *

Perhaps our over-strict family discipline would have prevented me from ever wholly clasping it. With us, holiday-tasks were real tasks. From half-past ten till noon, from two till four, I sat over my exercise-books which had a picture of the taking of Tananarive by General Duchesne in blue and red upon their covers. The cicadas would be scraping away outside the wooden shutters which had a fleur-de-lis cut in them through which the fierce sun darted 'a long beam full of dancing motes' (to quote a line by André Lafon).

Wasps would be bumping against the panes, and enormous blue-bottles against the ceiling. That immense summer hum of childhood I now hear only in myself. It seems to me now that summers no longer hum, and that the crickets, as I pass, fall silent that I may not be tempted to think of the youth of long ago.

★　　★　　★　　★　　★

No, it was not happiness. There is, in the experience of carefully sheltered children, an empty and very obvious place reserved for that visitor, with whose name they are familiar. Love was always cropping up in the stories of Zenaïde Fleuriot which my mother chose for me from the *Collection of Books for Young People*. But what, precisely, was this 'love'? I often hear talk of love between young people. Many of my friends have told me that they cannot remember ever having been 'pure'. But, for those of my kind, watched over as though they were called upon to live in a world of angels, nothing announced the coming of that unknown stranger. Flesh and blood were held in subjection by some celestial spell. No storm muttered over my early days. I knew nothing but the name of love, and heard only occasional allusions to what must never be openly mentioned. Merely to think about it was already counted as evil.

Yet now, after sixty years have passed, it is still that vague, that feverish waiting for the coming of *something* that, for me, most nearly resembles that magic thing called 'happiness', perhaps because no fulfilment could as yet define it, and that the mere waiting was a land without a frontier.

It is thus that a heart finds itself predisposed to God. Not that the best christians come from the ranks of children such as I am describing here, by whom the religious life is first felt as a state of sensibility. Had I to deal with the subject of priestly vocation, I should have much to say of this, and many a warning note to sound about precocity. All vocations should be late-flowering growths.

But what am I straining after? If ever there existed children like the boy whom I have conjured from the deep well of the years, his kind must long ago have vanished. Only the concatenation of very special circumstances, such as no longer exist, could have produced so over-sensitive a race. There can be, I imagine, very few protected childhoods of the type I have been describing, now left. What I can only think of as an obscene wind of words and images now blows about the world, bringing outrage even into the most austere of homes, and dinning into the ears of the young what grown men mean by happiness. But who can tell? So degrading is this rising tide that it may, for all I know, produce another generation of young boys, no less hungry, no less disappointed than the one who, sixty years ago, pressed to the railings of a school-yard, watched the workmen whistling at their task of putting up a platform from which, he thought, he would take flight into an immense and misty happiness which, so far, had no name.

II

WHEN I come back to this garden just before the grape harvest, it is the time of year, too, when the postman brings my first theatre tickets. Already, in Paris, the same people are once again occupying the same seats. The three blows have been struck, and, not for the first time, I shall miss the beginning of the play. And yet has this drama which I perform with only myself as audience, anything new to give? I have long ceased to be taken in by the old magic, and if, on waking, I lean from the same window as fifty years ago, and breathe in the mist which has the smell of the lost years, I mistrust my power to orchestrate the voices which reach me from a vanished world.

Mistrust? – that is an understatement. From these sad and empty days I seek distraction, not because I am bored – I do not any longer know what it is to be bored – but because they are too full. It is only that they seem empty, though, in fact, they are filled to overflowing with a muted and insistent life, against which I should like to defend myself, but cannot. The scarcely opened book falls from my hand. I put a record on the gramophone, but the music is in league with the very things from which I hoped to be delivered: what remains of life when the old hours of work are interrupted, if not ended for good and all, and the old desire to enchant or to convince is but a burned-out ember. The September day is overcast. The fields are all deserted. I see nothing but this hand, a little stiff and twisted, which I raise to the level of my eyes. I hear nothing but the whisper of my blood.

* * * * *

This is the moment of truth. The poet has grown tired of endlessly re-creating a world which does not exist. I am determined to see, as they really are, this house, this old courtyard and the horn-beam walk. I will strike the scenery of a play which has but a single character, for, from the very first line, it is myself who is speaking to myself. Nothing but a few pictures now remain to keep me from seeing with unblinded eyes this poor house sandwiched between half ruined wine-stores. Here, on the very spot where I am sitting motionless, I was photographed with my mother in '17 or '18, and, but a few feet farther on, is where that picture was 'taken', which, reproduced in one of my books, shows me with my arms round the shoulders of my little son. I should like to wipe memory clean of them. But that is impossible. I cannot separate these walls, these tiles, this modest, unpretentious building from all that is not here to see, and, for me alone, endlessly renew a beauty which is almost more than I can bear.

*   *   *   *   *

Houses live and die. Some have never lived no matter how densely peopled they may have been. Those of the living kind have nothing to fear from the dead whom once they sheltered, for every death enriches them. It is as though within these massive walls with all their multitude of cracks, the same blood pulses still as once showed bright in children's cheeks – that blood which had already drained from my mother's waxen face in the days, not long before her final sleep, when she could still climb on foot the slopes of Malagar. I cannot help it if now what is but matter lives again before my brooding eyes. The life that floods it comes from those eyes, and the love which animates them is something that I cannot overcome.

It is impossible for me to see these objects as they really are, as they would be if I were not here to see them. Even when I shall exist no longer, the life withdrawn from my heart of flesh and blood will still in secret flow in this 'great heart of stone' which is what Lamartine called his house.

Lamartine, and those many other poets, known or unknown, whose destiny, when they still lived, was as closely bound to one spot in all the world, as are their bones to the few feet of earth in which they now await the resurrection. They constitute a kind, a family, of artists very different from those who find in Paris all their inspiration.

*   *   *   *   *

There is a sharp dividing-line – which has become noticeably more accented since the time of Baudelaire – between the art of cities and the art of the countryside. I am quite clear in my own mind as to which side of that line I belong, not as a result of choice but of birth. I am not unaware that bucolic literature tends to be facile. I am deeply suspicious of the 'Rosa Bonheur' side of this type of art. I am careful not to indulge in it, and turn for inspiration rather to those purer sources which are dear to me: among others, to the purest one of all: Maurice de Guérin.

I have said that I belong to one particular school of literature owing to the circumstances of my birth. But to have been born in the country, or to have lived there is not enough. Little more than a mile from Malagar, from the front-steps of Malromé, where he died, Toulouse-Lautrec looked out upon the same landscape that I am seeing now. But perhaps his dying eyes were straining still, to see, beyond the blaze of sunset on the hills, the old, familiar back-stage world with its sharp and dubious smells, or he imagined himself at a table in a bar, gazing at a painted face with green shadows. Maybe a lonely horse, motionless in a meadow, turning its head and whinnying, set him dreaming of a spring afternoon in the paddock at Auteuil.

It matters little whether birth or choice have made me what I am. I know my invisible family, and will never deny my kith and kin in art. No fashion lasts, and I am well content to be a lonely figure in the rearguard of letters, provided that here, in a low chair beside the fireplace of a country kitchen, I may see again the boy who told himself the same story as I am telling to myself, watching the dying embers.

*   *   *   *   *

One by one the bedroom doors are closed. I push against the heavy shutter of the entry. It resists the pressure of my hand. That same sound of creaking hinges used to wake me when my mother opened it at dawn to let in the coolness of the night just past and hold it prisoner till evening between the walls of the self-effacing house.

I take a few steps: I stop: I listen. It is September. Gone is the vibrant buzzing from the fields. The noise of crickets which I hear among the vines is, perhaps, but a throbbing in my ears, or the murmur of past summers in my thoughts. A waning moon hangs in the sky, but still her light is enough to drown the stars. She has become obtrusive and an irritant. No longer can her ancient magic work on me. She has floated above too many bad, forgotten poems. Dangerous counsellor of poets and composers, mother of facile similes and overworked emotions, she now does violence to the constellations and the dark.

Not that I have ever learned to find my way among that nightly swarm. But here a few have been domesticated and stand out from among their crowding neighbours. It is as though my voice had grown familiar to them, as though they are running from the bottom of the meadow to eat out of my hand. I need the house as a point of reference if I am still to find it possible to name them – or those, at least, which, as a growing boy, I came to love, and they are few. I have forgotten where and when Orion the Hunter comes in view. But Aldebaran is visible, and Arcturus. Vega I cannot find because of the moon.

Cold now of heart and aimless, I move through the setting of a play which will never, in my lifetime, be revived. I have blasphemed the moon, but it is all the mystery of the night I now reject. I have reached the age at which the old magic of the dark is no longer an abettor. I have nothing any longer of myself to project upon that infinite screen. It is not from me only, but from the world, that youth has gone. Every child, though he does not know it, is an enchanter. So long as that power remains with us we paint the night with magic. She gives back to us only what we have already given her.

But what if I am wrong? Perhaps the night has no need of us to make her thrill and suffer. When I was young I knew the keywords invented by the poets, which merely to utter could bring our hearts in union with the spheres. Tonight, I say them over to myself, or so many of them as memory allows. I try them one by one, like rusty keys which will no longer turn in the lock. Romantic invocations to the moon, even the most famous of them, have now a foolish sound. They die upon my lips even before I have spoken them to the end.

Yet one comes back into my mind which was known only to a few friends of the poet who wrote it. I am, beyond all doubt, one of the rare persons in the world today who could recover those lines from the deeps of memory. Weak though they are, they radiate for me a strength for ever young, a power so undiminished that the sky, for the space of a few seconds, seems to have become once more what it was half a century ago: warm and living, like a breathing body:

> Si tu venais ce soir dans le triste jardin
> Doucement, comme en rêve, ayant peur que la grille
> Gémisse. . . .

I feel my way through the words which quiver, though scarce awakened, and spread their torpid wings: *Si tu venais* – I speak them – *Si tu venais,* until, all of a sudden, there flashes out the incantation:

> O nuit d'été!
> Tes astres, tes parfums, tes voix, tes voix sans nombre,
> Rien ne me serait plus que la charmille sombre
> Ou le temps pour jamais semblerait arrêté.

Here is the hornbeam tree, as dark as the one in the poem, and time has not yet stopped. Here is the terrace, an altar-stone which hands now dead once consecrated – a hornbeam this, like other hornbeams, a stone like any other stone, a night which is just night and nothing more, blind and deaf, without thoughts or memory.

The vast expanse of fretted galaxies has never sung for me of the uncreated love. It is but absence infinite. The night has never had another heart than mine, nor other passions. It speaks of God only to those whose hearts already brim with God, but they no longer need to make that détour of the stars to bring them to their Love. If I pray before the darkened distance, it is not on Cassiopeia that my eyes are fixed, although that constellation bodies forth in the night-sky the sign and symbol of the Son of Man. I look, not at the sky, but at the plain, where the vessel of a village church lies anchored in the mist.

I walk back towards the house which looks now like a piece of painted scenery, thanks to the limelight of the moon. Juliet might make her entry on the stage – or Werther, too, alas! I do not even turn my head. The creaking shutter banishes the night which now no more concerns me, since it is nothing, in my eyes, but old enchantment faded.

★   ★   ★   ★   ★

On the evening of which I speak, I had extinguished all the lamps but one, which stood by the sofa, far from the hearth which had lured and held me though the night-air was not cold. The blazing vine-shoots gave a gleam to rosewood and mahogany. As the flames died down – how can I explain what it was I felt? – the silence was not quite the same silence. There had been a shift in time. It was at that very moment that she opened the door, not by pressing on the latch, but, as her custom was, by pushing with the full weight of her heavy body.

I uttered no cry. I was not astonished. She smiled at me, her eyes turned inward to where those endless worries rioted which fed her deep anxieties. Not for a moment did I think of her as one risen from some strange abyss. At last she looked at me. It was my face when young that she saw then in the flickering firelight. How I knew that I cannot explain. Her voice, at first muffled, became more vibrant. That part of her preoccupation which had to do with me came from her lips in a confusion of words: but now and again a phrase broke through, clear-cut, peremptory: 'It is not a question of whether or no you have talent. What matters is that not through you should scandal come.'

I did not consciously answer. As when I listen to myself on the radio, I heard myself replying. The voice was the impatient voice of youth, held within bounds by respect and an exacerbation of tenderness. But nothing reached her of what I had to say about the demands made upon me by the work I had to do. The question between us was one, indeed, of vocation. A terrible Judge most truly lived. I should have to give an account of myself, the justification of a whole life at the mercy of a single thought, a single glance. And always there was that terrifying possibility that not all of us would be united for eternity in the everlasting Love: that one of us might fail to answer to his name at the great roll-call, one who had been thrust into the pit by the weight of a millstone hung about his neck, in the shape of a green-bound book with Grasset's imprint.

It was as though she had before her eyes two superimposed pictures. The same sort of anxiety had as its object another of her children. The *Action française* had been condemned. In Bordeaux, where reigned a cardinal who would hear nothing of compromise, we were in the lion's jaw. Country gentlemen who had led saintly lives were dying without the sacraments. 'They have done nothing, mother, but obey their conscience. . . .' . . . 'There can be no Christian conscience that is at odds with the Church.' . . . 'But the Almighty is not concerned about what paper we read!' The look she gave me was both sad and stern. 'God is not mocked,' she said. I protested that I was not mocking God, and reminded her of the saying that 'God is Love' . . . 'Not in the sense you give that word, my boy: otherwise it would make everything too easy.'

I hung my head. The silence grew more dense. Another wave of time toppled and broke. The words I was hearing now were eloquent of day-to-day anxieties. . . . 'Just between ourselves, I think it had a tubercular origin, but that we did not know. . . .' Addition sums were going on in her head. I saw, as though by magic, long columns of figures in an eternal ledger. 'There was no market for the wine, though, of course, the price of resin had never been so high. But ought we to have left the pine-trees standing? Half of the resin goes to the tenant-farmers, whereas the wood. . . .'

What I said then I do not now remember, but it brought me this reply: 'So long as you do not go without, a little generosity costs you nothing.' Illnesses, property, those minor troubles moved only on the surface, and she made me free of them. But I guessed that there were others, known only to herself. That noble and exacting spirit never dodged the irreparable, the irremediable. Her heaviest crosses she bore in solitude, under the eye of God.

There was nothing now but an incomprehensible susurration of low words until silence came again – a silence bearing no resemblance to that of my real life. It was the silence of an older time, and now I cannot tell by what sign I recognized it. And all the time her eyes were fixed on something that lay beyond the son whom she no longer saw, beyond the plastered walls, beyond the night-bound fields. She was looking . . . O God! I knew at what: at death, at the hour of her death which she knew was close at hand. I gazed at her, brimful of pity, as though the day would never come when I, too, should be compelled, in my turn, to endure that confrontation. My heart went out to that created being who knew that tomorrow, perhaps this very night, a hand would touch her shoulder – and it would be a sign scarcely perceptible, as though someone were saying to her: 'Get up, the hour has struck.'

But what madness to dread death for her! Why, in the eyes she turned to me, that questioning look, so full of fear? 'Mother, it is all over for you now. Your hour struck twenty-eight years ago. You are at rest at last, at rest in peace.'

The cry I uttered unloosed within the walls of that old room, like some tremendous eddy, a sound of moving waters, perceptible to my inner ear, though no woodwork creaked and no breeze ruffled the curtains, the sound of a vast ebb carrying that poor body out to the open sea. A few half-burned logs were glowing still. Deceived, no doubt, by the late-risen moon, a cock crowed. I had come back to my life of normal days and nights. Why did I not get up? Why did I not fall upon my knees? Why had I not laid that sacred head upon my shoulder, and covered it with kisses? Poor fool! your arms would have clasped nothing but emptiness, your lips would have sought in vain that ravaged brow.

It had been a dream which, by some miracle, you still remembered, though, as a rule, on waking, you saw your dreams slip through the net which never held what sleep had brought you from the depths. Once again this night, this dead house at the heart of darkness, resembled an empty snare which had caught and held, for one short drowsy moment, this dear, dear ghost before she fled from it. Nothing was left but the useless meshes spread beneath the autumn sky to catch the dead who do not come back, ever.

★   ★   ★   ★   ★

The layer of mist above the plain spares me, when I wake, the sadness of a farewell look. Good-bye to country sights and sounds! I am all haste now to be gone. The chaos on every side still has the feel of life. Yesterday's arm-chair is drawn up to the hearth in which a log has glowed all through the night. There are books lying about, and I lack the courage to put them back on their proper shelves. But as soon as I have shut the door behind me, the house will enter into sleep: and oh! how sound a sleep! The heavy shutters will leave no chink for the sword of sunlight, and the night within these walls will be such as only dead men know. In the portraits that I love, the eyes of my children, and those of the young man who was once myself, will remain wide open in unbroken darkness until one April morning when the Resurrection sun will rise again.

Then, God willing, I shall come back. 'I hope we shall see one another next Easter! One should always hope!' . . . says the good old caretaker when I say good-bye. But from the tone of her voice I guess that she has fearlessly faced the possibility that our parting may well be for ever.

Here, it is to inanimate objects that I absurdly attribute a sense of sorrow, from them that I have to tear myself. I, who from childhood on, have ever been impervious to the strange and the fantastic, who could never take much pleasure in tales of dwarfs and fairies, as though Christ had focused on His adorable mystery all my powers of dreaming and credulity, now, on this morning of departure, yield to the foolishness of thinking of all those several items of flotsam, one by one, left behind them by poor, forgotten lives when they withdrew, and wonder what their fate will be during the five months of entombment. In imagination I hear, as they will hear, the nights of winter trickling on the tiles. Those twenty weeks of thick, unbroken darkness will here create, I am quite sure, possibilities which my thoughts can ill contain, as though what I am leaving of myself within this empty house will brim its rooms with muted life, as though the power were mine to give a heart of flesh and blood to all these things whose only worth is to have been chosen, a hundred years ago, by the women from whom my own life is derived. God knows their taste was poor! But the opalescent glasses for which my mother blamed them, are held by modern taste to be 'amusing', with the result that they have been brought down from the bedrooms to do honour to the *salon*. I, who, as a rule, feel no affection for objects, who have collected nothing, and have never managed to keep anything for long, feel now such warmth for them that I dread, on their behalf, the silence of the winter nights.

Yet, through those five long months nothing will break the silence but the nibbling of mice, the scampering of hungry rats beneath the tiles and the whisper of rain which no human ears will hear, and no eyes see at noon, on those often so luminous winter days in Aquitaine, a patch of supernatural brightness on the empty hearth.

Yes, nothing else, I know, but do not quite believe it. Gently I shut the door upon a mystery. Here is the yard where the grass of oblivion is already sprouting. For a moment I lay my hands, I press my forehead and my cheek, against the lime-tree's trunk. It is all over. I watch the road ahead through my windscreen. The poplars, *our* poplars, keep me company as far as the first turn. I do not seek to find a presage in their swaying tops. Already, as in every previous year, on the outskirts of the villages, groups of children, with anxious, solemn faces are walking to school. At Saint-Denis-de-Piles each one of them is carrying in a tiny fist a bouquet of chrysanthemums. Maybe, one of their schoolfellows has died? But soon there are no children to be seen. The doors of all the schools in all the villages have shut behind them.

I look within myself to see whether, perhaps, a spark remains of that old fire which once burned high whenever I drew near to Paris. How intense a longing then laid hold on me, what soaring hopes, with each October. But no! All I can see at the far end of the great French road, driving onwards between the plane-trees, under the pure blue of the sky, are the pavements of the *quartier* where I live, which the city mongrels foul with such regularity and such abundance, that one might almost think them to be employed by some Public Service to exercise, in the 16th arrondissement of Paris, the privilege which no one would deny belongs to it, of amassing the largest accumulation in the world of dogs' urine and dogs' mess.

✶   ✶   ✶   ✶   ✶

This hideous image of the Paris soon to suck me in, brings to my mind horrors of a different kind, of which it is not my intention here to write. Not that living in a country-house has made me forgetful of them. But trees serve to protect us from our fellow-men. From dawn till dusk, the radiance of that patch of land which I have known and loved since childhood, conjures up for me a multitude of worlds unknown, endlessly recreated, peopled by beings whom I do not see, who do me no harm. And now the moment is at hand when the doors of the cage will shut on me.

How often, on my sleepless bed, I shall lie, thinking of the old house under the sky's dark canopy, of the shuttered windows, like port-holes battened down upon a cargo which for me alone is precious, each item of which has a history long known to me. I shall think of that house upon its hill as of an Ark aground on an Ararat cut to its measure. None sees it but the hunter Orion rising vast and lonely from behind the hornbeam tree and padding softly across the spaces of the winter sky.

III

A GHOST visited me one night at Malagar: I have described the episode in the last chapter. Another ghost appeared to me, a few days later, this time not in the lassitude of a lonely evening, but in Paris, while I was reading Alain's *lettres sur la philosophie première*.

Those letters had been written to one of Alain's former pupils, who, like all the rest of them (except Henri Bouché) was killed in the First War. Alain, in a posthumous fragment of autobiography, printed in last May's number of *La Table Ronde,* rather cold-bloodedly recalls this wholesale slaughter of his spiritual sons.

Speaking of himself in the third person, he writes: 'Bouché was only wounded: the others remained where they fell. Such accidents do happen, for disciples, after all, are but human, and the weapons of war do not discriminate. It will be realized that the authority of Professor Alain gained immensely. . . .' The tone of this passage would have revolted me, had it not been a sign of modesty – or so, at first, I tried to think. But there was worse to come. Alain had completely forgotten to whom the letters were addressed, even his name! He admits as much, quite shamelessly: 'I cannot recall what that young chap from the École Normale was called, who was so bursting with health and worked like a carthorse. He was one of the first to go to the war, but he did not get further than the battle of the Aisne.' That is really a bit too much, thought I to myself. Even in his master's memory, this young man, cut off in the flower of his age, was so completely dead that he had not left even a name behind him!

Then my attention was drawn to something added by Claude Mauriac: 'A note informs us that the young man in question was Philippe Borrell, one of the 1910 class, who was killed in 1915.' Philippe Borrell! Who was I to throw the first stone, I who had

31

known him long before he had become one of Alain's disciples, and had been his friend. We had been thrown together at Bordeaux, in 1905. I must have been his senior by three or four years. He was still a pupil at the *lycée,* and it was at the *Sillon* that we met[1]. I was more to blame than Alain, for I was guilty of a worse fault than forgetting a name. His very existence had slipped from my mind, as had that of so many of my youthful friends in the old Bordeaux days, who had been swept into oblivion by the surging currents of my life in Paris.

All of a sudden, I saw him there before my eyes, not bursting with health as Alain has described him, but a schoolboy, sturdily built, with a face not unlike that of the young Claudel, in the bust which his sister, Camille, made of him. Under the broad forehead blazed a pair of remarkable eyes. How it all came back to me! The *Sillon,* which had brought us together in 1905, soon became a cause of separation. I was filled with intellectual pride, as a young man so often is who has led an isolated existence in a remote countryside, deprived of the advantages of those Paris contacts which are such a valuable help in smoothing away the rough edges. I took violent exception to the fact that Borrell, whose precocity had dazzled me, should make a point of seeking the company of his fellow-workers in *Le Sillon* (instead of mine), whom I held to be incapable of discussing with him the things that I thought so important.

*   *   *   *   *

We must have taken 'the Paris road' in the same year, he to work at the Lycée Henri-IV for the entrance examination to the Normale, I for that of the École des Chartes. It suddenly came back to me how, one day, I had run into him outside the Carmelite House in the rue de Vaugirard. He was selling Sangnier's paper, *La Démocratie.* I pretended not to have seen him, out of no concern for his feelings, but because my first novel, *l'Enfant chargé de chaînes,* was just then being serialized in the *Mercure,* and was giving a good deal of offence to members of *Le Sillon,* because of one of my characters

[1] *The Sillon* was a group of young religious enthusiasts with a strong interest in social problems, who had regular discussion meetings. (Translator)

who had certain features in common with Sangnier. I decided that
Borrell must hate me.

That was the last I ever saw of him. He was to die, I was to live
on, and forget. And now, there he was, as I used to see him, coming
out of school with a heavy satchel of books, a rain-drenched cape,
and his bright blue eyes. Two lines from a poem he had once given
me, an imitation from the Greek *Anthology*, came back into my
mind. I looked at him: he looked at me. In him I saw one of those
judges whom I could not challenge, one of those whose place I
had taken, though I could not fill the empty seat, and knew that he
had the right to call me to account.

Some there are, trained in the Normale and still alive today, who
miss no opportunity of doing so. To me they solemnly address
their 'warnings', as they call them. The crime, in their eyes, of
which Mauriac is guilty, is that of not being Péguy, of not being
Bernanos, but of being Mauriac.

But that of all Alain's pupils, slaughtened at the same time, only
one, after fifty years, should come back from the grave, and that
his name, which was once so dear to me, should be recalled by my
own son, made me hang my head. I look at my record, and am, at
once, eager to counter his charges. What Borrell detested in me
when I was twenty, what obsessed him through the years, was
simply that I was possessed by the demon of literature, a demon
dressed in the fashion of the day. What I had brought into the small
world of the Bordeaux *Sillon* was a mind shaped by *Sous l'oeil des
barbares* and *Un homme libre* – a fact that those young men could not
but execrate. Borrell, the schoolboy, had detected at the very first
glance the inconsistency of my whole life: my pride was stronger
than the friendship he had inspired in me. To him I say farewell.

★　　★　　★　　★　　★

Nevertheless, all that I write today, had its beginnings, fifty
years ago, in the little club-room of the Bordeaux *Sillon*, close to
the Madeleine, which was the Marianite chapel. So far as one can
judge, without being unduly rash, what the schoolboy of 1905
might have become in 1955, whose ardent faith I doubt that Alain

could have influenced (Philippe Borrell was Spanish by origin), I am pretty sure that we should have moved forward side by side. It was not to utter a 'warning' that *he* came back, but to whisper in my ear that it is never too late, to beg me to make haste before I should be called upon to hand in my paper. I beg him to forgive the many things that mark the miles upon the road which I have travelled, and he consoles me with two lines from a poem by André Lafon, who, as he did, died in 1915:

Je ne dirai pas: il fallait, ni pourquoi?
Puisque c'est si peu nous qui faisons notre vie.

When we parted, he had only ten more years to live, and, in that brief interval, there was to be that formidable meeting with Alain (who in these letters to Borrell shows himself more hostile to religion than in his other writings), that struggle not to lose his faith, and to safeguard his love. He kept his faith: he saved his love: he gave his life. Yes, he was 'the first', as Alain said, the first of all that generation of sacrificial victims: Philippe Borrell.

✳   ✳   ✳   ✳   ✳

O inequality of fate! Philippe Borrell has forced me to question my own life, which has been protected and fulfilled. But he was not the only one....

One day in this rainy August, a 'Diversion' led me into unfamiliar roads. Entering a village, I caught sight of the name: Loisy. My wife said: 'It is Nerval's Loisy....' I had barely time to see through the misted windscreen a roof shining and wet with rain. Already it was Mortefontaine. Against the green paradise of Nerval's childhood loves, against a background of damp, dark leaves and soaking grass where Adrienne and Sylvie were dancing still, I saw with my inner eye, the dangling figure of a bald-headed corpse.

Rue de la Vieille-Lanterne . . . Paris was under snow: the day dawned darkly. Not only this hanged poet, but others, too, must have died that night in destitution. So ended, on the 26th January, 1855, with, perhaps, still in his pocket, the seven sous which he had borrowed from Asselineau, the man who had dreamed of dying in a garden *'au milieu des arbres, des treilles et des fleurs d'automne'*.

It is with astonishment that, in our old age, we ask ourselves how it has come about that we have gone through life without happening on shipwreck. Room enough there has been for misery, and the manner of our death has still not been determined. . . . No matter: the journey is no less precisely what it was. Why these divergent roads when many destinies seemed so much alike at the setting out? At dawn all poets are attuned to the same joy, have drunk of the same philtre. Nerval was one of the many companions of my early years. What romantic was not? Yet, I can clearly see that point upon the road at which we parted company.

The Nerval whom I loved – and humbly I confess it – was not the man who stands so high in the estimation of today. It is a far cry from the youth in love with Adrienne and Sylvie to the lucid madman of *Aurélia*. The pioneer, the precursor of a new poetic age, was then unknown to me, or rather, it would be truer to say that I ran from him, bolting for shelter, as I always have done, when faced by any attempt to use mental derangement, systematically exploited, as an artistic method. So repellent do I find anything that resembles the dream element in literature, that, almost automatically, I swim against the current of the whole surréalist movement. There can be nobody who fights more obstinately in the rearguard of letters. Of this attitude I am neither ashamed nor boastful. And yet. . . .

Dreaming lies at the base of all poetic vocation. I doubt whether any young man has ever transposed life more completely than I have done. To do so is an essential part of youth. But have I, at any point, cut off the current of that transposition? A poet is a man who has never wholly ceased to be a child, a child who has survived the passage of time without the protection of the guardian-angels of childhood, a child without a rail to keep him from falling, a prey to all the passions of the heart and flesh, to all the secret frenzies of the blood. When such a condition is carried to extremes, it ends, as in Verlaine's case, in the rue Descartes, on the floor of a prostitute's bedroom, or dangling at the end of a rope above the snowed-up pavement of a Paris slum which the cold dawn has emptied of life.

On the previous day, Nerval had written to someone: 'Do not expect me. To-night, when darkness falls, it will be black and white.'

*　　*　　*　　*　　*

What is it, then, that saves those who have saved themselves? All poets are subject to this madness. Goethe, Hugo were not exceptions to the rule, but examples of the tremendous victory of the will to live, to overcome the dark, satanic powers. It was the descendants of Hugo who, in the long run, had to foot the bill. What is it, then, that has saved those of us who still survive?

When a man reaches my age heredity becomes something more than a word. Not that it stands out clear and plain, but that in the grand total of our destiny, we come to see the part played by what is not 'us' – in so far as 'us' means the dreamer, the seer, in short, the poet. That sense of prudence, of the calculated taking of risks which we recognize in ourselves, that instinctive knowledge of what to do or what to leave undone – these, I now realize, have been handed down to me by people I have never known, whether in Bordeaux or in the country, all of them members of a long line of hard-working men and women – sugar-refiners of the rue Sainte-Croix, cloth-merchants of the rue Saint-James, or importers of wood for casks, like the tenant-farmers of Les Landes. They have never ceased to bring invisible pressure on my life, when pressure was necessary. Each time that an instinctive reflex brought me up short on the brink of the absurd or the irreparable, it was the secret expression of *their* will within me. It is they who have saved me, unless, of course, they have destroyed me, in so far as, for a poet, to save his life is to lose it. If Verlaine had written nothing after *La Bonne Chanson*, if he had died the Assistant Director of a department in the Prefecture of the Seine. . . .

*　　*　　*　　*　　*

This triumph of his ancestors in the life of a creative artist does not occur without some risk of back-fire. I sometimes wonder whether the change from poet to novelist, does not have in it as motive, some obscure longing for revenge. The poet lays rough hands upon the middle-class inheritance which, for so long, has bound him hand and foot, and uses it to keep him supplied with 'types'. In that way he gets his own back.

*   *   *   *   *

If the characters of his invention sometimes seem to us so horrible, it is that they are caricatures of his guardians drawn by a crazy and frustrated poet.

All the same, I am still convinced that the poet of whom I am thinking would, in the long run, have succeeded in raising the stone which a parsimonious and careful line of forbears had laid upon him, were it not for the fact that, to the extravagant foolishness of an adult who had never quite emerged from childhood, he opposed another foolishness which was just as bad. Gérard de Nerval most certainly had religious leanings, but can one go so far as to say that he was a christian? I know too little about him to answer that question. But was it not he (I hope that his adorers will forgive me if I am wrong), was it not he who, when asked 'what is your faith?' replied: 'I accept all faiths'? To accept them all is to pour oil, not water on the devouring flames. On the other hand, to cling to one only, especially if that one be catholicism, even if the practice of it is intermittent, that, more surely than heredity, serves to embank the thick and muddy flood, to direct its course, and, no matter how furious and irresistible the onset of the flood-waters, to lead it back, at length, into its eternal bed.

But no, that image of embanking is deceptive. The religious life does not curb, rather does it satisfy the poetic craving, not like a fairy-tale which might be true, but like a coherent vision of existence, while, at the same time, leaving a sufficient margin of uncertainty, mystery and darkness to maintain that element of disquiet without which there could be no art, if, as I believe, every great work is an attempt to provide an answer to that 'What are we? Whence do we come? Whither are we going? which Gauguin (I speak from memory) inscribed at the bottom of the triptych which, fifty years ago, belonged to a Bordeaux friend of Claudel and of Jammes, Gabriel Frizeau, and which was my first contact with modern painting.

But, most important of all, a living faith, rooted in love, brings to a fixed standstill in contemplation all that is wandering and aimless, and is manifested in a liturgy which is, at once, sublime and work-a-day. Did Gérard de Nerval ever have recourse to that? I have just been re-reading *Aurélia*. No lucid madman could have allowed ordinary mortals to advance so far into the deep caverns of unreason, where visions rise and mingle, not in chaos, for their sequence obeys some strange and unknown law. I do not remember that through all the dreams of all the religions the golden thread of catholicism ever ran so visibly as through the texture of that tapestry which Nerval wove. Not that that makes me feel inclined to draw the dreamer to me. It is only too obvious that what he most sought in Christianity was the promise of a personal survival. What enchanted him was that he would meet again, after life's final exit, his Jenny Colon, as he might, in life, have met her at the stage-door of the theatre at which she was performing. But mostly, in the christian hope, he looked forward to embracing the mother whom he had not known, by the thought of whom, until the end, he was as though obsessed.

This hope he incorporated in the dream that was his life. But life is not a dream. For the christian life is the very opposite of dream. It is from the first of all duties to accept life as it is, that the romantic is always trying to escape. In his heart of hearts he chooses madness, because he prefers it. He prefers what is not to what is. Therein lies the mortal sin of romanticism.

Joubert said: 'The Revolution has driven my thoughts away from the real world, by making it too horrible.' No historical event was needed to make Nerval turn his back upon the real. The real in itself, the real as it appeared to him, he had to change and re-invent. . . . By a derangement of all the senses? How close Nerval is to Rimbaud! – and to Maurice de Guérin, as well. I do not see, so much as feel, it. If I were a critic, I should dearly love to seek for, and to find, the signs of that deep fraternity between three inspired beings who never knew each other in this world, but whose common madness took the form of thinking that they could at once recreate and flee from it.

IV

A FEW hours' drive by car, and life becomes a slate from which I have wiped all it has recorded, from day to day, of human history. What I take note of now is a flight of cranes, uttering their cries and laboriously, against the blue, setting a course for the north; a sudden squall: the sun shining through the falling rain enveloping the white foam of the flowering pear-trees and the just unfolding leaves in a steamy radiance. An artless rainbow, stretched from hill to hill, seems but the crude painting of a child.

This, perhaps, is the only record God requires, this pastoral, year by year renewed, for it alone is without evil. True, in nature as among men, the internecine war goes on, but it is free from guilt. How great a blessing is this power bestowed on me to break away, in the course of a few hours, from all that my calling forces me to scan and annotate, and to rejoin my fountain-head.

But is it here that I shall find it? Of the young creature who, beneath this hornbeam-tree once bore my name, I find no trace. Nothing of him remains. The child, the youth, the young man of that distant past is nowhere to be seen, not even what is left of him. It is as though he had never been.

Or are, perhaps, those remnants living still? They must be, since my life continues. The slow wastage of the flesh makes it hard to credit that the child within me is, in some sort, permanent, that now, after fifty years, he is still what he was and what for ever he will be.

Under the hornbeam I accept the illusion of escape from life, from that old and stranded barge which can no longer cheat itself with the hope that any tide will ever again set it afloat. Though each hour spent within view of the silent stretch of country, has a different colour, the days are all alike. They are confounded one with the other, and their uniformity creates an eternal present.

Since, too, the vines laugh at our mechanical progress, there is no sound nor smell to remind me of motors or of petrol. There is a complete absence of machinery. In me the faithful oxen find their last, most loving friend. In the muffled afternoon my ears catch the sound of dialect words from distant centuries, words which must endlessly enfold these heavy beasts before they will consent to take one forward pace and then another, the same words which my great-grandfather would recognize were he to open the door and stand suddenly before me. It is I who would 'appear' to him. It is the living who 'appear' to the dead.

At any other period of my life, I could, had I so wished it, have been alone. I could, as this evening, have stood motionless till darkness fell, master of the night, or seated in the old *salon*, my hands upon my knees, a Pharaoh in his tomb. The spring rain on the roof is the drip, drip of the centuries.

I could have, but the idea never came to me. The Solitude, which is now domesticated, was the enemy of my young years. In October, during the grape harvest, I had, however, to accept it. What I am now free to choose was then obligatory. Even when no thoughts of love are in his mind, a young man alone thinks all mankind unfaithful to him by their absence. He demands that others shall be at his disposal, in order that he may feel himself to be alive. It matters not who they may be: he is afraid of none of them. Not yet do others fill his heart with terror because his very youth disarms them, and has power to cast a spell even on monsters. But now they terrify the old hare who was once a youth. If the Bacchantes had not torn Orpheus limb from limb, the old man he would have grown to be would have lost the power to charm wild beasts.

The old hare crouches between two hummocks, and blends the colour of his pelt with the surrounding earth. With feelings of relief he hears the barking of the hounds die in the distance, and, if he is an old hare capable of knowing God, then the form in which he lies thinking becomes a shelter where he prays.

But he mistrusts himself. The machine has invaded his home, in the form of a pick-up which he has himself installed. Not all music, now, is favourable to that peace which has, with so much difficulty, been achieved. Probably there is none to which he would not find silence preferable, though some there is with power enough to bring the gift of life again to the old Pharaoh in his tomb, so that the heart which ceased to beat ten thousand years ago begins to move again.

Just so, the other evening, did Schumann's *Fantasia,* picked out at random, suddenly let loose in the old *salon,* I know not what despairing angel, who began to bump against the walls. I could hear one of his wings fluttering on the window-pane. Not until the record had ceased to turn did he find the way out and was swallowed up in the horrible darkness of the spring night.

*   *   *   *   *

Not all the music loved by me since childhood, with which I have been familiar for as long as I remember, has the terrifying power of that *Fantasia* which is ever linked, for me, with the rags and tatters of a dead passion. And so it was, that on my last evening in Paris, I went to the Opera where I could listen once again, with an emotion quite untouched by bitterness, to *Tannhäuser,* all the most famous airs from which my mother used to sing.

And, as I listened, I reflected that those Parisians of 1861 who, like Baudelaire, fought doughtily in defence of Wagner, knew almost nothing of the works on which his fame has since been built. At best they could have heard a few fragments of the *Flying Dutchman, Rienzi* and *Lohengrin* (unless some excerpts from *Tristan,* which he had just completed, were included in any of the three concerts which he gave in Paris at about this time). But genius is indivisible. The whole of Wagner is potentially present in the opera which foundered under the catcalls of the gentlemen of the Jockey Club.

It should be difficult for us to have a clear view of this early Wagner – minus *Tristan,* minus the *Meistersinger,* minus *The Ring,* but not for me, because that was all I know of him between the ages of ten and sixteen. 'Star of Eve' from *Tannhäuser,* 'Elizabeth's

Prayer', and the 'Pilgrim's March', formed part of the ritual of our summer holidays. 'Elsa', from *Lohengrin*, did not join the company until somewhat later.

I rather think that my mother – God forgive her! – did not hesitate to sing Elisabeth's great aria, *O Blessed Virgin,* in church. But we children preferred – *But thou appearest, sweet and lovely star* – because it was earmarked for the hour which brought relief after the stifling August days in Les Landes. A mist was rising from the fields, and we looked for the star between the crowded summits of the pines.

O thou pale star, night's fiery harbinger . . . Wolfram's song was a link for us with yet another 'marvel', included in the Abbé Ragon's anthology, which was my introduction to romantic poetry, as, a few years later, a similar volume, edited by Léautaud, was to that of the *Symbolistes.* This 'marvel' was Musset's invocation: *Pâle étoile du soir, messagère lointaine.* . . .

The music and the poetry of the romantics made up, for our delight, one single and immense nocturne. I am inclined to wonder whether childhood is not better attuned than the years of maturity, and, still more, of old age, to the stars. At least, it was so for us who knew nothing of the galaxies, and were not frightened by the eternal silence of infinite space. The night made manifest a mystery which was not frightening at all, but adorable. It declared the glory, not of an unapproachable God, but of a God welcomed and possessed. The silence of the night was one with the silence of the God within us, and only a line of poetry or a song could break it without being guilty of blasphemy.

Maybe I wrote *Asmodée* simply and solely for the ironic pleasure I found in making the children in that play sing the air from Gounod's *Cinq Mars: Nuit resplendissante et silencieuse* which, too, belonged to our ritual of the dusk. The faint ripple at the bottom of the meadow sufficed to bring Lamartine's *Lake* before my eyes – it was included in the Abbé Ragon's collection, though with the more passionate verses omitted – and to make me hear, at the heart of an immortal darkness, the sound of water broken by a boat's prow.

This close connexion between night and romantic music was not the product merely of a child's imagination. In Wagner, as in Shakespeare, darkness plays a prominent part, though not always. But *Tristan* most certainly caught and held the silence of those nights in Venice when it was being composed. I have just been reading again, in Guy de Pourtalès' excellent book, some passages from the journal which Wagner was keeping at that time for Isolde, for Mathilde Wesendonck. On 29 September 1858 he listens while a gondola, with its load of musicians, draws away into the distant spaces of the Lagoon, and notes: 'It is as though the last echo is dissolving in the moonlight which seems to hold suspended a world of music made visible.'

A world of music made visible, that indeed is what Wagner reveals to us in the *Star of Eve* in expectation of which I sat, the other evening, at the Opera. And when, at last, it came, I could not agree that it is in any way unworthy of the genius which created *Tristan*. ... As I listened, the tears came into my eyes. It had participated in a mystery. When we were children, we did not make any distinction between it and the star itself which, with heads thrown back, we sought between the darkened tree-tops. It was no piece of stage machinery that made it twinkle, nor was the setting one of painted canvas. The trees with their slashed and wounded trunks were making moan. Their outspread branches did not interlace. No matter how close-planted they might be, each was for ever separate, and, at the lightest puff of wind, the high tops made a gesture of refusal.

One should no longer be a critic at my age, because the great works of art can no longer be seen as they are. We cannot free them from the sediment left by our lives as the years move on. What I was hearing at the Opera, no one but I could hear: the summer nights of childhood so filled with portents, are the kingdom of a passion as yet unknown. The pilgrims in *Tannhäuser* draw us after them, and we, too, take our way to Rome, there to seek pardon for sins of which we are guiltless, which, as yet, we do not feel the craving to commit.

*   *   *   *   *

Music has still the power to sway me: but how is it with poetry?
Certain questions which we ask about ourselves can long remain
unanswered. Then, all of a sudden, some unexpected incident sheds
light upon the problem when we least expect it. In my boyhood,
and all through my early years, I was a great reader of verse. Life,
in my case, drew its sustenance from books — perhaps to the detri-
ment of living – was, as it were, orchestrated by the poets. Prose,
even imaginative prose, was without value in my eyes unless it had
a deep top-soil of poetry. It seems to me now, looking back, that
the reading aloud of the poets, both in Bordeaux and in Paris,
played a major part in all my friendships.

But it is an undoubted fact that I have almost entirely given up
the reading of poetry. It is no longer a necessity for me. The same
is true of novels. I scarcely ever open them, except in the way of
duty, or because I still feel some faint curiosity about the craft of
fiction.

Is there, I ask myself, nothing left today of the youngster, drunk
on words, who could not imagine that there would ever be a day
or a night when he would not listen to the voices of Baudelaire,
Verlaine, Rimbaud or Jammes? Yet, old though I am, I do not feel
that I have grown dry and arid. I may have torn down much of the
theatrical scenery, but that does not mean that I am no longer
in a state of poetic grace, for genuine poetry is not the opposite
of the real. Poetry belongs essentially to what is. Only bad poetry
is a lie.

In the ageing man's detachment from all passion, in that 'never
more' which sounds in his ears when a young face comes into his
field of vision, in the distance which now exists between himself
and his fellows, as though, with every day that passes, he sees them
growing smaller on the bank he has already left, from which his
boat is drawing away, there is, it seems to me, sufficient matter left
to give lift to genuine poetry. The presence of death, too, should
be a help, for death is now a felt reality and not the theme of which
youth once savoured the dark enchantment, thinking itself safe
because death was something that came only to others. It is now a
close companion, a veiled shape which stands blackly at a distance

the extent of which we cannot measure. Its shadow is over us, and we know that we have only to stretch a hand to touch it, that all we have believed, professed, affirmed about the mystery to which it holds the key, is on the point of being confirmed or denied eternally.

This confrontation of each passing moment is unaffected by the hustle and bustle made by us as social beings acting out our parts upon the stage. Does not this inner drama of our lives, which calls for no rhetoric, create the very climate in which poetry lives? Why is it, then, that I no longer seek the poets, without whom at twenty I could not live?

*   *   *   *   *

For the answer to that question to be given, or, at least, for my thinking about the problem to move in a definite direction, it needed two accidents which led me, in the course of the last few days, to open once again several anthologies. One of those accidents was 'poetic' to the last degree: the other, the very acme of the vulgar.

Two extremely pretty young girls, one dark, the other fair, arrived unexpectedly at my house from the Basque country. These visitors, fresh from the land of Jammes, who might have stepped straight out of one of his 'Elegies', spoke much of him, and asked from which of his poems I had taken two lines which I am particularly fond of quoting:

> *On voit à l'intérieur pâle des métairies*
> *Les chapeaux de travail dormir près des tamis.*

I soon turned up the poem in question. I had to read it aloud, and then several more. No doubt I found the intonation which was mine, fifty long years ago. But, as I read on, I found myself having to fight down a sense of discomfort which was not unlike that which comes to me when I re-read letters received and written many years ago. In those lines a whole world of sentiment found expression which, I now see, was wholly unreal. The sunset of life reveals with its horizontal and relentless beams whatever falsity there is in sentiment. The poems of Jammes have kept their ancient beauty and, to that extent, are as 'true' as they ever were. But their truth is that of sensation, it is what is felt by a young faun held captive in the land of our South-West. His truth is the old villages where he is bored to death, of the great estates drowsing beneath a line of hills drowned in the blue of heaven, of Clara d'Ellébeuse's sun-hat moving above the vines. These poems remain, or should remain, eternally alive, but only so long as there are young men and young women, like my two visitors, who can still drink with pleasure of this icy stream which flows between the alder roots.

But I can no longer feel myself back into the attitude of the young Jammes or the young Mauriac confronted by that countryside where they endured the torments of adolescence. But to analyse still further what I felt, would lead me too far afield: to the condemnation of a certain type of romanticism which, at my age, seems to be the very height of absurdity and foolishness. And so, as soon as the young girls had taken flight, I shut the book.

*　　*　　*　　*　　*

But in the course of that same week, thanks to a less poetic accident, quite another reason was revealed to me for no longer reading the poets, and one which was the very opposite of that which had made me turn from Jammes. I scarcely dare put down in words what it was that led me to take from my library shelves the *Fleurs du Mal*, which, for so many years, has stood within reach of my hand without my ever, so to speak, having recourse to it.

What drove me to do so now was a crossword puzzle. The 'clue' concerned an uninflected word used incorrectly, in the plural, by Baudelaire. Since I flatter myself that I know the *Fleurs du Mal* inside out, I felt sure that I could go straight to the poem which contains this incorrect plural. But, no sooner had I opened the book than I completely forgot what I was looking for. I was caught up again in the old magic. Each line came alive to me once more, like a snake emerging from its winter sleep, even before I had read the poem through to the end. The long-forgotten spell held me enthralled, but with a queasy feeling from which I could not free myself.

Yet no young girl had asked me to read these lines aloud. If I submitted to the rediscovered power of incantation, it was not because constraint was put upon me, or, at least, such constraint as there was did not come from the outside. It was in the very poems themselves. I could not escape. But this time there was no question of a lie. It was their truth that made the reading of those words intolerable.

I confess that I have never been in agreement with the innumerable interpretations inspired by the *Fleurs du Mal,* nor have I ever recognized the Baudelaire who was my hero when I was a young man, in the 'case-book' figure analysed and psycho-analysed by so many critics and famous philosophers. Baudelaire is the poet of the real, so little romantic that the very language created by his poetry for its purpose is the nearest thing to prose that any poet has ventured to use, the most 'figurative' – to use the modern jargon, always strictly controlled by the object, whether that object be a little wizened old woman tottering along a Paris pavement, or a decaying carcase with its feet in the air and its belly alive with swarming maggots. But whatever its nature, Baudelaire saw it with an unswerving eye, smelt it, touched it, and showed it *sub specie aeternitatis* as Van Gogh did his kitchen chair.

When we were young, we allowed ourselves to be held fast by the enchanter at the very centre of this world-as-it-is within which he had imprisoned himself, and us with him. His attempts at escape, all the drugs of the spirit and the flesh, could not free him from that hermetic circle. He stayed within it till the end, whereas Rimbaud, after him, could not persevere beyond his nineteenth year, and then rallied round him the herds of the blind and deaf.

★　　★　　★　　★　　★

I have become neither blind nor deaf. But I know that this world in which Baudelaire suffered, is not a closed system. I have escaped from the magic circle of smells and colours and forms. I have found the way out. Baudelaire, too, knew where it lay. He struck the window with a powerful wing, and then fell back on to the dirty carpet of his poverty-stricken room.

Ma jeunesse ne fut qu'un ténébreux orage
Traversé çà et là par de brillants soleils.

Into these shadows pierced through, here and there, with sun-rays, the *Fleurs du Mal* can still plunge us for the space of a reading. But how insufferably long that space must seem to those who have opened their minds to the light, and their hearts to peace.

It is to the man, now, that my thoughts turn, to the stricken poet, incapable of speech, except to mutter 'crénom' over and over again, with a prolonged chuckling. 'It is a torment inflicted by a hand not human but almighty, and only the almighty could endure it.' It was of Christ that Pascal wrote those words. In the order of humanity, the poet, too, is cruelly armed against himself! Baude-laire, until the last day of his life, was, at one and the same time, both knife and wound.

A prize subject for the psycho-analysts. What disciple of Freud has not 'had a go' at General Aupick's stepson? There, plain to see, was the wriggling Oedipus. Complex offering every kind of satis-faction to the 'prentice practitioners, though, God knows, they cannot have found much pleasure in their work. And then, after the demonstration had been so often repeated that nobody, one thought, could have the heart to start all over again, and hoped that at last the body would be handed over to us christians, who are his spiritual family, for decent burial, lo and behold, along comes a philosopher and puts in a claim for it! His name is Sartre, and, once again, poor Baudelaire has been put back on the trolley and wheeled into a different dissecting-room.

The man's poetry has left the professor unmoved. Now, at last, the secret is to be revealed. And what is the secret? – no more and no less than that Baudelaire had willed his own destiny. He had insisted on having that destiny, and none other. He, alone, had played the role of Fate. No disaster had come to him that he had not summoned. How very remarkable! – including, I suppose, aphasia at forty-six? Why, of course, seeing that he had come into that legacy of syphilis which he had been seeking, for twenty years, in the company of all the most squalid prostitutes whom he could find.

> *Vice beaucoup plus grave, elle porte perruque.*
> *Tous ses beaux cheveux noirs ont fui sa blanche nuque.*
> *Ce qui n'empêche pas les baisers amoureux*
> *De pleuvoir sur son front plus pelé qu'un lepreux.*

This youthful adorer of monstrosities had fully made up his mind what he was going to be, without, for a moment, being the dupe of the character he had elected to play: 'for no man is ever anything but a swindle.' That is Sartre speaking, and he is right to make his point *if* there is nothing in a man that does not transcend the man: *if* there was no power in Baudelaire other than that of self-destruction, which Sartre denounces, and was undoubtedly present in him.

Here the christian finds himself beaten before the battle has been joined. There is nothing he can oppose to the findings of the philosopher, no proof of what he believes, of what he knows, of what Baudelaire believed and knew, which gives to his self-inflicted torment a very different significance than that which is assumed by the voluble dialectician who has now taken possession of the remains. No discussion is possible between us, any more than it would have been possible with the poet on his death-bed. Even if his tongue had not been tied by aphasia, Baudelaire could have said nothing in reply to Nadar when that happy and untroubled atheist paid his last visit to the man lying under sentence of death, and kept on savagely repeating: 'There is no God!' But I must quote Nadar's own description of the scene, in his book – *Charles Baudelaire intime:* 'The last time I went to see him in the home of Jeanne Duval, we argued about the immortality of the soul. I say "we" because his eyes spoke as eloquently as his tongue could have done had he been able to use it. "Look here," I said: "how *can* you believe in God?" He moved away from the window-rail on which he had been leaning, and pointed to the sky. In front of, and above, us was the full splendour of the setting sun, putting the whole sky in a blaze, and outlining with gold and flame-colour the powerful mass of the Arc de Triomphe. "Crénom! Oh! Crénom!" he exclaimed once more in a fury, shaking his fist at the sky.' How weak those fists striking on the door of his Father's house! – and how quickly it must have opened to let in the returned prodigal!

At this point Sartre would argue that Baudelaire was not really a believer, that it was only when he was weakened by disease that his resistance broke down, that *Mon coeur mis à nu* has no more importance in his work than has *Num quid et tu* in that of Gide, that he boasted more than once of his lack of faith, especially in *La Fanfarlo*. But we, his brethren, know that this sinner was no less one of us than are the saints. The sinner and the saint, according to Péguy, together form an integral part of the Christian system. No matter how often Baudelaire denies, his denial turns always to blasphemy, in other words, to the act of faith. In point of fact he had never, for one moment, ceased to pray. It matters little that he did not believe in the God of the philosophers, of the scientists, or even of the theologians. He is for ever speaking to *somebody*, and, since he speaks to him, he must believe in his existence. Of the answer made to him, he, like each one of us, can be the sole judge. That it is beyond the reach of any analysis, I agree. The nature of his prayer, however, emerges clearly: it is never the product of a vague emotionalism.

When Baudelaire prays, he does not cease to be the artist who marked the end of the romantic era, and wrote that the poet's highest claim to honour is that 'he has accomplished precisely what he set out to do.' And so it is to Him that he says very plainly and clearly what he had made up his mind to say. When he wrote *Les Phares* he was well aware that each of the eleven verses was evidence of the presence of the divine in Man – evidence which no dialectic could destroy.

That, at an interval of space and time, there has appeared upon the surface of the earth's crust a mould containing the germ of those human spirits, to whom he gave the name of *Phares* or *Beacons*, and from among whom he picked out a few of his favourite painters, is an obstacle which he never attempts to side-step, in the shameless manner of the philosophers. He forces us to hear that 'cry repeated by a thousand sentinels', as, at dawn, from farm to farm, the crowing cocks call to one another and reply. He never doubts that Somebody is listening to that 'ardent summons': Somebody with whom he knows that he is closely linked, who has marked him from his earliest childhood, as one disinherited yet predestined.

The child that Baudelaire once was:

> Il joue avec le vent, cause avec le nuage,
> Et s'enivre en chantant du chemin de la croix;
> Et l'Esprit qui le suit dans son Pèlerinage
> Pleure de le voir gai comme un oiseau des bois.

Just before he was struck down, in one of his short prose poems: *Mademoiselle Bistouri*, Charles Baudelaire all of a sudden addresses himself to God, but not with supplications and with cries. Each word frames a question and demands a reply: 'Life is aswarm with innocent monsters. O Lord, my God, you the Creator, you the Master: you who made both Law and Freedom: you, the Sovereign who lets things go their way: you the Judge who pardons: you who are filled with motives and with causes, and did, perhaps, put within me a taste for the horrible that you might convert my heart, as a surgeon cures with the sharp incision of his lancet: O Lord! have mercy on mad women and mad men! O my Creator! can there exist such things as monsters in the eyes of Him who alone knows why they exist, how they have *made themselves what they are,* and how they could not have made themselves differently?'

Vain is all controversy! If what Baudelaire believed is true, then his destiny escapes the dialectic of the atheists, and psycho-analysis cannot reach below the surface manifestations. What can take us apart save only the angel's trumpet at the last day?

On one point only are we, henceforward, his brothers in religion, convinced that we are right: the poet of the *Fleurs du Mal* belongs to us, and who shall contest our property in him, the lover of Jeanne Duval whose friendship brought the blush of shame to Sainte-Beuve's virtuous cheek? Nothing is stranger to the moderns, nothing more distasteful to them when they come across it in its last, christian possessors, than the metaphysical knowledge of evil.

> *Ah! Seigneur! donnez-moi la force et le courage*
> *De contempler mon coeur et mons corps sans dégout!*

Who, in these days, feels the need for such strength, such courage? The moderns look at themselves with assured complacency, and, if they have learned how, they describe themselves. The crawling human insect need excuse himself to no one for having followed the law of his species – need render no account of all those bodies and those hearts which he has used for his own purposes, and then rejected.

But this attitude cannot but have its consequences in the world of art. Entomology has its methods. If applied to human history, will they bring new life to fiction? If Man is nothing but a 'swindle', if that is all there is in him, then, we cannot escape the conclusion that the so-called psychological novel has, up till now, been living on a lie. There can be no future for the novelist except to be the portraitist of nothing.

But, perhaps, the poets and the saints were not, after all, either swindlers or dupes. Maybe there really does exist in us that kingdom in which we have believed on the word of those travellers who have brought back what they have found it in, that something which has its echo in what we have discovered in ourselves.

Charles Baudelaire had so great a passion for the thing-in-itself, and for the word that perfectly expresses it, that, no matter how hideous it may be, he forces us to touch and feel it. The horrible old Jewess like a living corpse, the old woman mocked at by the urchins in the street, the carrion, the vampire, here testify no less than the giant-winged albatross, or the young woman leaning on a balcony moored in the rosy mists of a Bordeaux evening. The greatness of the human spirit in spite of all its hateful blemishes! 'You have convinced yourself of that, but it is a lie.' If it is a lie, then what is art? Whence comes that mirage which so enchanted Baudelaire and all the artists of the ages; for which, indeed, they lived?

*   *   *   *   *

On the 4th of February, 1857, Baudelaire sent his manuscript to the printer. On the 25th of June, *Les Fleurs du Mal* appeared. Meanwhile, on a quiet May night, Alfred de Musset had been visited, not by his muse, but by death. To his brother, he said: 'Sleep . . . at last I am going to sleep.' Perhaps he was thinking only of the sleep of this world, as some believe that when the dying Goethe said 'More light', all he meant was that the shutters should be opened – so does the most ordinary word expand its meaning at the approach of the final agony.

What was Baudelaire doing on that night between the first and the second of May, and what were his thoughts when he learned that Musset was no more? Perhaps that his destiny would compel him to bring a second death to this dead man who was still so very much alive, who had bodied forth in poetry all that he himself most hated. In some jottings found after his death (he had been playing with the idea of defending Heinrich Heine about whom Jules Janin had written a stupid article) there is this, which dates from 1865: 'Musset . . . poetic gifts, but a bad poet, only to be found now in tarts' bedrooms cheek by jowl with ornamental glass dogs, and bits of china won at the Asnières lottery . . . a superior sort of café ballad-monger, a sentimental undertaker's mute.' But as early as 1857, the reasons for his contemptuous attitude to Musset, had exploded in a letter to Armand Fraisse. 'Except at about the time of my First Communion, that is to say, at an age when everything that has to do with prostitutes and silk-ladders, has an almost religious significance, I have never been able to endure that darling of the dandies. His impudence is that of a small boy invoking Heaven and Hell when he's just brought off a pick-up at some table-d'hôte, and all he produces is a muddy stream of grammatical mistakes and faults in prosody. He is completely incapable of that slavery which alone can turn a daydream into a work of art.'

Each word here must be carefully weighed. Never was a genius more clear-sighted than Baudelaire. Never did poetry so merge with criticism, never was inspiration so closely linked with that lucidity in which there is no place for kindliness towards what the poet was determined to destroy, and did, in fact, destroy. From

Rimbaud to Mallarmé and Valéry French poetry has never deviated from the road opened up by *Les Fleurs du Mal,* in other words, has never ceased to move farther and farther away from *Rolla* and *Les Nuits.*

Had it been merely a question of technique taking priority over inspiration, that would have been nothing much to boast about. But what Baudelaire did was to make rigour of thought get the better of go-as-you-please. Generally speaking, he was a living proof that a poet loses nothing by being intelligent.

The fastidious, however, have shown their readiness to pardon the shortcomings of the author of *Le Chandelier* and *Les Caprices de Marianne.* There are others, too – of whom I am one – who feel an affection for him on grounds about which I will say something later. The fact remains, however, that Musset has received a wound from which he will never recover. The poor pelican of *La Nuit de Mai* carried the sharp baudelairian arrow in its side. Even had it been less sharp, it would have pierced him all the same. Alas! what flabby stuff it all seems when one goes back to it. 'A young man with a heart of wax' was how Lamartine described Musset. The trouble is that his work, too, was soft as wax.

Did Musset have forebodings of the fate in store for him? Did he hold any views about Baudelaire? I very much doubt whether the needy and vaguely tainted dandy ever attracted the attention of the rich dandy who was his elder by ten years, the idol of French youth, already on the point of being ranked by the school manuals as the equal, in poetry, of Lamartine and Hugo, and ultimately destined to become a member of the Académie française. I have read the speech he made when he was admitted to that illustrious body. From it I learn that Duranty, whom he succeeded, was one of the great glories of Bordeaux, where he was born.

The name of Baudelaire must have made the illustrious poet of *Les Nuits* shrug his shoulders. I am inclined to think that he took his departure from this world without having had the slightest presentiment that, only a few weeks after his death, a dangerous enemy of Ninette and Ninon would arise. He was spared that revelation which overwhelmed certain novelists of the old school, in 1920, when Marcel Proust appeared in the zenith, and they realized (I am thinking in particular of Boylesve) that it was like him they had always wanted to write, that they, too, had been seeking Time Lost, but in the wrong direction, A newcomer had Regained it, and, in doing so, had cast them into outer darkness.

Musset, for his part, fell asleep with his mind at rest, an object of adoration to all France. He had been granted the homage of Sainte-Beuve, of that 'oncle Beuve' very dear to Baudelaire who had never received from him so much as an encouraging word. Poetry takes curious revenges. Re-reading the *Lundi* devoted to Musset, I came across this forgotten pearl: 'One of those poets who will endure, Béranger. . . .'

If I still want to break a lance or two for Musset, it is not only on account of his plays, whose chief weakness is that they never for a moment let us forget Shakespeare, for indeed I am not greatly enthusiastic about them (though that does not alter the fact that, in the hey-day of youth, I quite literally *gargled* the 'Respire, coeur navré de joie!' from *Lorenzaccio*). But I still find the Musset of *Les Nuits* disarming, as also the Musset of the *Lettre à Lamartine,* of *Une soirée perdue,* of the *Stances à la Malibran,* and even of the beginning of *L'Espoir en Dieu.* There are moments when I can bring myself to love him, and can actually go so far as to accept *Namouna's* warts and *Rolla's* boils.

The strange thing is, if I may be allowed the comparison with my humble self, that, in the days when I was writing poetry, I was moving deliberately in the direction of Baudelaire, and trying to find the secret of a certain recipe for an alloy, for an element of hard matter. It was this that produced my poem, *Atys,* which is still to me the least disappointing of anything I have written. I may be the only person not to be disappointed; that does not matter. What I was trying then to find and to capture was precisely the passion which still sits in the poem, caught in a close net of words which, for me, at least, are irreplaceable.

How comes it, then, that though I am hostile to Musset's poetry as a whole, there is something in him to which I cannot but remain loyal? I don't know whether there is any truth in the story of the man who jumped to his feet, with a deadly white face, during a lecture by Paul Valéry (who was castigating Musset) and started to stammer out a protest. He was certainly the spiritual brother of that other young man who, one evening at the Opera, in 1840, on the day after the publication of *Rolla* in the *Revue des Deux Mondes,* picked up on the steps, the butt of a cigar which Musset had just thrown away. I might well, God forgive me! have been one of those two young idiots. But if I had jumped up in the middle of Valéry's lecture, what should I have said? How should I have explained the contradition between my loyalty to Musset and my predilection for a type of poetry which sounded the death-knell of his?

I should have had to ask the audience to bear with me while I told them the story of my youth. But that would have been impossible for the simple reason that my youth contains no story. I should have had to begin by describing the two thick volumes of Musset's Works, one of which had been left forgotten on a bench and been soaked by the rain on a night of the summer holidays, and was still, as it were, starred by the drops. This edition dated from Musset's lifetime, and was a left-over from the library of a great-uncle whom I had never known, an old loose-living bachelor. My elder brother remembers how the baking-oven had been lit for a holocaust, and how he had seen his governess burning great-uncle's books, and how the leaves had writhed and twisted like souls in hell. How came it that *Faublas* was spared? Perhaps its small size saved it. It was hidden away behind the volumes of Guizot, where I knew well that I could find it. I am amazed that from the library thus handed over to the secular arm, three collections of drawings by Gavarni managed to escape, and came into my hands – I have them still: they were published by Hetzel in 1846 – in their original bindings.

Musset, too, was saved. Perhaps, after all, my mother had had an affection for him when she was a girl of twenty. I did not hide away in order to read him, but then I was past the age of my First Communion which, according to Baudelaire, is the only one at which it is excusable to like Musset. True enough, Musset is the adolescents' poet. He belongs to the years when the tyranny exercised by one's family, by one's duties, and by the fact that one is always a child to one's mother and one's teachers, becomes an intolerable burden. There is a stirring in the blood, there are dreams in the mind, and these things condemn us to be perpetually engaged in creating a world which, though we do not know anything of it, we feel to be essential to us if we are to make good our escape. This visionary universe takes on substance in the vagueness and the falsity of Musset: it provides a setting for would-be gallants seated on a milestone on a night of carnaval, feeling the beating of their hearts beneath their hands, or setting their spurs ringing under the high vaults of churches, or on the stairways of brothels where virgins are theirs for the taking. . . . But seraphims are shaking the light gossamer of lilacs, Lucie's fingers are skipping lightly on the key-board of a piano, bathed in moonlight, and the evening star, a messenger from far away, rises over our childhood, and watches it fade and vanish in the mist.

None of these images seriously disturbs the absurd world of our sixteenth year. At that age Baudelaire repels us because in him poetry and the real are intermingled. His inspiration springs from the very heart of that reality from which the youth averts his eyes. When the moment comes for him to face it squarely and comply with its demands, he ceases to be a child, and becomes a man. If the poet in him survives the period of adolescence, it is then that he turns to the *Fleurs du Mal*. But what truly belongs to Musset must be left to him. He satisfies the vague onset of suffering and desire which come to such a child as my backward look can see imprisoned behind the bars of scruples, of the bans imposed by relations and sunken-eyed instructors who do not understand, being held captive in an arid and a burned-up land.

Yet these two poets, separated by a generation, belong to the same race. Both were libertines and dandies, representatives of two different types of dandyism, two different types of immorality. Both had retained the ability to discriminate between good and evil. But Musset was a product of the eighteenth century, deriving from Parny and even from Béranger. His deism was very far removed from Baudelaire's profound experience of the catholic mystery.

That did not prevent the preachers of my youth from liking to quote Musset. They made great use of *'malgré moi l'infini me tourmente'* from *L'Espoir en Dieu:* and even of *Rolla!* During the Lenten sermons of 1875, in Notre-Dame, Father Monsabré had given them a dangerous example by making that illustrious pulpit ring with lines of which the apologetic value seems today to be more than doubtful.

> *J'aime! voila le mot que la nature entière*
> *Crie au vent qui l'importe, à l'oiseau qui le suit!*

The religious of those days were not, as are ours, the very spearhead of the *avant-garde*. They did not know that it was better not to quote Musset.

But this is a grave reflection on our poet, from whose work Father Monsabré could not have borrowed a single line without offending against the sanctity of truth. There is nothing genuine but suffering, in Musset, and that is not enough to make me love him. I count many friends among the dead, such as Maurice de Guérin and Benjamin Constant, whose least word has the power to move me even now . . . but not Musset! The pelicans of literature who are so free with their heart's-blood no longer appeal to men of my age. After all, perhaps it is not to Musset that I have remained faithful, but to a collection of poems bound in green leather and left on a bench at the end of the holidays of my sixteenth year, into which the rain of an autumn night had soaked slowly and marked for ever.

V

A FEW evenings ago I took down, at random, as I often do, a volume of Balzac. It was *La Muse du département,* and I opened it at the scene in which Lousteau and Brianchon are rather patronizingly discussing the novels written under the Empire. 'The literature of the Empire,' says Lousteau, 'went straight to the point without bothering much about details. It had ideas, but did not express them. It observed, but did not impart the results of its observation.' 'Today,' he goes on, 'the novelists are concerned with character-drawing. They describe the human heart. . . .'

The Lousteaus of today (for his type is eternal) know that genuine novelists no longer indulge in character-drawing for the simple reason that there are no characters except in the idea we form of them, and no longer unveil the human heart, since reality provides us with nothing in the least resembling the human heart as portrayed by the writers of tragedy and the psychological novelists, to satisfy the requirements of their calling. The novel has become life itself, and not that 'chart of moral anatomy' which Paul Bourget thought that it could draw from life.

In this matter, I am inclined to side with our modern Lousteaus. But a sudden thought has struck me. I have taken down the Balzac with a gesture that has long been familiar to me, and at once I find myself in a house every room of which I know by heart. In the days of my youth I spent whole nights in each of them, and, if I went into the garden, could find my way blindfold to the lime-tree on the bark of which are still visible the interlaced initials which I carved there many years ago.

I wonder whether the works of Kafka or Joyce, to mention only two names of writers now dead who are the masters of the rising generation, can be said to have that quality of being 'habitable' which was the distinguishing mark of those who were the treasured favourites of the one to which I belong; books so deliciously 'habitable' that, at no matter what age, we can come back to them even though they give us nothing but fictitious reality re-created by authors who intrude on every page. Balzac, for instance, a simple-minded lump of humanity, with his megalomania and his elephantine graces, is for ever coming between us and what he claims to be pointing to and commenting on, instead of making us see and feel it, in a discontinuity which breaks every logical rule of well-constructed narrative.

I don't in the least mind confessing that for me, a real novel is a book to which I can return again and again with pleasure, and not one I must work my way through and get out of, as though it were a nightmare. To be perfectly honest, Proust is about the only novelist who can give me, to the same extent as Balzac, a sense of complete familiarity with the author and the world he has created, which one can enter and leave without even having to go back to the beginning of a chapter. Apart from Balzac and Proust, I know only *War and Peace* which I can enter in just that way, merely by pushing open the first door I come to.

Most of the other great novels have to be re-read from the first page. Which are the novels I have returned to oftenest in the course of my life? They are not, I am sure, the same ones as those my juniors read and re-read. But then what *do* they read more than once? My list contains *Adolphe, Bovary, L'Éducation,* the *Mill on the Floss, Middlemarch, Dominique* . . . among many others. But do my juniors really love what they love? Do they, I mean, pay constant visits to their favourite books, and *live in them* as we used to visit and live in those novels of manners and character written in accordance with aesthetic principles which they condemn, or think outmoded?

That is the question I ask myself. I am quite prepared to believe that the young writers of today have a greater apprehension of reality than there has ever been since human beings appeared upon this earth and story-telling began. But I cannot help wondering whether that reality which is so hard to grasp, does not, in fact, evade our grasp more completely, the greater the effort made by the reader to hold it fast. The firmly outlined characters of the traditional novel, and the arbitrary psychological deductions which were the special province of the old-fashioned observers of the human heart, will perhaps enjoy a longer lease of life in the feelings and the memories of men than the work of their modern counterparts.

*   *   *   *   *

'And what about this one? Is it really suitable for her?' The 'her' in question is my granddaughter. I remember how sixty years ago that same question had a way of being asked, almost every day, by my scrupulous mother: 'Is it suitable for him?' I always dreaded what the answer, dictated by my mother's high sense of responsibility, would be, and had a horrible feeling that I should be condemned to a course of Zenaïde Fleuriot. The general view was that I 'positively devoured books'. I am not, however, sure that I really lost much by cheating my youthful appetite with food of such poor quality. In those days I still had, to so high a degree, the gift of transfiguring, that I could endow one of Zenaïde Fleuriot's heroines, Armelle Trahec, with as much beauty as I later found in the Natasha of *War and Peace,* and so convincingly that now, at the end of a long life, I can still see her green eyes shining in her small, thin, freckled face.

'Is this book suitable for her?' No: a young girl could never really *get into* the story through which I am glancing. I have just rediscovered it: the old magic is at work again, and, from now on, I shall never fail to have it within reach. I am speaking of *Les Hauts de Haute-Vent, Wuthering Heights* (translated by the Lacretelle brothers, as *Haute-Plainte*). How tremendously alive I still find the dwellers on that bleak upland which is surely one of the gloomiest landscapes in all English literature. I have only to read the names of those tormented creatures to see them, each and all, vividly before me. The wild Heathcliff stands head and shoulders above the other characters. Orpheus was not more beset by suppliant ghosts than am I. But I push them aside in my eagerness to reach another, or, if I let them delay me for a few moments, it is with no intention of listening to their story once again, but because I want to question them about Emily Brontë, the embittered young woman who conceived them, and could not but carry within herself all that was gnawing at the inhabitants of Wuthering Heights, since she lived most of her short life in the Yorkshire vicarage, the windows of which looked on to a graveyard, and, beyond that to the wind-swept moors where she wandered as often as she could break free from household duties, while her dissipated brother, Branwell, got himself gloomily drunk at the inn.

As a child, I used to make short work of a story. I read *Wuthering Heights* in a single day of the summer holidays. Now, I re-read it in a series of little sips. I pause on every page in an attempt to get on the track of a very secretive young woman who died one hundred and eight years ago. But if there ever has been a book which can stand in isolation from its creator, and impose itself upon the reader in its own right, it is surely this, with its catastrophic world in which are imprisoned a small number of damned souls each one of whom is delineated with a fine, hard line. I know that it is foolish to pretend that one can separate passions from their physiological context, from the indeterminate confusion of circumstances. But I have never, on the other hand, doubted that a great book like this has been slowly built up by the successive alluvial deposits of a life, and enriched, day by day, with the author's desires and agonies.

Perhaps, after all, I have no right to be called an artist – as that word is understood today – I, who find nothing to interest me in a book divorced from its writer, in an autonomous production which is just language and nothing more; I, who try, without allowing myself to be discouraged, to feel my way back to the primary source to a work of art, to that spirit from which it leapt fully armed, and in which my young contemporaries do not believe. I obstinately continue with my search, buoyed up by the mad hope of some day holding it quivering between my hands, like the baby hawk which Emily Brontë once found upon the moor, and took back with her to the parsonage. I know that I shall find nothing, but that does not stop me from endlessly circling round Emily's secretive face and tight-pressed lips: not round a book but round a living being.

I burrow, but detest the burrowings of others. I push from me the weighty volume published by Mrs Virginia Moore twenty years ago, which deals at length with the secret of Emily Brontë. She makes use of a key which always more or less turns in the lock when one is studying a human creature who never confided in anybody. According to this author, Emily was obsessed by a strange and gloomy passion which ate away her life in the Haworth parsonage. Since she left a number of poems which, even in translation, sound a note of harrowing despair, there is nothing easier than to attach to them this particular meaning, which is only one of a hundred possible others.

*　　*　　*　　*　　*

In collaboration with her sisters and her brother, Emily had invented an island to which they gave the name of Gondal. For years the Brontë children were engaged in writing a history of the Gondalians and many of Emily's poems have to do with this cycle. Perhaps she wanted to cover up her tracks. Perhaps she helped to create this imaginary world for the sole purpose of setting it between herself and us so that we might lose our way in it.

I do not intend to take any part in this debate: to do so would need a book. I very much doubt whether Mrs Virginia Moore has found out anything about Emily. But I am resuming the search in my own way. I am setting off again, as I once did many years ago, to follow her trail through the creatures of her imagination. I have my own interpretation of the despairing note which sounds in her poems. I know the precise places in *Wuthering Heights* where it is she who is speaking and making a direct confession. I recognize her voice: a moment more, and I shall be pressing her hot and feverish hand.

It is this attitude of mine which shows how old-fashioned I am. I cannot rest content with the surface, and the fact that I shall find nothing to bring back from the depths does not deter me from making the descent. According to M. Maurice Blanchot, if I am to believe his commentator, M. Gaétan Picon, writing in the last number of *Critique*, the language of art gives us access to the ultimate truth of Being. 'And this ultimate truth is only the transcendence of Nothing. The movement for the annihilation of language is evidence of the ontological truth of Nothingness. . . .' The mistrust of, the contempt for, the 'psychological' has its roots in this adherence to the Nothing. All very well to say that it is just a question of technique. It is not technique that divides us. I belong to a generation which believes in man, and in Him of whom man is the unchallengeable witness.

I am not prepared to say whether 'great thoughts come from the heart', but this I know, that great novels like *Wuthering Heights* most certainly do. There is more to it than that. They are the confused projection of that heart which it is given to all of us to confront with our own enigma. For all reading is comparison, confrontation. The little that we know of ourselves is sometimes what has been suggested to us, in a low voice, by some character in a book. The autumn moonlight shines down on the roof of my house, damp with mist, and on that graveyard at Haworth where Emily Brontë was laid to rest on 19 December1848 after having looked at it from her window all her life. There she rests, 'incomparably beyond and above all of us' – as it is written of a young woman, newly dead, in *Wuthering Heights*.

These novels have something more to tell me than what they say. Somebody is hiding behind them. Will the gloomy Heathcliff give into my hands that part of Emily which she wanted to conceal? The psychology of invented characters tells me something about that of a young woman who actually lived. Or, at least, I try to believe that it does. I act as though I believed it.

That is why I feel so far removed from the generation of writers which dates from immediately after my own, for which the word 'psychological' has taken on so pejorative a meaning that any work to which it is applied automatically becomes disqualified. When I was twenty-six and felt irritated by some pronouncement of, some denial enunciated by, Barrès or Bourget, I said to myself: 'When I am their age, I must be careful not to resemble them. I must learn to see and to judge men and things from the angle of the new generation.' That resolve I have not forgotten. I have tried not to be false to it, and perhaps, in matters other than art, I have succeeded. But now that I am a writer who is approaching the end of his days, I find myself alone imbued with that saying of Lacordaire which was graven in my mind when I set out: 'Sooner or later one reaches the point where one is interested only in souls.' I should have preferred him to say 'human beings', because it is the heart of flesh and blood that really matters to me. Through the creatures of *Wuthering Heights* it is the heartbeats of Emily Brontë that I count.

Yet where the essential is concerned I agree with my juniors. For a long time now, ever since the days of my youth, when Dostoievsky occupied the first place among our gods, I have seen clearly that only the simple-minded would think it possible, as Bourget did, to establish a 'chart of moral anatomy'. I knew that the passions of the heart exist in a pure state only in the classical tragedies, and in novels like *Adolphe,* which are so many blue-prints and diagrams.

*　　*　　*　　*　　*

I have been re-reading *Wuthering Heights,* and I shall do so again. I enter, I emerge from, I return to the books of my youth. But I have grown too lazy to make much effort to force an entry into any piece of modern fiction, any one of the 'latest things'.

I am told: 'You really must read it. It's bound to be the next Goncourt prize-winner.' I take it in my hands and weigh it. How thick it is! almost five hundred pages at a rough guess! In order to stimulate my appetite, I ask, as I would have done when I was twenty: 'Is it a love story?' 'No', comes the answer: 'it is a story about elephants.' I could not have sighed more deeply had love been upon the bill of fare. I open it, read ten lines and shut it again. The truth of the matter is that, faced by one more novel, I catch myself in the act of being quite unable to read.

Who would have thought it? Who would have dreamed of saying such a thing? For if, somewhere outside this world, an account has been kept of the number of hours I have wasted in the reading of novels, it would point inevitably to the conclusion that, for a very long time, I preferred fiction to reality.

I remember how, when I first settled in Paris, as soon as I could escape from the École des Chartes, and from all that turned young students into slaves, I never budged from my fire except to eat a hurried meal, and, even then, did not lay aside my book. It was not always one of 'the world's great books', not necessarily a Dostoievsky or a Balzac. The dreary novels of the Naturalist School, such as Huysmans' *En Ménage,* presented no obstacle to my voracious appetite, nor did even the Goncourt brothers' *Charles Demailly* and *Manette Salomon.* I was not particularly discriminating. With me, at that age, an author's name decided me for or against a book. I had a great respect for names, and being both an honest and a credulous reader, I was prepared to treat with reverence all 'geniuses' properly listed as such – and others, too. For I did not miss many of the marginal quotations in the official Market Lists of fame.

I crept out from my reading at dusk, rather like someone waking from a deep sleep, seeking some form of transition which would enable me to pass, without too painful a wrench, from the world of imagination to that of reality. Ahead of me lay night-time Paris with its unending streets.

What, then, has happened to me? In many other ways I find myself not so very different now from what I was half a century ago. What is the obstacle that has plumped itself down between the world of fiction and me, making all future access to it impossible? 'The novels you yourself have written' . . . yes, that, at first sight, seems to be a reasonable explanation. One's own work is substituted for the work of others, one's own characters for their characters. But, on second thoughts, no, since the appetite for novels lasted all through my years of maturity when I was already busy writing books. The reading of fiction continued to eat into my days. It was still the anticipated compensation for my labours. I pushed aside the story I was writing and took refuge in the stories of the masters. Today, I would rather read anything else – a periodical, or any newspaper which could provide me with facts and figures. 'Perhaps it's your age?' No doubt that has something to do with it, but merely to acknowledge the effects of age does not get one much farther.

The truth of the matter is that the invented characters of fiction, like recorded music, come to life only through some element which we ourselves supply. It is we, the readers, who give to these imaginary creatures a setting in time and space somewhere within ourselves, which enables them to move freely and suddenly, to impose their destinies. I realize that, at least in my own case, this time and this space were part and parcel of the life which was opening before me when I was a young man of twenty, the life I had not lived as yet, but was about to live. Novels gave substance to my as yet half-hidden future, and lent to it a succession of different faces. Through the medium of their heroes, I tried myself out in a variety of parts – the successful man, the squalid failure, the lover or the criminal. They revealed to me my own possibilities, I never, at that time, suspected that the play had already begun, and so wasted much time in reading. Such meetings as might have come my way in the outside world would never now take place, because, sitting by a coal-fire in a fifth-floor room in the rue Vaneau, I was substituting the destinies of fictitious persons for my own.

I was not, however, growing any younger. The expanse before me was narrowing, yet, however restricted my life, it was now peopled by living persons and real things. My private destiny was beginning to be intermingled with the universal history of mankind. All the same, the creatures of fiction continued to move and breathe in me, but no longer as prefigurations of my own life. By this time they had turned into points of comparison. How far, at my age, had Rastignac got, or Lucien Leuwen or Dominique? Was I fated to be a failure like Frédéric in *L'Education sentimentale*? For a man approaching maturity, and already producing work of his own, the reading of other men's novels is a way of getting himself into focus, of taking his own measure.

*   *   *   *   *

But as the years pass, and the temporal future shrinks, when the stakes have been laid, the work finished, the copy shown up: when the human adventure is drawing to its close – it is then that the characters of fiction no longer find in us sufficient room to give them freedom of movement. They are caught between the hardened, solidified mass of our past which nothing, from now on, will ever penetrate again, and the death, more or less imminent which will, for such time as remains, be our constant companion. Its shadow is upon us, and the farther we go, the denser does it become.

What purely fictive creatives could spread their wings in so thin an air? They lived upon the hopes of our young years. It was our blood that had flushed their cheeks, and they had thrilled with passions that were ours.

I have reached the time of life when Julien, Fabrice, Dominique and Lucien, brought back from the gulf of the years, have nothing now to give but tedious tales. As I had occasion to point out in connexion with Emily Brontë and *Wuthering Heights,* it is the writers, rather than their books, who still for me have the gift of life, and even then only in so far as they express themselves through the medium of direct confession. I feel drawn to Benjamin Constant, not because he attracts me as a man, but because his *Journal* gives him to me entire. Having come only late in life to D. H. Lawrence, I have never been able to read any of his novels to the end. *The Plumed Serpent* and *Lady Chatterley's Lover* dropped from my hands before I was half-way through them. Yet I greedily devour the copious literature which has grown up round him, the revelations of Catherine Carswell and Dorothy Brett, everything, in fact, which can inform me about the machinations of that ridiculous prophet.

Only creatures of flesh and blood still exist for me in that no-man's-land between the ending of an active life and the nothingness which goes by the name of old age. That is why the doctrine of 'commitment' seems to me to be basically false. I feel no more 'committed' now than I did in the old days. All that has happened is that I can no longer interpose a fiction between myself and reality. No amount of reading can any longer take my mind from what remains to me of life, from the presence within me of the advance-party of death, from those political activities which, day by day, bear witness to the savagery and stupidity of mankind. To be sure, it is still possible for me to find some quiet siding where I may vegetate and forget, like one of those 'veteran' locomotives which are still kept under a low head of steam, or used to push empty trucks. No matter . . . nothing can alter the fact that old men are irremediably forced back on what is happening now, or what really happened in the past (which explains why it is they are such gluttons for books about history). They can find no refuge in the future, because for them there is no future, and because that void so suited for the proliferation of the seductive inventions of the novelist, which constituted their natural field of activity, has become the unalterable past.

There is nothing for the ageing man to look forward to but what he has believed, or pretended to believe, if he calls himself a be-liever: nothing but that unimaginable reality which is like the sea, hidden by one last dune, the muttering of which he cannot hear. If there existed anywhere a world of fiction which took account of eternity, I would still have recourse to it, and it is true that even now I find myself re-reading Huysmans' *En Route*. But that book is little more than a journal thinly disguised as a novel. What other names come to mind? Bernanos? Graham Greene? But all fiction, even when it does admit the active presence in this world of Grace, merely has the effect of cheapening a truth which is not the product of invention, and is beyond the power of words to communicate.

It is the poets, really, and only the poets who are in tune with the closing years of a life, the reason being that poetry, like religion, breaks through appearances and goes straight to what *is*. Not that I am readier to open the poets than the novelists. In my case, memory is a substitute for books. My needs are met by all that I have harvested in the course of a long life, by all the poetry that echoes in my brain, by what I have collected for myself, from the 'Selections' of my boyhood, on. There are poems in that Treasury completely forgotten today, which have, for me alone, a secret resonance which will endure for as long as I am capable of thought.

The people we have known in novels are not wholly dead for us: they, too, belong to our past, but have been eclipsed by the men and women of flesh and blood whom we have known and loved. In even the least fulfilled of lives there are more Natashas, Dominiques and Luciens than in the complete works of all the great novelists, and they have this advantage over the Natashas, the Dominiques and the Luciens, that they have been, and still are, not the products of the imagination, but real persons. The past wraps us round in a darkness starred with the faces of those who have actually existed, and the source of that light which has made them shine, may, perhaps, still burn brightly on the further side of death.

Thus, the nearer we come to our latter end, the more do we detach ourselves from faces and from riddles that we may attain to the reality which words once both expressed and concealed. If it be nothingness, then we realize that the silence into which our modern poets seem to be drifting is but the harbinger of a nothingness in which all appearances are doomed to dissolution. If, on the other hand, those loved ones who have preceded us into the domain of death, still live eternally, if each passing minute brings us nearer to them, in that case we gladly accept the disappearance of all fiction. Now is the time to shut the books and, if ever there is time to look at films, now we must put an end to all that pullulation of images. In youth art is nothing but the shadow of things to come: but, in the evening of life, when there exists for us no longer any earthly future, can art speak to us of that eternity which already we are contemplating? To this contemplation only music is attuned. But it, too, will soon give place to silence, to that living silence which, here below, is the beginning of eternity.

★ ★ ★ ★ ★

If I no longer make my way into any tale invented by my contemporaries, I have an insatiable appetite for their published recollections. Their memories are mine.

If I have found a bitter pleasure in André Salmon's *Souvenirs sans fin,* that is because the journey he describes is the one that I was making, at about the same time. We must, to within a very few years, be exact contemporaries. I greedily devoured his memoirs, as I do all the log-books of the same voyage which I am near now to completing. What a resurrection of ourselves is the record of the lives of others!

God knows I am about as far removed as anybody could be, by the circumstances of birth and education, by beliefs, friendships and tastes, from the author of *Calumet* and *Tendres Canailles*. That does not matter: what does is that we have, both of us, floated on the surface of the same period, and been spattered by the same breaking rollers. The things of which he tells, I too have seen, but from somewhat farther off, and, as it were, through the window of a first-class compartment, from which I have, now and then, descended, though without prowling over-much around Montmartre, or entering very deeply into its bohemian world. I remember that once, but only once, I crossed Max Jacob's threshold in the rue Gabrielle, and was horrified by the spectacle which his room presented, not because it was poor, but because it was sordid, a suspect place, if ever there was one, the sort of lair into which the female ushers the prey she has picked up alive and kicking in the street.

It is not the possession, or lack, of money that dictates the material setting of our lives. No one could well have been more poverty-stricken than André Lafon, no lodging more stark than his. But even in a basement-room, at the Lycée Carnot, with the help of a few odds and ends of curtains and coverings, a stoneware jar, a few reproductions of his favourite pictures and a brass lamp, he could construct that universe of silence and dreams outside which he would have been unable to breathe. Our social environment does not always impose its atmosphere. What lies deepest in every man secretes the kind of universe he needs.

In Salmon's book, Alain Fournier provides another example of this truth. Salmon knew him well. They worked together on *Paris-Journal*, but it would be an understatement to say that their lives were very different and their friends poles apart. With his starched collar and his neat tie, Alain Fournier was not much addicted to the company of 'bad-eggs'. For the half-dreamed, half-lived idyll of this son of a country schoolmaster, somebody like Clara d'Ellébeuse or Nerval's Sylvie was a constant necessity. Le Grand Meaulnes, the peasant lad, sets out to conquer, first the middle-class home of the narrator, then the ancient château deep hidden in its enchanted park. He presses his face to the window of the *salon* where ancestral portraits brood eternally over the children grouped under the lamp round an album of Gustave Doré's pictures. Le Grand Meaulnes, his back turned on all that was sordid, vulgar, tainted, moved through his elaborate and magic world to the holocaust of 1914.

Very different – but I am thinking now of an earlier period, between 1894 and 1986, the year of my First Communion – was Jean de Tinan (I have been reminded of him by another book) – that son of a patrician family, who showed his origins in a thousand and one little refinements, but spent most of his time in the Latin Quarter, with what his master, Barrès, called 'a proletariat of students and tarts'. The aristocratic Tinan delighted, as did Pierre Louÿs, in the company of the prostitutes of the rue d'Harcourt, that same rue d'Harcourt which Colette Willy also frequented, jealously kept to heel by her forty-year-old husband for whom every young writer was a possible 'nigger in the wood pile' (Jean de Tinan was one of them: *Maitresse d'esthètes* and *Un vilain monsieur* are by him). Colette remembered how she had admired, and been half in love with him, and describes him in that luscious style of hers which endows young people with a fruity succulence: 'Sensitive and gentle, with hands rather more delicate than are proper in a man, and black curly hair above a forehead which gave an air of nobility to his whole face. . . .'

I have taken that passage from Colette's volume of memoirs: *Mes apprentissages*. There is a very special pleasure in reading, at one and the same time, the recollections of one's several contemporaries. We follow the same person through the *Memoirs* of one writer and the private *Journal* of another, and see him at various periods of his life, and in different lights.

It was just about the time when I was finishing Salmon's book, and turning back to *Mes apprentissages,* that I discovered in Jean Delay's study of Gide's early life, some fragments of an unpublished journal kept by Pierre Louÿs. The adolescent of the Alsace School, who dazzled the young Gide, and was, in turn, dazzled by him, is shown to us by Colette as he was three years later, when he and his dear Tinan were, both of them, objects of adoration to the ladies of the rue d'Harcourt.

That nocturnal progress from tart to tart, described for us in *Penses-tu réussir?* brought Jean de Tinan to an early death. Rue Bréda, Place Saint-Georges, rue Nôtre-Dame-de-Lorette, rue Faubourg-Montmartre, rue Drouot, rue de Richelieu, Place du Carrousel, the Quays . . . down all those streets Tinan walked every night, just before dawn. Discreet and prudent though I was, how often have I not followed that same route, in my thin evening pumps. Between the banked roof-tops flowed the river of the paling sky. I would hail a passing bus if its lamps were blue, knowing that its stables were at Vaugirard, and that it could drop me on the way home.

But to go back to what I was saying: it is our own temperaments, our own characters, and not the possession or the lack of money which determine the background of our lives, and create the environment the young poet needs in which he utters his first newborn wail. If I have not myself belonged to the Bohemia of letters, if I remained a prudent young man, that, I know, is not a reason for boasting. I have no intention of repeating the Pharisee's prayer. For this withdrawal, this need to dwell apart, to set a defensive wall between ourselves and others is due not to any virtue, but to weakness.

Barrès found that out, infrequently though he let his fine eyes rest on me. 'Hesitation about pushing out from the shore,' he wrote, after reading my *Mains jointes:* 'a vague feeling of regret for an easy, padded, warm childhood, filled with affection. . . . But a time comes when it is necessary to escape from that uncertain April of the feelings, to become a man. One has got to take a line, to move freely where it leads, and not stagnate.' Have I ever stopped stagnating? The enchanted house and park of Le Grand Meaulnes was my native homeland, and I have never broken the bonds that tie me to it. All through my life I have changed from one garden to another, replacing with a new and modest paradise the lost Eden of childhood. Even today I only leave the beech-woods of the Seine et Oise to seek again the refuge of my native Garonne hornbeam. I shall leave the mahogany furnished room in which I am writing these lines only to have once more about me the shelter of that rosewood drawing room where, in a month's time, I shall be breathing once again the vinous fragrance of the casks waiting to be filled, and be reminded of the grapes that were harvested long, long ago. Between myself and life, between me and my fellow-men, in spite of happenings and wars and bereavements, I shall endlessly rebuild like a laborious ant whom no amount of destruction can discourage that safe refuge from which, at intervals, I distribute criticism, advice and blame to others.

The fact remains, however, that it was in Max Jacob's wretched room, one day, that the Lord appeared, and that from it, every morning, Max climbed to the Sacré-Coeur for early Mass. From it he went away to Saint-Benoît-sur-Loire where, in due time, French gendarmes came looking for him.

★ ★ ★ ★ ★

I fled the grandeur and wretchedness of Montmartre, though never unmindful of what it had to give. Thither went Picasso, driven by an inner need, that he might be fertilized by those who, before his time, had suffered within the leprous but invigorating squalor of its walls: Van Gogh, Toulouse-Lautrec. It is with no patronizing eye that I presume to judge the Bohemia which was Salmon's homeland. No real frontier divides those who have made the same journey. Salmon conjures up few, if any faces, with which I am not familiar. There is scarcely an incident in his life which does not sound an echo in my own.

Whether products of Bohemia, or children of the comfortable classes, the poets of any one generation show, in their twentieth year, much the same colouring, and, if I may say so, share much the same sufferings:

Ce n'est ni la nuit ni l'aube
Mais cette heure où, dans Paris,
Les rôdeurs et les chiens maigres
Errent dans un brouillard gris.

L'heure amère des poetes
Qui se sentent tristement
Portés sur l'aile inquiète
Du désordre et du tourment.

Thus sang the young Carco. Turbulence and torment were the common patrimony of all of us, bohemians and bourgeois alike, of fifty years ago: and those who still survive squat round the same dying embers.

VI

MAN SOON grows accustomed to his own miracles. I find it not at all surprising that the great virtuosos, an Yves Nat, for instance, or a Walter Gieseking, who have departed from this earth, or rather have returned to it, there to sleep for ever, can now come back, responsive to my wish, and play for me alone, as once they played to hushed crowds in all the capitals of the world. Their inspired hands create the enchantment I demand of them, fleshless hands today, a congregation of light bones, still crossed perhaps above the hideous emptiness in which a heart once beat, though of that heart nothing now remains. Yet, I can hear it beating once again, as I sit writing in this room (Yves Nat is playing Schumann's Fantasia in C major).

The presence of those authors whom we love, who have been our life-long companions, whose books will be our help and comfort until we, too, are no more, is of a different order. They are not present as the musician is present. No matter how often we read a dead author, he is no longer there. His work survives, becomes a substitute for him. It is a record, in which the various entries turn often to his disadvantage, and accuse him, according to the hands into which he falls. No matter how great the posthumous fame of a writer may be, he is no longer capable of speaking in his own defence. Even if the radio can still make us hear him, it is a ghost who speaks, as defenceless as he would have been had he lived before the invention of the phonograph.

Had Benjamin Constant's voice been recorded, that would not have saved him from being at the mercy of those who, today, accuse him. He is given into their hands by reason of that very work which sides with his accusers; above all, by that *Journal* in which he so constantly gives evidence against himself. We who love him for his lucidity of mind, and all the more because he brought that clarity of vision to bear upon himself and tells us only what it reveals, because such unimpeachable evidence leaves us disarmed before those who hate him.

For a number of years before his novel was published, he was in the habit of giving readings from *Adolphe* in the *salons*. Those readings, had they been captured and inscribed upon a record, would have been of no service to him now. On the contrary, could we hear his voice the effect of it would be only to add to what his accusers have to bring against him. So – they would say – it wasn't enough for him to betray both his mistress and himself in his book. He must take pleasure in retailing these matters to a listening public! I imagine that the grandiloquence proper to the age in which he lived, restored to us through the medium of a gramophone, would make his character seem only the more odious. We should remember that, at Coppet, he took the role of Pyrrhus to Madame de Stael's Hermione in a performance of *Andromaque,* and that almost before the make-up was off, they resumed that same argument which Racine had helped them to transpose for the guests – now perhaps listening at the door of the room in which the two illustrious lovers were beginning once again to bandy their horrible abuse.

The fate of the writer, delivered after his death into the hands of his enemies, holds no anticipatory terrors, because he does not realize how much his work will reveal to his disadvantage when he is no longer there. Besides, he is a bad judge of his own work, and unaware that it contains, not only what he had so carefully prepared for publication, but everything that has come from his pen, all the secret confidences, all the letters written when he was least himself, when, as we say, he had let himself get out of hand.

Fortunate the musician to whom I am listening! True, I thought first of the interpreter, now dead, but still alive for me, thanks to a record. But records are fragile things and can deteriorate. Sooner or later they will disappear, even though technical improvements now make it possible to re-record them. No doubt the physical presence of Schnabel, of Gieseking, of Yves Nat in this room in

77

the country where those who are no longer alive still play to me, is the most wonderful of all the miracles of our time: but it makes me overlook another, which belongs to all the ages – that peculiar privilege which music enjoys of not surviving as a poem does, or any other literary product. In fact, it does not survive at all: it goes on living.

A book is delivered into our hands, and, with the book, its author. In the case of music, however, it is we who are delivered. The music enters into us and acts upon us like a developing fluid and 'brings out' all that is most secret in ourselves, but without any sense of heartbreak, or, if heartbreak there is, it is sweet.

We do not call Mozart to account. If his letters reveal to us someone who bears no resemblance to his music, who has not the same dimensions, that matters little. The music is what matters. It wipes out the account to be rendered, it dismisses the case against him. That is so with all musicians, or at least, with all pure musicians. It does not altogether hold true for Wagner, who in his own way was a theorist, a philosopher and a poet. But it is only in so far as he is not a musician that he becomes vulnerable. Almost all the other great composers slip through our fingers. It is we who never manage to slip through theirs.

* * * * *

No injustice lasts in music. What great musician has ever been exposed to the insults heaped on Racine? I know of none who runs the risk of being treated as Benjamin Constant or Vigny have been treated. When I was a young man, we spoke rather slightingly of Beethoven. Cocteau (I think it was) made fun of music 'to which we can listen only with our heads in our hands' – which is precisely the type of music I have always loved. I must confess that it is only by making a considerable effort that I can enjoy that other sort which tries to make me hear or see things other than myself: fountains, clouds or gardens in the rain.

Music must be listened to with one's head in one's hands, because it compels us to see nothing but what it has discovered in ourselves, which is always the most secret, the most deeply buried, part of us, to which it sometimes leads us from outside. Mozart plays on us this trick in his work which is all vibrant with the *Kleine Nachtmusik*. But the garden path along which he directs our footsteps lies far from the torches and the festival, beneath a canopy of sleeping leaves, so distant from the serenades that we no longer hear them. A little while, and we shall go back. We know how the music will end in a wild saraband, but for the moment we are alone with him and with ourselves. Someone in the darkness is sobbing on a bench; it may be Mozart, it may be we ourselves. It is both. We should like to stay there for ever, though the music is almost unendurable. But already he is leading us by the hand, back to where the masked figures are playing at hide and seek, chasing one another through the night-enveloped garden. An enormous statue looks down on them, but they do not see it: a pale colossus, the Commander. The sound of hunting horns reaches us through the maze in which we are lost, and their notes are intermingled with the wailing of the *Requiem*. No matter what Mozart may do, no matter whither he leads us, we follow hard upon his heels. He escapes from our clutching hands, but how shall we escape from him?

If death took almost all of them in the flower of their youth (Mozart was still far from his fortieth year, Schubert was barely thirty, Weber and Schumann and Mendelssohn) . . . that was perhaps the price they had to pay for the privilege they now enjoy. They live on in our midst, more invulnerable than the angels, and we, from below, look up at them with humble adoration, we, the poor writers whose destiny unfurls under the double sign of insult and oblivion.

*　　*　　*　　*　　*

Poor writers, indeed! My friend Henri Guillemin was created and brought into this world to cure us of the absurd ambition which most men have, not to be forgotten after they have left this world. He has so cruel a way of dealing with the illustrious dead, that we should all feel little envious of their doubtful immortality. But the dread of one day falling into the terrible hands of a critic of his type is not sufficient to rid my contemporaries of their obsession, for it can scarcely be doubted that it is the hope of living on in human memory that leads so many young people of both sexes to yield to the temptation of scribbling.

No matter how small may be their chance of producing work that will outlive them, it is that they have in mind, even when they believe that they are thinking only of the next Goncourt Prize. They would not sweat so much blood were it not that they are buoyed up by the hope of becoming immortal. That, really, is what releases the never-ending flood of manuscripts and printed matter which swamps the publishers' offices, pours over the critics' tables, and is responsible for the tide of books with uncut pages which inundates our homes.

And this is where Henri Guillemin comes in. He is not like other critics. He is less concerned with airing his views on the work with which he may be dealing, than to give us his reasons for the love or hatred which a specific author may arouse in him. He has invented the *critique-passion* which is comparable with *amour-passion*. Since he excels in his chosen field it never occurs to us to blame him, until the moment comes when he lays destructive hands upon some great dead author whom we happen to venerate. When that happens, we hit back.

His books make me reflect on the fate in store for us when we shall be no longer here to defend ourselves. When I think of what people dare to say about a living man who has plunged into the sea of politics, even though he can use a pen to advantage, and is known to be a doughty fighter, I cannot but shudder when I think of what his adversaries will do to him when he has left the stage, and his 'act' is over.

I am well aware that politics are not much concerned with the dead, and that party hatred is soon deflected from the buried. The writer, however, who has stirred angry passions in his lifetime, is still a target even when he is in his grave. What a temptation to his surviving foes is a man who remains still vulnerable after his death! He leaves a trail of written evidence against himself, not only what is known already, but other evidence as well which becomes the happy hunting-ground for sportsmen of the type of Guillemin – private letters, personal note-books, jottings of every kind, all the accumulations from childhood to old age which pile up in the drawers of those for whom writing has been a natural mode of expression.

Those who join with enthusiasm in this game of literary exhumation frequently do so out of love. Love was the driving force in the case of the Stendhalian Martineau or the Balzacian Bouteron. But Guillemin, who is also capable of being inspired by love (Rousseau, Lamartine and Hugo were, turn and turn about, the recipients of his favours, though the latter has been the victim of a number of atrocious indiscretions from his pen) Guillemin it is who has invented the sport of hunting down manuscript material from a desire to strike at the reputations of certain men, now dead, who, like Alfred de Vigny, had good reason to think that they would be for ever out of the reach of scurrilous attacks.

My friend, no doubt, would protest that the search for damaging manuscripts is not, in his case, inspired by hostility, but, on the contrary, creates it. It is not because Vigny was antipathetic to him that he has presented us with certain discoveries which he has made: it is those discoveries, rather, that have made Vigny odious. The point is arguable, but I, personally, do not believe a word of his defence. The antipathy pre-dated the researches. It was political in its origins and pointed the way for Guillemin the hunter to the documents of which his hatred felt the need.

This is crystal-clear in the case of Vigny. No other critic would have found in Guillemin's discoveries the slightest reason for reviling the poet. This is the danger that lies in wait for us beyond the grave: we may fall into Guillemin's hands – we and our lives: not our lives as we have known them, as they have emerged for us in memory, but that vast expanse of them, unknown even to ourselves, which has been lost in oblivion.

For of what we have done, even of what we have been, almost nothing now remains in our memories. This can be proved by an experiment which it is open to anyone after the age of fifty to try for himself: let him re-read some letter, chosen at random, which was written to him fifty years ago by a mother, a fiancée or a friend. He will find in it allusions which no longer have any meaning for him to persons and events about whom and about which he now knows nothing.

Only the other day I read in a bookseller's catalogue, a letter of mine, there reproduced, which was dated 1913, that is to say forty-six years ago. I recognized the handwriting as being mine, beyond any doubt, as also, alas! the turgid style in which I was then luxuriating. But of the addressee I have not the slightest recollection, nor of the reasons which had led me to write the letter. Before an author gets to the point of saying to himself: 'Be careful, now! anything you put on paper may be published some day!' he must have achieved some degree of notoriety. What may he not have accumulated from the days, especially, of his early youth?

Oh, well, we can afford to laugh. We shall no longer be there to suffer from these indiscretions. The worst that can happen is that no Guillemin should feel prompted to embark upon the necessary research!

★   ★   ★   ★   ★

This sort of risk makes us writers sensitive to another aspect of our failure to impose ourselves. It is not our work that has survived, but our persons, our lives, in so far as these things are likely to provide the erudite with an occasion for amusement or for scandal. But in the case of Vigny, it is his work which has remained alive and provides a triumphant answer to the charges made against him by Guillemin. The author of *Eloa* and of *Destinées* could not conceivably have been a police-spy, and, of course, never was.

It is not Vigny's admirers who throw down the most effective challenge to his accuser, but *La Maison du berger*. The worst of fates for a writer is to survive *minus* his works, *minus* 'the best evidence he can give that he is worthy of respect'. The true glory is to be blotted out as a person by the effulgence of the work we have done, and thus to escape from the clutches of a Guillemin. That true glory has been accorded to Shakespeare, who is invulnerable because his identity is unknown.

★   ★   ★   ★   ★

Benjamin Constant is, I agree, more open to attack than Vigny. He wrote, on one occasion, that he was impatient to be 'done with life, and so be free from my fellow-men.' He forgot that for a small number death is no protection, and that of the small number he would always be one, perhaps the most exposed of them all and the most helpless. Others had been careful to prepare in advance – and how cleverly! – their posthumous reputation. For Rousseau, for Chateaubriand, for Gide, this was their chief concern – apart from physical pleasure. If they laid claim to having confessed everything, to have underlined the worst in themselves, it was in order to make themselves invulnerable, to leave nothing behind them for the literary excavator to ferret out.

Rosseau was the first of these pharisees to realize that the pharisee's prayer was his best defence. Gide developed to perfection the technique of glorifying all that blackens a man's life. On the eve of his death, Benjamin Constant, famous and misunderstood, cared nothing for posterity. 'He eats his vegetable soup, sets off for the gaming-house' – and then dies, heedless of what he may be leaving behind him in the way of evidence for the prosecution, first and foremost of that *Journal,* kept for his private eye alone, and filled to bursting with all those things which the common run of men most execrate in one of their fellows.

We can dredge, almost at random, all the sixty years of his existence and be sure of bringing to the surface something squalid, something shameful. Helvetius, Laclos, Restif had been the first masters of the little motherless prodigy whom one of his tutors introduced into a house of ill-fame. As far back as he could remember, there was no time he could recall when he was pure. A scandal and a disgrace since his earliest childhood, Benjamin Constant never had the protection enjoyed by other victims of Henri Guillemin, and, notably, the most recent of them, Alfred de Vigny, the protection given by those incorruptible presences who stand guard over the memory of all great poets. In Vigny's case these were not only the figures of Eloa and Satan, of Moses or of Samson. The vast stretch of silent country lying outside the doorway of the 'house on wheels', the dense heath in which the *Maison du berger* sinks almost to its springs, the same heath on which the wolf in *La Mort du loup* stretches himself out and dies without a sound (I think I know the precise spot, and whenever I drive back from Malagar I salute it: it is on the borderline between Guyenne and Angoulmois) – that world I know so well keeps safe his sacred memory from every outrage, every insult.

But who shall protect Benjamin Constant from his eternal enemies? They belong to a race which hates, and will ever hate, him through the centuries. Who will stand up against his judges? Certainly no one of comparable genius, that is very certain: no one but himself, since Adolphe is still he. But who is he?

Among the trophies of the chase brought back by Guillemin, is a letter written by Benjamin to the Directory, demanding the banishment of the curé of Luzarches (but asking that he shall not be arrested, still less deported. On the contrary, he insists that no harm shall be done him. And who, if it comes to that, dear Guillemin, has told you that the priest ever was deported or that Benjamin did not intervene to save him?). So mean an action does not ring true of the man as we know him, at every moment of his life, in his *Journal intime,* the only journal, to my knowledge, with the single exception of Stendhal's, which does not contain a single thought set down deliberately for the eyes of posterity. The author of that horrible request bears no resemblance to the dazzling young man who was loved by so many women who had one common feature, nobility of heart and superiority of mind. Benjamin could hardly have lacked the same characteristic, he who was understood and pardoned only by creatures formed in an heroic mould. I do not deny that the young rake was a believer in that dissociation of pleasure and love which Gide later elevated into a doctrine. No matter. The women who haunt a man's life are its best judges. I do not shut my eyes to the fact that some were prostitutes, but it is those who truly loved him that count: Mme de Charrière, Julie Talma, Anna Lindsay, Mme de Staël, Rosalie de Constant. Tell me by whom you have been loved, and I will tell you the manner of man you are.

What, then, was Benjamin Constant? We complain that literary criticism today has been invaded by the theorists. We must admit, however, that the author of *Adolphe* and the *Journal intime* does force us to consider, from the very beginning, the mystery of personality. Against whom, Guillemin, my dear friend, did you think you were fighting when you declared war against Constant? No man has ever delivered himself to the same extent into the hands of his enemies. When at every moment of his life he looks at himself, questions himself, at whom is he looking, whom is he questioning? Anyone in particular? I should hesitate to say: he is no one, yet his name is legion.

At certain periods when he and Mme de Staël were making themselves a laughing-stock in the eyes of all Europe, he regarded himself as a monster. 'When I return to Paris, I draw up the windows of my carriage so as not to be pointed at.' This erratic trifler, this sentimental Buridan's ass, who let himself die between Minette and Charlotte, Germaine and Amélie: he who could write: 'So whimsical is that wretched thing, the heart, that we turn, with a feeling of terrible desolation, from those to be with whom should spell delight . . .' – and again: 'There is something sacred about the heart which suffers because it loves . . .' was also the Huguenot patrician from Lausanne, calculating and astute, who, after a succession of failures, ultimately raised himself to an eminence far above anything he had dreamed might be possible, and died in an apotheosis of fame. But when we look at him in the evening of his days, what do we see? The renowned champion of political liberty, the great aristocrat who was once an object of worship to the poor and unprivileged, neglected and gloomy at the end, transformed into the living image of My Lord l'Arsouille. I cannot forget the terrible thing he said in the last year of his life – 'I eat my vegetable soup and set off for the gaming-house.'

This was the youthful reader of Helvetius and Laclos; this old man who had set all Paris on the wrong track, taking off, at night, the mask he had so carefully modelled, trying to get the feel of life in a shady gambling-hell.

Sainte-Beuve briefly dismisses Benjamin Constant's duplicity. Multiplicity would have been the better word. When he writes to

Mme de Charrière: 'Do not let yourself be made uneasy by my situation. I assure you I get as much amusement from it as I should were it another's' – he shows that he is already conscious of this infirmity. His life is never wholly his own, and his destiny remains external to himself each time he looks at, and submits to it. This very inconsistency explains his frantic efforts to become 'somebody'. Because he is endlessly engaged in taking himself to pieces, he must be continually re-adjusting, well or ill, the social framework within which he undulates and drifts. This young and ambitious man has to obey the law of self-preservation. If he is not for ever moving forward, he becomes diluted. That is not peculiar to him: nobody *cuts a figure* in the world unless he can indulge the illusion that he already is one.

Guillemin presents him to us as a man greedy for money and speculating on the *biens nationaux*, whereas, in fact, no one was ever more contemptuous of money than this gambler. He lent it, borrowed it and lost it with complete irresponsibility. Money was certainly necessary to him even if he had to wheedle it out of his mistress, because there was no political career to be had in Switzerland, and since he could bloom only in the atmosphere of high politics, he had to become a French landowner and acquire French nationality. With him the question did not arise of choosing between Paris and some other capital: there was no other theatre built to his measure. Only on the banks of the Seine was that drama of politics played which still goes on after a century and a half. But it is a long time, God knows, since a Benjamin has been a member of the company.

*   *   *   *   *

If he foreshadows the Rastignacs and the Marsays of the *Comédie humaine,* it is only very superficially. There is a vast difference between him and the beasts of prey of Balzac's jungle. He who wrote: 'Circumstances count for very little, character is what matters . . .': he who could say of Adolphe that he 'was the victim of his own character, and had wasted his gifts by letting himself be guided only by whims and fancies of which nervous irritability was the sole motive-power' – knew, and always had known, that it was, for him, a question of life or death not to resemble *Adolphe* in this, but to lay down a line and follow it, to fix on a career and see it through to the end. There was one thing he never did, and that was to confuse himself with his ambitions. He had always been aware that there was no choice possible between 'being a some-body' – as parents say to their sons, and being nothing.

And become somebody he did. But was he ever convinced that he was really the character he had set up to be '*dans les siècles et dans les cieux*'? Did he believe that he had become himself, or that, on the contrary, there was another Benjamin Constant, very different from the man whose bier the people of Paris escorted through the streets?

Our belief in personality is closely bound up with our idea of the soul. Towards the end, this young atheist was beginning to catch a glimmer of light under the heavy door which had always stood between him and God. But did he ever really believe that he had a soul? Our souls exist from the moment of our birth, but it is for us to keep them alive, to make it possible for them to expand, or to debase and lose them altogether. Our souls are both what we are and what we become. In the case of those who do not believe in the light, I cannot say where that kernel is situated round which their personalities take shape, nor do I know what process of crystallization allowed Benjamin Constant to make a convincing blend of the sorry Adolphe, the illustrious personage he played in Paris, Mme de Staël's hangman-lover, the tormented adorer of Mme Récamier, and the womanizer.

Yet we who love him know that he was a very definite person, one, moreover, who had made himself proof against all the poisons of the eighteenth century in its decline, though they had been injected into his blood from his earliest years. What of nobility and feeling survived in Benjamin Constant demands the respectful attention even of those who have no love for him. Of Guillemin I would ask: is it for you, a scorner if ever there was one, of political Christianity and fashionable catholicism, to wax indignant over the hatred inspired in this child of those religious dissidents who had been driven from France by a church which he had never known from the inside, of whose secret sanctity, seemingly disgraced by the many flagrant examples of simony under the French monarchy on the eve of the Revolution, he was wholly ignorant? You know as well as I do that what Benjamin Constant hated deserved to be hated, and that it was impossible for him, without the miracle of Grace, to see behind the golden glitter of the crumbling façade, the countenance of the living Christ.

All the same, in 1822, he publicly denounced, in terms to which today Guillemin might well have appended his own name, those 'ultras' who had made themselves oppressors in the name of Christ: 'What the whole of an enlightened nation is demanding, these men are opposing, and denying in the name of religion. They are invoking a belief which is primarily the champion of equality and justice, and using it to the advantage of privilege and iniquity.'

A piece of play-acting? Who is in a position to say that? The great book, now forgotten, which he regarded as his life's work, that *History of Religions* at which he had laboured, at intervals, for so long, is proof that however licentious, Constant had never been indifferent to God, nor had ever despaired of finding Him. From the years of his maturity onwards, he had shown himself to be the enemy of dogma, but only because he believed that it prevented men like himself from finding their way to the Divine. Besides, we should not forget that on at least two occasions, once when he met his Langalerie cousins, and once when he was with the Baroness Krüdner, he gave evidence of tolerance for religiosity even in its crudest form.

If Benjamin Constant, as I have said, was to believe in himself, it was essential that he should believe in his soul. And he did believe in it. He, who had never encountered God upon his road, at least once in his life encountered a human soul. He saw it emerge, living, from a body in ruins. This incident took place at the bedside of the dying Julie Talma on 8 May 1805.

*   *   *   *   *

Here, I think, I must repeat all that the *Journal intime* tells us of Benjamin Constant's *tête-à-tête* with death. All I hope is that

Guillemin will meditate upon it, and also upon *La lettre sur Julie*. The strangest feature of the whole affair is that Julie Talma, a true child of her times, was a militant atheist, and that the spectacle of a pagan death-bed should have produced in Benjamin the sensation of a spiritual presence which was quite independent of the body. Julie passed from life to death without her spirit being in any way damaged. 'Her organs are destroyed, her eyes no longer see, she breathes only with the greatest difficulty. She cannot so much as raise her arm, and yet the intellectual part of herself is entirely unaffected. But why, if it comes to that, should death, which is only the complement of her bodily weakness, harm it? ... I have looked on death unafraid, for I have seen nothing sufficiently violent to shatter that intelligence.'

All Julie's other friends had gone away. Only Benjamin was with her. 'She was incapable of speech, and indicated by signs such help as she thought it still possible for me to give her. She pressed my hand in token of her gratitude. It was thus that she breathed her last.'

This noble woman gave back to him in her death more than she had ever received from him. To this sceptic, so brilliant, so defenceless, so detached from everything and so greedy, to this feeble tormentor who could not bear the sight of tears which he himself had caused to flow, who had no faith in ideas, in human beings or in himself, and who felt for himself almost as much contempt as other men inspired in him, Julie offered the evidence of a soul hesitating and trembling on the brink of the already abandoned flesh. On 8 May 1805 Benjamin saw what it is given to very few of us to see: that a corpse is quite literally an empty shell. The body knows corruptions as soon as the spirit leaves it – the spirit, that part of ourselves which is different from the millions of human beings who have preceded, and will come after us, the soul which can be saved or lost, but not destroyed. We are individuals only in so far as it exists, and as we are aware that it exists. Man is spirit or he is nothing.

* * * * *

I have had to concede something to the implacable Guillemin!

I am forced to the conclusion that Benjamin Constant did denounce to the Directory, and cause the arrest of, the *curé* of Luzarches, who had opposed his candidature. I had argued that there was nothing to prove the deportation of the priest, or that Benjamin Constant had not intervened on his behalf. It did not take Guillemin six weeks to snatch from me even that soft cushion of doubt. He has flaunted his triumph. 'The abbé Oudaille' – he wrote to me – 'was most certainly sentenced to deportation. His name appears on the list of priests who arrived at Rochefort between the 6th and 17th Nivoise, year V, and died in Guiana on the 7th Vendémiaire, Year VII.'

★   ★   ★   ★   ★

After that, I am prepared to believe anything of anybody. That Benjamin Constant was capable of doing the most unpleasant things, I already knew, but did not love him any less on that account. Admittedly, there is something peculiarly horrible in his behaviour on this occasion: all the same, I intend to look this denunciation straight in the face. It was abominable, but it was not unparalleled. We have, all of us, lived through a time when this type of vileness was only too common. The four years of the Occupation, and those immediately following it, showed very clearly what hatred, whether political or racial, combined with self interest and greed, can make men write and do who pride themselves on their integrity.

The same holds true today.... There are colleagues of mine, far from being 'swine' – as Sartre would call them – who have condoned the most cowardly and hypocritical judicial crimes known to history. In all countries, including France, Stalin found philosophers, writers and professional 'wise men' who, knowing what he was doing, gave him the approbation of silence and, so far as I know, not one of them has even now repented.

In the year VI, Benjamin Constant knew nothing of historical determinism, but a good deal about 'reasons of State'. What, after all, was this *curé* called Oudaille? A conspirator who had come within reach of the law. That, no doubt, is true, but it is also true that it would be to Constant's advantage to see him out of the way.

It is that I cannot forgive. He was not carried away by political fervour: he was just getting rid of an obstacle. Somebody was in his way, and he had him sent to penal servitude and death. Yet, the author of his crime was none other than Benjamin Constant, a man I hold dear, who said to his cousin, Rosalie – 'The only thing in life that I really respect, is suffering' . . . the friend who, when Mme de Staël was made almost distraught by the death of her father, wrote in his *Journal* that passage which Charles Du Bos so loved to quote: 'I know nobody but myself who always tends to feel more for others than for himself, because pity pursues me, and because the pain which would soon die down were only I concerned, becomes increasingly intensified when I think that someone else needs consolation.' He forced himself to weep over the death of M. Necker, and refused to enjoy himself 'because I feel that Mme de Staël has need, not only of my consolation, but of my sufferings.'

Did the man who wrote that, and really meant what he said – he can be very hard on himself in his *Journal,* and is so lacking in charity towards himself that we find it difficult to believe him when he exhibits the nobler sides of his nature – never let his mind dwell on the convict with the consecrated hands whom he had denounced and destroyed? Did the poor priest of Luzarches sometimes walk in his clumsy shoes through Adolphe's dreams? Who can say? The *Cahier rouge* deals with a period well anterior to the year VI, and Benjamin Constant did not begin, until eight years later, to keep his *Journal intime.* I have felt compelled to re-read it in the hope of finding some trace, as it were, of those half obliterated footsteps. So far, I have come only on this. Under the date, 20 April 1804, Constant describes the hanging of an Englishwoman. He writes: 'There was, in the details of her sufferings, from the start of the proceedings until their end, such a depth of human misery, that I felt as though I were being held fast in an icy grip.' He deplores 'the iron hand of an implacable society'. I wonder if, at that moment, he remembered how he, himself, had, on one occasion, furnished the victim?

* * * * *

The few letters, or fragments of letters, from Constant to Rosalie, which date from the year V, show us a Benjamin uniquely concerned with acquiring French nationality, and worming his way into the political life of our great country. 'To be or not to be.' He would never be anything if he did not accomplish something in politics.

With what fury and frenzy did he who could so quickly detach himself from anyone or anything, pursue the prey until he had run it down! Woe to him who might try to bar the way! What was this outlawed priest to him? A mere impostor whom the Directory was fully justified in destroying. Benjamin, at that time, was just thirty, which is for most men the age of ferocity. Ferocious was, in any case, what he seemed to be even to the woman who was fondest of him. During that year VI, Julie Talma wrote to him: 'There is something of falseness in you. You are not so good as you have tried to persuade me.'

But, once sated, disgusted, detached, once himself again, the plaything of the women who loved him, and disarmed by their sufferings, he may sometimes have spared a thought for his victim. How could he who wrote, when talking of the prisons of Venice, that he was in a hurry to be done with life that he might the sooner escape from his fellow-men, live comfortably with the memory of a certain *curé* of Luzarches who had not escaped from the young Benjamin Constant? He could be moved to pity by the sorrows of his mistresses, but not by that ignominious death. He could reproach himself for those tears, but not for that blood. What are the torments of love compared with what a reviled and tortured prisoner endures in his flesh and in his heart? Romantic despair no longer touches me. When a man grows old, he finds that to suffer through those we love is, in the order of humanity, a form of happiness. He no longer commiserates with Werther, but with the persecuted innocent.

*   *   *   *   *

The corpse which, thanks to Guillemin, floats, after a century and a half, upon the surface of an illustrious life, rises, in fact, from depths within ourselves. We believe that we are capable of benevolence, because we are capable of tenderness. Desire and lust we cover up under the name of love – but we have been accomplices, many and many a time, in the martyrdom of the *curé* of Luzarches, even if we have not, in our own persons, denounced him and handed him over to the authorities. The transient censure of so great a part of the human race has only too often had no effect on those who communicate with us only through the heart. I cannot help remembering Bourget's outburst to Paléologue during the Dreyfus Affair: 'I could spit on justice!' The novelist, who was beside himself because a young diplomat had told what he knew in defence of a Jew unjustly accused, was the same man who waxed lachrymose, in his books, over the fate of nobly-born adulteresses, and claimed, in the closing lines of *Un crime d'amour*, that the only faith he professed was 'the religion of human suffering'! But that equivocal attitude lies deep in all of us, and we only forgive Benjamin Constant for what he did, that we may have the right to forgive ourselves for what we have allowed others to do.

No Guillemin will ever be able to adduce proof that the *curé* of Luzarches was waiting for Benjamin Constant, one night, when he came from the gaming-house, or that the author of *Adolphe* sometimes walked in company with that sad ghost along the muddy pavements, in the darkness of the Paris of those days. . . . But we can rest assured that the *abbé* Oudaille prayed for his executioner. The corpse of the priest has floated to the surface, but who knows whether his soul did not remain deep drowned in the destiny of Benjamin Constant? It was, maybe, that soul which inspired Constant to write, in a letter to Prosper de Barante, ten years later: 'My religion contains just two points: to will what God wills, that is to say to do homage to Him in my heart, and to deny nothing, that is to say to do homage to him in the spirit.'

I am wrong. If Benjamin had written that under the inspiration of the *curé* of Luzarches, he would have added a third: 'to know oneself a sinner and a criminal in the eyes of God and to live in hope of His grace.' But that was something of which the master of self-knowledge was least capable. It avails nothing to feel horror when we look into ourselves if, at the same time, we do not look at the marks in the hands and feet, and side of the innocent victim who died upon the Cross which the convict of Rochefort and Guiana carried with him to his death.

VII

WHEN I was young I used to take much pleasure in the Goncourts' *Journal*. Why is it, then, that I had no sooner opened the new edition, than I let it drop from my hands? I was well aware, in the old days, that there was a silly side to the brothers, that they were capable of swallowing any story, no matter how 'tall'. Long before Proust produced his pastiche of the *Journal,* I was in the habit of reading it when I wanted a good laugh. The highly self-conscious and precious style which the Goncourts invented, shimmers on the surface of things and links them with a certain type of painter, of which there has never been a shortage, who sees everything and understands nothing. Still, they were the authors of *Charles Demailly, Manette Salomon* and *Germinie Lacerteux.* What should I think of those novels if I were to read them again now? I cannot say. Forty years ago I found them highly original, as I still find brilliant their idea of assuring their survival through the medium of an Academy, unparalleled anywhere else, which is mainly recruited – believe it or not – from the ranks of professional men of letters.

But all this does not alter the fact that I have shut the *Journal,* never to open it again. One flounders and splashes in its shallows, and only too soon touches bottom. And then, there are all those Gavarni stupidities, not one of which we are spared.

*   *   *   *   *

So much for that. What I find a great deal more interesting is that in the very same year in which the two young magpies began accumulating their treasure of flashy and bogus facts – most of them trivial and untrue – another young man, just back from his travels in the East, 'entered', as another might enter an enclosed

Order, the novel which he was determined to write, and had decided never more to leave. *Bovary* was no sooner started than it became a monk's cell, an ascetic discipline.

At first sight, Gustave Flaubert may not seem to be very different from the Goncourts, whose elder he was by only a very few years. Every period has its own peculiar silliness which is shared by those born into it, big and small alike, even when some of them have genius. Our own is magnified to infinity by magazines, the radio and the movies. Yet, I cannot help feeling surprised that the Goncourts' record of their second-rate orgies was so exactly like the pictures conjured up by Emma Bovary and Homais the chemist, of student life in Paris. It comes to this, that 'reality' in 1851 was precisely like what those fools imagined it to be, and as stupid as they were. Certain utterances of Flaubert in that year, taken very seriously at the time, might well figure in a 'Dictionary of Commonplaces' for use by artists of his general type. To me they seem no less nonsensical than the statements he put into Homais' mouth.

All the same, to pass from the Goncourts to Flaubert at thirty, is to cross an immeasurable gulf. We take off from the world of 'literary gents' and land in the story of a man who was about to enter into a six-year long struggle with sentences – the story of a human destiny.

★   ★   ★   ★   ★

I had opened the first volume of the *Letters* with the idea of refreshing my memory about the sources of *Madame Bovary*. Perhaps I should have gone further back than the letter of October, 1851, in which he writes to Louise Colet: 'It is the very devil of a job to get my novel going. I am worrying like mad, and all to no purpose, and a word-itch has got me scratching like the devil. . . . What a clumsy oar a pen makes! . . .' But these letters of his are not just documents meant for consultation: they have the breath of life: a flesh and blood man speaks in them, and not merely a man-of-letters, though their writer never claimed to be anything else, and was primarily concerned in getting on with *Bovary*.

The all-in wrestling bout with this, that or the other sentence, the moiling and toiling far into the night, the intervals of exhausted collapse after sweating blood over fifteen lines which he would then delete just as dawn was breaking, the whole ridiculous ascetic paraphernalia – was the only form of self-discipline possible for him, just as Croisset was the only monastic cell in which he could live the life of a recluse, because he was one of those unfortunates who can reach perfection only in the manipulation of words. At a later date, *Salammbô* and the *Temptation* were, like gigantic tumours, to be the outward and visible sign of the disease of a mysticism without an object.

I know, of course, about the 'thorn in the flesh' which necessitated this life of solitary confinement. 'The devil's blow' which struck down this handsome young man when he was driving one day along the Pont-Audemer road, was nothing less than epilepsy, according to the perfidious Du Camp, 'that accursed evil, that nervous collapse which Paracelsus called "the human earthquake"'.

Long before that, in the days of puberty, he had suffered from strange obsessions. He remembered the exact spot in a Paris street, the specific shop-window in front of which he had, like Atys, determined to castrate himself, he, the young god who, when at the age of seventeen, he had attended the first performance of *Ruy Blas* in the Rouen theatre, had, by his appearance, laid a spell on all the eyes turned to him!

At the time when he was getting into his stride with Bovary, he had just become reconciled with Louise Collet, after a long estrangement, though Croisset was still forbidden ground for her. Their meetings at Mantes took place only every other month. How can we avoid being led to the conclusion that his unending battle with words, the spisodes of which filled his letters to her, served as a pretext for keeping that insatiable Muse at a distance?

When this strange creature – who had counted the heart-beats of many famous men, and loved to rest her beautiful head on the breasts of all the Institut – dared to defy the injunction and, in 1855, forced her way into Croisset, Flaubert drove her out of the house, and out of his life so brutally that Mme Flaubert, who had never consented to meet her son's mistress, was shocked and scandal-ized. 'This mania of yours about words has sucked your heart dry!' But she was wrong to reproach him in this way. His heart was still what it had always been. Such love as the young Flaubert had been capable of feeling was not of the kind that can ever become the be-all and the end-all of a life. Words had not sucked him dry: but, to a heart hungering and thirsting for the absolute, they could offer only a shadow of that purity, the phantom of that perfection, to which he aspired, for which he was born and which, so he thought, did not exist.

*   *   *   *   *

When we think that we have drained to the dregs an author who has been our life-long companion, though we may never open again the books which have, in some sort, become a part of our-selves, scattered passages from them still live on in our memory where all the pleasure that a much-loved writer has given us lies hoarded and condensed. Of this hard and scornful Flaubert it is those passages expressive of tender affection which float like clouds in my private sky, high above *Salammbô* and *Saint Antoine* – those gloomy reconstructions, those opera-settings, those dead cities which have never been alive. What passages? Those, for example, which occur in the letters which he wrote after the deaths of the two beings he most loved, Alfred Le Poittevin, and his sister, Caroline – and one in particular from a letter which, in the early days of their liaison, Louise Colet received from him. It was written on the night of the 8th August, 1846. 'The sky is stainless, the moon is shining bright. I can hear the sailors singing as they raise the anchors in readiness to sail on the next tide. Not a cloud is visible, not a breath of wind is stirring. The shore is white under the moon, black in the shadows. The moths are fluttering round my candle-flames, and the night-scents are drifting through my open win-dows. How is it with you? Are you sleeping?'

Even more than his letters, the last chapter of *L'Education senti-mentale,* which I once knew by heart, glows in my mind with a fire which time has not diminished, but, on the contrary, has strength-ened.

It is in the meshes of that chapter that the true Flaubert is caught and held. He who had determined never again to give himself away through the medium of an invented character, who was Madame Bovary only in spite of himself, and without deliberate transposition on his part, because *L'Education* was flesh of his flesh and bone of his bone, because there, in that final cry, that final sob, he was drawing on the feelings of his own heart, substituted himself for Frédéric, and Mme Arnoux for Mme Schlésinger, the adoration of his youth, a woman older than himself, mistress and mother, on whose breast he had always hoped to find a refuge from the hated world. When he could no longer count upon that hope, what was there left? Writing. But what exactly does that mean? No man can screen himself all his life long with words from a gloomy world from which God has withdrawn. All that the receding tide has left upon the barren shore is a mass of dead jelly-fish, the residue of a humanity which has lost its soul: Bouvard and Pécuchet. There is nothing left to do but dine with the Princesse Mathilde, to enjoy oneself at Magny's, to throw tall stories to the Goncourts, like pilchards to a couple of seals.

*　　*　　*　　*　　*

There is nothing left but silence. It has always been a matter of surprise to me that people should find anything mysterious in the fact that Racine fell silent after *Phèdre* (*Esther* and *Athalie* were commissioned pieces), and Rimbaud after *Une saison en enfer*. Surely this refuge of silence when an author has no more to say than he has said already, is the most natural thing in the world, the most reasonable, and not worth wasting a moment on. Yet we look upon these poets as oddities, almost as monsters.

We men of letters too often get into the habit of forgetting that it is many years since we had anything of value to communicate to others. The old mills go on turning in a vacuum long after there is no grain left to grind, if, indeed, there ever was any. All that remains of us is a mechanical ticking which the ear no longer notices, which only death will stop.

The ear no longer notices it, yet so accustomed have we grown to the sound, that the silence of a single man of letters produces a shock. That is an understatement: it gives rise to a scandal which never dies down. Rimbaud stopped writing eighty years ago, and we have not even yet got over it. The fact is that writing is our job – and what a job! The author who chooses to write no more tramples under foot the privilege, the wonderful prerogative of keeping himself fed and fat (provided, as the saying goes, he has 'made a name for himself'). It is his duty to write, irrespective of the quality of the work he produces, or even of its reality. The sower is paid for making his 'majestic gestures' even though he scatters no seed.

'We who work to please the public' . . . that phrase of Racine's in his dedicatory letter to Madame, shows how far we have come since his day. It is no longer a question of pleasing, or not pleasing the public, but of keeping alive. That is something the public understands. It thinks it reasonable enough that those whose job is writing should go on writing, even if the content of their work is emptiness, for no better reason than that writing and publishing are their means of earning a livelihood. After *Phèdre*, Racine had reason to fear that he was giving less pleasure to his public. That is a problem which we, today, do not have to face. What crowned and laurelled author would deny his right to go on producing books and making money out of them?

There was a time, it is true – I am thinking of the 'century of enlightenment' – when the writer no longer wrote to please, but to instruct. Since then there has been no fear of silence on Parnassus. It is difficult to imagine Jean-Jacques, or Voltaire or Diderot ever getting tired of telling men what they should think of Man who is born good, of society which corrupts him, of laws, of the advances of science, of superstitition. The Encyclopaedists produced children who, even today, rally to attack certain abuses. Every period has its Calas scandals. Nevertheless, the type of literature which demands and denounces is less and less practised among us. This is not the place to ask why, but it would be a mistake to feel too confident that the Muse of Indignation is incapable of giving those who are eloquent about nothing a chance to say something.

But do they say nothing, or what goes by the name of nothing? To maintain that, would be to exaggerate. Most modern authors find in themselves the matter of their books, and I am underestimating the prevalence of that passion for self-portraiture (warts included), that aftermath of romanticism, which is now in its last, 'post-gidian' phase. When other subjects fail, there is always that to fall back on, that 'I' from which we can always squeeze a few more drops, though the fruit has been pressed so hard and so constantly that there is little left but the rind.

If writers of this type lived a thousand years, it is doubtful whether they would ever stop talking about themselves. It sometimes seems as though the very fact that the subject has been sucked dry acts as a form of stimulant, so that the amassing of so many piles of books with so little in them is, for them, in itself a pleasure. It is as though this very emptiness entitles them to claim the rank of great classics.

But it is time for me to remember that there does exist another branch of the writing family which is a living contradiction of what I have been saying, because it manifests an aggressively professed vocation of silence. This is especially true of the poets. They are moving towards silence. From poem to poem the words are becoming progressively more widely spaced upon the page, and it looks as though this process will continue until there are no words left at all. The volume of blank pages, which Virginia Woolf described as 'my best book', was not the product of an author who had nothing more to say (those who have nothing to say, go on for ever saying it) but of one who had too much, and when I say too much, I mean in terms of quality rather than quantity. It was from Stéphane Mallarmé that the poets caught this sickness of retention, and the infusion of cherry-stalks which poor Francis Jammes administered, has not provided a cure. Since Mallarmé died we have been presented with the spectacle of his descendants making a series of nose-dives –

Sur le vide papier que la blancheur défend

– and so successfully does the paper defend itself, that their lips have become permanently sealed. That is what comes of being an idolater: that is the dead-end to which the cult of the word which is no Word, leads. But is not anything better than the creaking of outworn engines running in a void? Should we not prefer this sterility rich with intention?

It is essential that we discriminate between *varieties* of silence. In poetry, silence is not a state to which the poet finds himself reduced: it is the source of his inspiration. Every great work is born of silence and returns to it. Even in the case of an old writer who has outlived himself, and can no longer produce anything of importance, his work, in so far as it may be said to exist at all, lives on in his silence. A *roman fleuve,* buzzing with inspired chit-chat is, nevertheless, born of silence, and is gorged with it. To be sure of this, one has only to read the first words of *Du côté de chez Swann:* '*Longtemps je me suis couché de bonne heure . . .*' – which at once plunge us into the accumulated silence of the sleepless nights and waking dreams of childhood. Just as the Rhône runs through Lake Léman, so does a river of silence run through the Combray countryside and the Guermantes' salon without mingling with them. That is the miracle of Proust.

With many poets, the work never breaks wholly free from silence, but remains more than ever caught up in it. In Maurice de Guérin each word is heavily charged with an inner silence. In his *Journal* he notes: 'What every man of a certain temperament, withdrawn rather than superior, guards with the greatest vigilance, is the secret of his soul and the inward habit of his thinking. I love the god Harpocrates with his finger to his lips.'

With Maurice de Guérin, the work is both a breaking and a confirmation of silence. When I was a young man, I found in André Lafon, a poetry which sprang from a self-communion and an interior contemplation as carefully sustained and as jealously guarded as in Maurice de Guérin, though his lyric outpouring, obscured, as it were, and muted, bore no resemblance to *Le Centaure* where de Guérin's tone becomes a crystal goblet for the retention of the precious liquid of a certain kind of silence.

The solidity, the hardness, the transparency of Racine's and of

Valéry's poetry, has silence at its very heart. It is that which separates the verse of both from that of the romantics, which is noisy, whereas theirs is heavily loaded with silence. The same is true of Maurice de Guérin's prose in which we hear a young man holding his tongue. This may seem absurd, but it must be said. Even if death had not closed his lips before he was thirty, the 'finger of the god Harpocrates' would alone have sufficed for his song to be broken off short, or, rather, to become identified with that murmur deep within himself from which it would never again be detached.

External circumstances do nothing more than provide a pretext for the poet who has chosen silence. The failure of *Phèdre,* the *Affaire des Poisons,* Jansenist scruples, the ambition of a historiographer – which, according to the literary pundits combined to put an end to Racine's career as a dramatist, probably weighed no heavier in the scale than did the squalid Brussels episode in the life of Rimbaud. For, not only did they cease from writing, but disowned (this is true especially of Rimbaud) what they had written already, as though that part of themselves, their work, had betrayed them. It is as though by disowning it, they were hoping to recover their integrity, and to restore to the inner self its true identity.

'You have had the great happiness of being able to express yourself' – people frequently say to a writer: 'your work will be your witness.' But is that true? Who can say with certainty whether what we have externalized, what we call our 'work', has not left us for ever the poorer, whether, in fact, the writer is not a being who has been irreparably mutilated? Perhaps Arthur Rimbaud, when he lapsed into silence, was really searching for that part of himself which he had wrenched from its roots and thrown for fodder to our generation. A writer is, fundamentally, a man who has lost his shadow, or, rather, when he has outlived himself and is nothing but an old mill churning out words, he has become a shadow which has lost its man.

*   *   *   *   *

The law of silence was operative in the destiny of Proust.

If we are to believe M. Bernard de Fallois, between the moment when Marcel Proust's first attempt at novel writing, *Jean Santeuil*, dribbled away into the sands, and his starting to work on *Du côté de chez Swann*, there was a period of despair. He had abandoned the book, of which the high spots, even at a time when he was concentrating all his attention on Sainte-Beuve, were beginning to be apparent. In any case, his despair cannot have been absolute. Had this abandonment been final, and without hope of remission, then, undoubtedly, he would not have survived the shock. The internal analysis of his work reveals distress rather than despair. The wonderful landfall was very close, and he could already sniff the wafted scents of a country which would for ever have remained undiscovered if the sickly little Marcel had not exerted himself to reach it. How could he have taken the failure lying down? After all, the years of discouragement were the years of gestation, more than half unconscious though it was when things were at their worst. But he must, very soon, have felt stirring within himself the world to which he was to give birth.

I feel sure that he could not have borne to go on living had he abandoned for good and all his struggle to regain time lost. It will, no doubt, be argued against this that others *do* resign themselves to the necessity of abandoning a pet scheme, and put up with that necessity until their dying day. 'How many remarkable men there must be about whom we shall never know!' Actually, there can be few things rarer than a great work still-born. I have never yet, myself, experienced any such misgiving. To be sure, I get letters, almost every day, in which I can detect something similar. But it is rarely that the writers of these letters are concerned about the creating of some specific work. What mostly worries them is the thought that they may fail to 'make good' in a literary career. These 'prentice-writers are mostly obsessed by the idea that they are incapable of fulfilling their own appointed destiny, and not by the feeling that they may fail to bring into the light of discovery virgin lands which will otherwise vanish with them, unrevealed, when they die.

To the question: 'Why do you write?' – it was (I think) the

young Paul Morand who replied: 'Because I want to be rich and famous.' As is almost always the case with this sort of a 'wise-crack', the answer served the purpose of making palatable a truth which was too bitter to be swallowed without sugar in the coating. Even with the greatest, if we look closely enough, the revelation of a world in the Balzacian or Proustian sense is not at issue. André Gide never revealed anything but André Gide. From the very first line of *Les Cahiers d'André Walter* to the final confession of *Ainsi soit-il,* he explored no other continent than himself.

Every human being is, of course, a world to himself – a world, unfortunately, in which he soon gets bored in the case of Y or Z, but not of André Gide. This comment of mine does not in the least diminish his stature. It is impossible, however, to deny that there is a difference in size. The Proust who says 'I', in *A la recherche du temps perdu* expresses himself in that work no less completely than Gide does in his. But he is not the sole object, nor is he just one character among a host of others. He should, rather, be compared to a developing-tray in which the faces and the passions of a whole society already three-quarters engulfed, come to the surface, his own among them, not in isolation but incorporated in the magma of a family, of a world, of an epoch, dead in time, but caught and held in the continuum of a masterpiece.

Gide was too clear-sighted not to be aware of this difference. When he started on *Les Faux Monnayeurs,* he persuaded himself that he was at last getting away from André Gide and creating a universe peopled by other beings than himself. That does not alter the fact that if we turn back to *Les Faux Monnayeurs* now, we have only to read the first few pages to realize that the book gets what life it has only from the character of Edouard, who is Gide, and from the young adolescents at whom Edouard looks with Gide's eyes. The fascinating *Journal d'Edouard* winds like a stream of living water through a world of puppets.

The intelligence of the novelist observes but it does not reveal. Proust, who was no less intelligent than Gide, does not, as he does, try to see clearly in order to understand clearly. Proust's world, held suspended in flavours and in smells, is not so much understood as regained. Even when he turned from these mysterious processes of discovery, a tangle of secret paths led him back to them all through the days when he was despairing of ever becoming a novelist. It was enough for him to recover a whiff of scent, the hint of a particular sound, the jolting of a cart, a vague glimpse of light under his bedroom door. This sick man, confined within four walls, is the nodal point of a thousand invisible avenues along which the living past moves back into the present.

During the whole of the time when he had abandoned the pursuit of his destiny, and was writing of Balzac or Sainte-Beuve, everything combined to make him aware of all that part of his work which did not derive from his critical intelligence. Though he had come to believe that he would die without having said what he most wanted to say, that the secret which he held in trust would vanish with him, he was all the time asserting that the desired revelation could be brought about only by acting in obedience to those laws which only he could apply. Nothing was farther from his mind than the idea, so prevalent today among novelists, that there exists a method and a system of disciplines which are of value in and for themselves. He held that the solitude of the novelist is total. He has no precursors: in him everything begins again. When, at last, he was ready to write the opening line of *Du côté de chez Swann* the first day of a creation dawned which no one else could ever repeat: because the novel is not a science, and contains in itself no law which is universally valid.

Proust wrote 'The End' on the last page of *Le Temps retrouvé,* and then he died. Had he lived on after the completion of his work, what would he have done? Since he had an admirable critical intelligence which might well have been enlisted by the research workers of two continents, he could have embarked on a new career, but it would have been on a wholly different level from that on which he had set out on his search for Time Lost. Certain great creative artists there have been who, like Balzac, could extend their work indefinitely, since there is no final stopping place in the Human Comedy. Had Balzac lived for a hundred years, he would have gone on writing, if his creative faculty had remained undiminished, because the matter in which he was working was a river for which there could be no end except in death. But when the creator has within him, as Proust had, a completed monument, on no matter how vast a scale, with its proportions, its balance, its harmony duly established, then, the work once finished, there is nothing for him to do but to take refuge in silence. True, he might have gone on providing his book with fresh nourishment by injecting new elements into it – that would have been in accordance with the Proustian method of composition – but in that case his work, contained as it now is within banks, would have become an enormous river in spate.

But for the writer who has completed his creative labours, there is always the possibility of putting his pen to good uses if he has other interests than those of a purely aesthetic kind. The older I grow, the less discrepancy do I find, in a writer's life, between the work to be done and the side to be taken. If he is so fortunate to outlive his fictions, then is the time for him to choose either retirement, which is something to which everybody has a right, and which I should never blame anyone for preferring – or to become a fighter if he believes in a truth which calls upon him to defend it, at every level and in every way, no matter how mixed with impurities it may seem to be.

As I see it, the only thing that should be forbidden to the superannuated writer, who has chosen neither retirement nor the taking of sides, is that he should consider 'talking when he has nothing to talk about' as a reputable way of life. To do that is to transgress both the law of silence and the law of commitment. The harvest is gathered in: the grain is stored – if grain there be – but the old threshing-machine goes on whirring. The printed columns appear and disappear, achieving the miracle (for it is a miracle where words are concerned) of meaning absolutely nothing, meandering like rivers of nothingness through this age in which we live – an age crowded with happenings, revolutions and crimes. Our world is obliterated in them.

VIII

EACH AUTUMN I go back to Paris a few days too soon, so that I never see the netting of the wood-pigeons. Saint Luke – whose feast is on 18 October, presides over the great round-up. But my cousin, the sportsman, has more confidence in Saint Simon – not the author of the *Mémoires,* but that Canaanite, one of the Twelve, whose day is the 28th.

That does not alter the fact, that by Saint Michael's day, at the end of September, my cousin has everything ready, the decoys all planted in the tree-tops and connected with the hut by an arrangement of long strings within easy reach of his hands. Already he sits perched on the raised seat from which he can command the whole of the oak plantation. With his face turned to the north, he gazes patiently at the vast avenues contrived among the pines, long strips of sky down which the wood-pigeons will come. These rivers of sky all converge on the patch of ground where everything is prepared to attract the birds, who will be thirsty after their long journey. Grain and water they will see; but the treacherous nets remain invisible. The decoys, operated by a method brought to perfection by generations of sportsmen, produce a sound like that of the wings of a pigeon alighting and settling. Down a tunnel connecting the hut with the prepared patch of ground, a bird, called the 'poulet', trained and held ready, but, above all, kept hungry, will be released to attract the hesitant visitors who will see him peaceably pecking.

The wood-pigeons have not yet put in an appearance. But my cousin is the type of lover who arrives first at the rendezvous. He is far too early, but he does not mind. To wait for what one loves is already to possess it. Does he never quit and go home? He has spent the winter months in lopping the young oaks which might otherwise obscure the watcher's field of vision.

No, waiting never bores him. Nothing bores this sportsman whose whole life is spent in watching. It is not yet day when he gets up. He goes down alone into the dark kitchen, the smell of which I can conjure up in imagination, the accumulated odours of everything which has been cooked there, over a slow fire, from generation to generation. He makes coffee with his own hands, and waits for the dawn.

I doubt whether he ever reads. One book, and one only, takes the place, for him, of all others – that small world of underbrush from which he never raises his eyes. When I walk at his side, I watch him. He can read that world of his like a printed page, or, rather, like a musical score, each note of which he can interpret. Not a creature can move, not a wild-boar, not a buck, not even a wood-cock, but he knows and recognizes. His eye can detect the black-headed mushroom when it is barely visible above the drifts of dead leaves.

If he raises his eyes, it is because the time has come to consult the sky when it becomes the road down which the first of the loved ones will show themselves. These prowlers of the first days work singly. They are daring birds who have gone ahead as an advance guard, and their capture is precious to the sportsman, who is always in need of decoys. No sooner has he encouraged them to settle, than he imitates the throaty cooing of their kind, and so lures the travellers on to captivity and death with a song of tenderness and passion.

I have never been a sportsman. As a boy I did not care much whether the pigeons came or not. I had a book in my game-bag, almost always a volume of Balzac, in an edition which had be-longed to my father, and dated from Balzac's life-time, with titles not all of which appear in the *Collected Works*. Our own bird-catching was a much more rustic affair than my cousin's, and also carried on at a far greater distance, in the depths of a remote and wild stretch of heath, under ancient oaks, the praises of which I remember that I have sung in *Le Mystère Frontenac*. They disappeared in the last of the forest fires – 'started by ill-disposed persons'. Men murder trees as well as their fellows.

My books preserve, for me alone, the memory of certain very secret places where, in the autumns of my boyhood, I experienced that waiting and that watching which allowed me to share in the instinctive life of primitive man.

My cousin, as I have said, when he stayed from dawn till dusk in his listening-post, opened that score which spared him the necessity of ever reading anything else. Smells and sounds, clouds, the barking of a dog, a whistle, all had for him a perfectly definite meaning. The divinatory science of the Augurs has passed to this last heir to a tiny world which I greatly loved when I was a child.

My cousin does not know the extent of my knowledge about him and his son. One Thursday, sixty years ago, I went to the Fair at Villandraut, and stayed with my great-aunt, who was his great-great-grandmother. I know from which side of the family the son came who did not inherit his father's passion for sport. He does not realize how many of the dead I recognize in him! He is no more than twenty, but he rises from the great deeps of the years.

This starting of the pigeon-netting before the 15th October – at which I have never seen a single bird caught – becomes for me, therefore, a 'trapping' of a quite different order, or, rather, not a trapping at all, but a descent into the underworld from whence I bring back that Eurydice who is for ever being lost again, the childhood which is still a living thing, and will be till I draw my last breath.

The day on which I turn up in response to my cousin's invitation, I leave behind me a torrid Malagar where the sounds of the grape-harvest and the heady smell of the vats are also things that rise from the depths of my childhood. . . . But Malagar is still closely linked to my present. It was no mere accident which led the Academicians of Stockholm to see to it that the name of my old home should figure on the Diploma of the Nobel Prize. At Malagar the garlanded writer occupies a very much larger space than the adolescent who many, many years ago sat on this same bench, writing the verses of *Les Mains Jointes*.

* * * * *

No sooner have I left Langon and taken the Villandraut road leading to Sauterne, than I enter a very different world. It was once mine, and is so no longer. I have to take only a few steps where my cousin lies in wait, to feel myself caught in the old enchantment. I whistle to announce my coming, fearful lest a flight may have settled. The cry of the sportsman tells me that I may move forward. I make my way to the very centre of the magic, the perhaps baleful, wood. How can I be sure? This forest does not know me, not I it.

When I pluck up courage enough to push on as far as Saint-Symphorien, and to enter the park, now somewhat neglected, where my schoolboy holidays were spent, I no longer fear that an evil spell will fall upon me from the black branches stretched above my head in blessing. Many of the pines in the park have long been dead, and more are dying every day. The equinoctial gales lay low those of them whose hearts have been eaten away. But the survivors know me, and the oak which was the adoration of my youth, remembers the warmth of my hand, of my lips, of my cheek when I repeat those lines which my brother the *abbé* addressed to it when he was young, which no one knew but I: *Old oak which often saw me seek the comfort of thy shade, weep muted tears for all the love that will not come again.* . . .

✶   ✶   ✶   ✶   ✶

But my cousin's forest knows nothing of me, or not that part of it where he goes trapping pigeons. For more than one 'property' contained within his innumerable acres, comes from 'my side' of the family, and my father, as a child, spent his holidays not far from Uzeste, in the shadow of the oaks, hundreds of years old, at Pieuchon, which is so dear to my cousin, and once belonged to a common ancestor. There he has maintained a strange and sacred grove where he forbids the cutting of even the smallest branch. A very deep-seated religious feeling, surviving from long buried ages, has inspired in him this primitive cult which the christian in me does not oppose.

If I could choose the place of my death, I should like, as soon as the priest had given me the Sacraments, and gone away, to stretch myself upon the ground, not far from the sacred oak in the park at Saint-Symphorien, and feel beneath my hands, for the last time, the dry bracken, the moss, the carpet of pine-needles and bark, the new-thrusting mushrooms. The sounds of the cow-bells and the Angelus would reach my ears above the mournful ground-bass of the pines which never cease their moaning. For the forest of Les Landes echoes the sea's vast turbulence, and will do till the day comes when fire destroys it.

Back once again at Malagar, I look from the terrace, in the evening light, at the forest I have so recently left behind me, and at the immense army of dark trees standing ranged against the sky. At this very hour, no doubt, my cousin is bringing his decoy birds down to earth, and making them drink and eat their fill.

I think that if I set out to find the spot where, as a schoolboy, I went bird-trapping well beyond Saint-Symphorien, hard by la Teychouère marsh, I almost certainly should not recognize it. The pines have probably grown up again, unplanned and ragged, where the ancient oaks which long ago, perhaps, watched the flocks of my shepherd ancestors pass by, stood sentinel above our rustic hut. But they have since been burned alive, and nothing of them now remains but those last pages of *Le Mystère Frontenac* which they inspired, and still are dear to me because of them.

*　　*　　*　　*　　*

Back in Paris. On this Day of the Dead it is a note at the bottom of a page in Daniel Halévy's *Mariage de Proudhon,* which gives direction to my thoughts. Burgille-sur-Ognon, the village of Franche-Comté – where Proudhon's mother was born, and he had still kept a cottage – today contains no more than a hundred and thirty inhabitants. Like so many of the villages of the old France, it is slowly dying.

One of my colleagues who recently paid me the customary call of those who are candidates for the Academy, has the good fortune to live in a small Béarn commune. He tells me that the population has been halved since he was a child.

There are some *départements,* for instance, Gers and Ariège, which are rapidly becoming deserts, deserts inhabited by the dead. The abandoned graveyards of old villages crowd about the churches which, too, are dead. Some there are which, perhaps for the first time in a thousand years, see no one any longer kneeling at their graves. No one ever more will visit them. The decline of our countryside is primarily due to the drying up of that peasant source from which Proudhon came, and, for that matter, all of us. Such little genius as we have has been its gift.

If these deserted fields no longer nourish men today, it is not because they have no nourishment to give, nor because peasant frugality is a lost virtue. But their fruits rot where they lie. In the Gironde, the little riverside ports where the English once came for the wine they loved so much, have nothing any longer to show but a few decrepit landing stages now left high and dry. That 'ease of communication' of which the free-traders of the nineteenth century hoped so much, no longer serves the cause of trade. Consequently, the populations have drifted away, not always Paris-ward, nor even to the local market town. There is always to be found, some kilometres from the villages, a saw-mill, a cartridge factory, or, as in my own district, an American camp. The small-holders leave their vines to 'make a living out of the Americans', at Poteau, in the great stretch of heath bordering the road from Bazas to Mont-de-Marsan, where mysterious activities are carried on behind barbed-wire fences.

'La Terre qui meurt' is the title of a book by René Bazin. But the abandoned fields do not die. They are waiting for the men to return. A day will come when the page written by the generations before our own through many centuries of history will be scarcely legible. The humble little romanesque churches, already falling into disrepair, are the capitals which will long stand out from a text now half effaced. It will take many more hundreds of years for the earth to cover them, but, when it does, their stones will be mingled with the bones of those forgotten fathers who will never again be remembered at any Day of the Dead.

★　　★　　★　　★　　★

To damn the present and to praise the past is one of the absurdities which comes with increasing years. God knows, I have little liking for the 'golden age' in which I grew up, the songs of which I used to hum when I was twenty. Even then, I found them ugly. I was always, I confess, unresponsive to the Montmartre poetry of Dorgelès and Carco. Montmartre seemed to me, even then, to be a dirty, sordid quarter of the town, though I remember making, as we all did, a pilgrimage to Max Jacob's room.

The source of poetry did not bubble up for me from those slum pavements. Young Parisian though I was, the holidays, as in my schooldays, sent me back to the two-faced Cybele who had born and suckled me. I loved with an equal love her radiant face, which was that of Malagar, and that other, soiled with ashes, which she turns to the moaning, suffering pines.

Uprooted, 'a deraciné' I most surely was, and took pride in the fact, since it was Barrès who had first used the term in this sense. But a young uprooted tree still keeps its roots and the lump of earth in which they are embedded. It seems to me that the provinces of the old days loosed their Rastignacs only one by one upon the capital. But loosed is the wrong word, for the young men went to Paris and returned to the country in the fine months of the year with a rhythm as regular as that of the circulation of the blood. There was nothing remotely resembling the monstrous vacuum-cleaner of today which sucks in human beings in the mass, and so re-establishes a desert where the wolves of the old France, if they came back today, would find no lambs to prey upon, since the flocks have vanished with the men.

★　　★　　★　　★　　★

I have recently been re-reading Hawthorne's *The Scarlet Letter*.

Julien Green, who made the translation of this book, assures us that Nathaniel Hawthorne at eighteen was so beautiful that a gipsy-woman once asked him whether he was an angel or a man. Julien Green, at the same age, had a sombrely angelic look, and that is not the only point of resemblance between the translator and his author. Hawthorne, like Green, lived in a world which was not altogether the one we know, and when in his Introduction to *The Scarlet Letter* he tells us of the mysterious torpor of the life he led, peopled by the persons of his invention: – 'late at night, I sat in the deserted parlour, lighted only by the glimmering coal-fire and the moon . . .' – the picture conjured up might be that of Julien Green at twenty, with his face showing clearly, or fading away, according as the room is drowned in shadow or touched by a brief flicker of firelight, which sets the mahogany armchairs gleaming.

Truth gone mad, and savagely mad, is the best description of the republic of bitter hypocrites who inhabit Hawthorne's story – hypocrites who look backwards to the farther side of the incarnations of the Son of Man, instead of taking it as their terminal point. It was the God of the Jews: not the loving and compassionate God of whom Abraham, our father, spoke, and whose loving-kindness overflows in the Psalms, but the inexorable Being, re-created in their own image by the hair-splitting Jews who abode by the letter of the law whom they worshipped; the God of the bad pharisees – for there were some who were just – the only men whom Christ denounced with a sort of despairing fury. For He who knew all things, knew that the pharisees were, no less than Himself, immortal. He saw them making use of Him down the centuries for the purpose of establishing their reign. *The Scarlet Letter* provides a sinister illustration of how the spirit can be exploited by the pitiless letter.

In the little town, which later grew into Boston, a young woman, whose husband has been absent on a journey for a year, becomes pregnant. Found guilty of the capital crime of adultery, she escapes the death sentence, but not the shame of having to stand in the pillory on the main square of the town. She is also condemned to wear on her breast, for the remainder of her life, a large 'A' which will expose her to the scorn of her fellow-citizens, and be the symbol of a shame from which there can be no escaping. Her seducer had been the most saintly pastor in the community. He lives choked by the secret he cannot reveal, until finally he confesses it and dies. Though it has been a torment, it has also sanctified and transfigured him.

What gives this terrible story its true significance is that, in it, the letter of the law gone mad not only takes no account of the spirit, but flouts the very word of God. For, in the Gospel according to St John, we are told of Christ's meeting with an adulteress. On this incident the Puritans were the less free to put their own interpretation, since the Lord's teaching was perfectly clear and admitted of no ambiguity. Who can fail to remember the eternal lesson delivered to us there? The woman has been taken in adultery, and the scribes and the pharisees bring her to the Master. 'Now, Moses in the law commanded us that such should be stoned: but what sayest thou?' But Jesus, making no answer, wrote on the ground with his finger. Then He uttered the saying which has, ever since, sounded in the ears of men: 'He that is without sin among you, let him first cast a stone at her.' And again he stooped down and wrote on the ground. And they that heard it, being convicted by their own conscience, went out one by one, beginning at the eldest even unto the last. When Jesus had lifted up himself, and saw none but the woman, he said unto her, Woman, where are those thy accusers? hath no man condemned thee? She said, No man, Lord. And Jesus said unto her, neither do I condemn thee: go and sin no more.

So what the pharisees had not dared to do, the Puritans in *The Scarlet Letter* did, and gloried in it. But what is even worse is that this falsification of the Gospel, though in the Puritanism described by Hawthorne it may have reached its extreme limit, is still to be seen in all the Christian sects, and even in the old Mother Church. We can follow its ravages from century to century. Which of us has not suffered from it, whether at the hands of the posterity of Port-Royal or at those of the disciples of Calvin?

How strange a mystery that men should reject, in the Gospel, the very thing that constitutes the good news, and should be the very heart of hearts of human hope: the pardon indefinitely renewed, the remission of sins declared anew each time that Christ saw a human being prostrate before him. 'Thy sins are forgiven thee.' Whence comes this hatred of good fortune? In *The Scarlet Letter* we can catch a glimpse of the answer. For the harsh law of

Moses, Christian theology, in its madness, has substituted its own law, which is no less harsh, no less pitiless, since, fundamentally, it is the same. But I will not pursue the subject further here.

What is really astonishing is that Hawthorne's novel, which stresses all the most odious distortions of the religious spirit, and should be a satire, carries a very different message. Unlike Molière's, this American Tartuffe initiates us into one of the least known secrets of true religion. The pharisaism of the Puritans creates, not only in the heroine who wears the scarlet letter, but also in the guilty young pastor, condemned to live a lie by reason of his cowardly silence, a genuine sanctity. I do not use that word only in the sense of Augustine's *etiam peccata*. That even our faults are an element in our sanctification is a commonplace with every writer of sermons. But *The Scarlet Letter* goes much deeper.

The young pastor, held a prisoner by his lie, passes for a saint in the town, as did Tartuffe in the eyes of Orgon. But he *really is* a saint, in spite of his hypocrisy: the crime he has committed condemns him to sanctity by transforming him within.

Here I touch on what, to my mind, gives so great a value to *The Scarlet Letter*. This book furnishes us with a key to what seems the most impenetrable of all mysteries, especially to the believer: the mystery of evil. Evil is in the world, and in ourselves. Yet, 'all is Grace'. Those are the last words of Bernanos's country priest. The very principle of our regeneration is to be found in what is worst in us. From this point of view, *The Scarlet Letter* is a document of supreme importance which I have frequently brought to the attention of the troubled and despairing. In it we are shown a guilty pastor who passes for a saint: 'To the high mountain peaks of faith and sanctity he would have climbed, had not the tendency been thwarted by the burden, whatever it might be, of crime or anguish, beneath which it was his doom to totter. It kept him down on the level of the lowest; him, the man of ethereal attributes, whose voice the angels might else have listened to and answered! But this very burden it was that gave him sympathies so intimate with the sinful brotherhood of mankind: so that his heart vibrated in unison with theirs, and sent its throb of pain through a thousand other hearts. . . .' What follows, must be read in its entirety.

It is not only because he humiliates himself, because he sees his own abjection and beats his breast, that the guilty pastor draws near to God: his very sin becomes in him a principle of total renewal before his brethren, but also before God. Similarly, the scarlet letter fastened to the breast of the young woman guilty of adultery, makes of her, in the eyes of the whole town, an authentic and venerated saint. What we are shown is pharisaism transmuted into the creative element of sanctity. Grace turns to its own purposes the worst canalizations invented by Tartuffe and Orgon. Its waters flow through them to reach and fertilize the hearts of men. The spirit makes use of the letter, no matter how despicable the letter may be. That is the moral of this sombre tale.

Some may hold that a novel which interests us mainly because of its theological implications can scarcely claim any very considerable degree of importance from the literary point of view. But the fact that, in spite of an outmoded technique, it still, after a century, has so great a power of suggestion, does, so it seems to me, bear witness to the richness of a literary form on which certain modern practitioners would impose their own narrow code. The genuine novel can afford to laugh at their 'art of fiction' just as the genuine poet can laugh at 'the art of poetry'. A novel can express anything and everything, and can achieve, as does *The Scarlet Letter,* the remarkable triumph of turning a cruel caricature of Christianity into an apologia which opens a door upon the mystery of evil.

IX

TO WRITE is to remember, but so, also, is to read. And it is to draw comparisons. *'Longtemps je me suis couché de bonne heure. . . .'* No sooner have I taken in those opening words of *Du côté de chez Swann,* than I get ready to accompany a child upon his pilgrimage, as far as he will lead me, to measure the distance which separates his road from mine, and to be amazed to find how often they meet.

But age brings a change in the perspective of such confrontations. When we are young we greedily question the invented characters of fiction, as if they held a secret which would enable us to lose none of our gifts, which would protect us against our shortcomings and mask our patches of emptiness, as though they prefigured the destiny awaiting us.

When we have turned the final corner of our lives, the curiosity which once kept us poring over books becomes retrospective. What matters then is to know whether our image, finally fixed in a number of our attitudes and in our work, differs from, or corresponds to, that of the masters who have preceded us. It is no longer the characters of fiction and ourselves whom we bring face to face. We go straight to their creators. It is they whom I question and not their imagined heroes. It is with them that I compare myself, that self still in the land of the living though, like the dead, I have completed my task, but not yet 'shown it up'.

It is this which makes me so fond of Henri Mondor's little book: *Maurice Barrès avant le Quartier Latin.* In it he comments upon the unpublished letters of Barrès in youth with a respectful lucidity, purveying neither praise nor blame, truth and tenderness. That is the only attitude worthy of the literary historian who is dealing with those who, on our journey through this world, have been our escort till the end, whose torches flicker still about us who so soon will join them. How dearly I love Pierre Reverdy for having written in a recent book: *En vrac* (a detestable title for a collection of thoughts, through which break, on every page, magnificently, the confidences of a rent and secret life) that: '*The great dead must be approached with care. I mean with decorum. We should not batten on what remains of them, eager for nourishment, like voracious insects, with too much manifest delight and greed.*' In just such a way does Mondor invite me to interrogate the schoolboy and the student, my senior by twenty years, who, after doing more than any other writer to mould my character, intervened, so miraculously, in my career, and launched me upon it. I am amazed to find how long it was before I knew anything about the beginnings of a writer who is so close to me in temperament. It was not until I read the first volume of Barrès' *Cahiers* published in 1929 (it begins with the few pages of his memoirs which he had time to commit to paper during the last weeks of his life) that I got any precise idea of what the small boy from Lorraine was really like. The generation immediately anterior to Gide's still had some degree of reticence left. The time had not yet come for undressing in public, of parading start-naked before the eyes of the world. Nobody then thought himself of sufficient interest to undertake a task which more properly belongs to the specialist in literary history.

But since, at eighteen, I had always kept *Sous l'oeil des barbares* within easy reach of my hand, I had learned to read between the lines of that book all that Henri Mondor has to tell me, the more easily because there is scarcely anything in Barrès the schoolboy which I was not to echo twenty-five years later. How often, in my bedroom in Bordeaux, did I not repeat that invocation in *Sous l'Oeil des barbares:* 'O Master, I remember how, when I was ten years old, I used to cry my heart out against the left-hand pillar of the lean-to at the far end of the junior play-ground. . . .' There was not even a physical suffering (including chilblains) which the young Barrès had endured in that icy yard, which I could not match from my own experience. More especially do I recognize as mine, that shrinking, not so much from masters as from school-fellows, that feeling of weakness intermixed with strength. The young Barrès, sickly and bullied, determined that he would be top dog. What he said to himself, then, white faced and clenching his fists – 'one of these days I'll show them!' – I, too, said later.

And the same sufferings threw both him and me into the arms of the same comforter. Barrès says that the only good thing about his school, Malgrange, was that it was in the country. He lived there in close communion with sky and trees, in tune with the changing seasons. That is what I, too, loved in *my* Malgrange, which was called Grand-Lebrun, and was situated not at the gates of Nancy, but on the outskirts of Bordeaux, where, fifty years ago, its park still contained a few corners which were almost wild. School did not interrupt the dialogue which the uncommunicative school-boy conducted at holiday time, with the countryside of his birth.

The countryside of his birth . . . the pictures it evoked, the dreams it brought, were very different in the case of the boy from Lorraine, from that of a little Gascon lad. I say Gascon, because there is no adjective corresponding to Guyenne – that land of with-drawn and misty contours which I like to think I share only with a chosen few. Here there is a divergence and a contrast between our two destinies. We did not learn the same lesson. What Lor-raine taught to Barrès was strengthened by the disaster of '70, through which he lived when he was eight. In that unobtrusive, undistinguished country, history showed like a tuppence-coloured picture, crudely daubed, which Barrès pinned up, once and for all, in his bedroom, and from which he never after took his eyes.

But where I sat with my back against a pine, feeling the burning sand against my palms, or looked out at the valley of the Garonne, filled with light and over-charged with fruit, lying at my feet, no human history was interposed between me and Cybele, any more than between me and God. True, wars had ravaged our Guyenne in other ages, and traces of them were to be seen everywhere. But the castles of the Black Prince which were pointed out to me no longer spoke of forgotten massacres. The church porches mutilated by the Huguenots, the battlements destroyed during the last revolt of Guyenne, meant nothing to a boy. The dead of those old wars no longer showed upon the surface, as in those frontier provinces where, not so long ago, burial mounds and crosses were still to be seen in the fields.

Not that the lesson taught me by my province was in any way either mediocre or base – rather was it religious, and that in a double sense, both Christian and pagan. And so it is that there has lingered on, in the secrecy of a few poems, the only part of my work which is still dear to me, truly inspired, as though the fact that I was born among the contrasting scenes of the rich river-lands of the Garonne, and the Landes – that desolate world of heath – in two-faced Guyenne, had left an indelible mark on me.

It was a very different lesson that Barrès learned in his Lorraine – a history-lesson all of battles, in which God played no part, or only in so far as he was an element in that continuous slaughter, and a part of the common inheritance. The sole living divinity was the nation of France, the service and cult of which was incarnate in the army.

The young Barrès was predisposed to listen to what Lorraine had got to teach him. If I had been transported, as a child, to Charmes, I should not have absorbed that same lesson. How strange it is to see him, at the age of seven, sharing passionately, like all of France, in the drama of Victor Noir, murdered by Pierre Bonaparte, and violently taking sides, as he was to do thirty years later, in the civil war unloosed by the Dreyfus Affair! But in those early days, when the people of Paris, almost to a man, followed behind Rochefort the funeral cortège of Victor Noir, it was to the prince-assassin that the little Barrès had given his heart.

The thoughts which all this has prompted in me are still confused, and must be brooded over at leisure. Barrès had this in common with Gide, that he was a sign of contradiction – and so has a chance of surviving. For me, who loved them both, neither the ideological armour of Barrès, nor the frightful nudity of Gide, has, in the long run, proved beguiling. Every creator must cut a way for himself, a personal track which did not exist before he came to open it. Will it still be in use when he shall be no more? The great high-roads remain, and a few paths preserved by a miracle. Perhaps our own? But we should not attach too much hope to that possibility. Though we may set out books as mile-stones on the path that leads to the grave, if no one uses it, the grass will choke it, and the briers of oblivion.

*   *   *   *   *

On the 18th October, 1897, Maurice Barrès entered in one of his *Cahiers* the following words: 'The great idea of setting a shield of deliberate politeness between me and those whose unfathom-able ignominy I recognize – they are as they are because it is their nature to be so) has been slowly growing in me: just systematic politeness and no motion of sincerity. *That* I must suppress, stamp out underfoot.'

There is nothing of the young romantic in that, nothing of the country lad who intends to get to grips with Paris. This is a man of thirty-five making the choice between two roads, or, rather, be-tween two opposing camps. It is a man of letters with a passion for politics, who, deep down, finds pleasure in nothing but politics. They, for want of something better, furnish him with his literary themes, but what he really wants is to be an actor on the political stage: everything else bores him.

Our life, and especially our public life, is dominated by the idea we have of men, beyond which we have, quite deliberately, never moved, even though we may not have remembered, and fixed in our minds, as Barrès did, the actual day on which we made our choice. For obviously, we *have* a choice. The ignominy of men is a fact, but goodness, kindliness, sacrifice, even of life, are also facts, which Barrès at thirty-five does not deny. This, too, he knew even better, seeing that he knew himself, had worn away his youth in that knowledge, and had begun his career as an author with a book on the 'cult of the self'. Everything is true about men except what Barrès had written of them. It is not human ignominy that is un-fathomable: that would make things too easy. What really escapes our powers of comprehension is the secret of that contradiction which is an essential part of human nature. It often saddens me to find the literary historians reconstructing the whole of an illustrious life round one single pronouncement which merely has the effect of debasing it, and is of importance to the critic only because it has never before been made public, and because it is his own private discovery. I am saddened because in this order of things every simplification is a calumny.

The 18th October, 1897 was for Barrès a landmark. In his declaration of contempt for the human race he was not announcing a discovery, but making a resolution – namely, from then on to treat human beings, in the battle of politics, as though they were basically ignoble and capable of the worst excesses. True, ever since the Panama scandal, a blinding light had been thrown on his religion, but it was in that year that his decision was to be made, though he still seemed to be hesitating. Zola had dined with him at Durand's, and made a great effort to win him over to the cause of Dreyfus. Barrès' first readers, those who had come under his spell, belonged to the Left. Blum was one of them. How much happier they would have felt if Barrès, and not Zola, had written *J'accuse*. But that still lay in the future.

In 1897 this leader of French youth was a man already defeated. After his dazzling entry into the arena in 1889, when he had just turned twenty-six, the year of *Un homme libre* and of his triumphant electoral campaign at Nancy, everything seemed to collapse under him. In 1893 came his first defeat at the polls. He had been caught up in the liquidation of the Boulangist adventure, and swept out of politics. In 1896 he was again defeated, this time by a younger man, at Neuilly-Boulogne, though the death of his opponent in the very moment of victory gave him a bitter revenge. Many are the pages in the *Cahiers* inspired by that young corpse.

Boulangism was a thing of the past, but the Dreyfus Affair was just beginning, and it is true to say that just when Barrès was taking the measure of human baseness, the Dreyfus Affair was getting into a rare tangle. This Barrès of thirty-five, this Barrès of the lank hair who had lost one battle, looked at his watch and decided that the time had come to start another. This time it would be a battle without quarter, a battle in which it would no longer be a question of treating men as an end in themselves. So as not to let himself be tempted by what remained in him of youthful confidence, just as

Pascal had written on a scrap of paper from which he was never parted – *the greatness of the human spirit* – so now did Barrès write in his secret note-book that human ignominy is unfathomable.

We often ask ourselves what constitutes the essential difference between Right and Left. An important line of division is at once obvious. On the one side are those who have a fanatical belief in mankind, the followers of Rousseau: on the other, the prudent men who mistrust it, but whose mistrust quickly turns to contempt. All tyrants, all dictators, the best as well as the worst, Bonaparte or Hitler, have frequently declared how little value they attach to human beings. In 1897, this contempt went so far, with some, as to lead them to the conclusion that the possible innocence of a man condemned for treason weighed less in the scale than those superior interests in the name of which the sentence must be upheld.

We have no reason to think that at this time Maurice Barrès had any doubts about Dreyfus, or that he had believed in his innocence. What is clear is that he deliberately took sides with those who thought it a matter of no importance to find out the truth, or to seek justice and ensue it. To Barrès it was simply and solely a question of taking a stand against those evil forces which might exploit the Affair for their own ends. The only thing of importance to him at that moment was to thwart their plans, no matter by what means, or, at least, to shut his eyes to the means employed by others – and to avenge the defeat of boulangism.

Thus the internal affairs of France became an interminable settling of accounts. Fifty years later, another 'affair' brought the same 'sides' into open antagonism. The pretext may change, but it is always the same Capulets who cross swords with the same Montagues.

That 18th October must have been, for Barrès, a time of armed vigil. The year just ending had brought Lieutenant-Colonel Picquart into the lists. The example given by that officer might have revived Barrès' faith in human nature. Within a month, Mathieu Dreyfus was to denounce the real culprit: Esterhazy. Surely, that 'connoisseur of souls', as Barrès called himself, should have smelled that one out? But no: he was already committed to a battle in which ignominy was to be the rule, and the interest of the nation the only consideration. What did the fate of one wretched man matter?

It is true that this inhumanity applied only to politics. These Macchiavellis of literature, journalism and material interest were, for the most part, fair-minded and kindly men in private life. That does not alter the fact that what strikes one most forcibly in the entry which Barrès made in his note-book, is his insistence on a code of good manners. For him, good manners were to be nothing more than a system, a suit of armour, a weapon for use in a world where all men move masked and wary.

Already, Barrès as a young man had said, in the first of his published books (I remember the phrase, because I copied it out): 'Always show to others a smooth exterior, and be withdrawn.' Though I may have a weakness for good manners, though human contacts, where good manners are absent, seem to me to be less and less tolerable, though I find it more and more distasteful to have to deal with mannerless boors, I no longer have illusions about that systematic politeness which Barrès, at thirty-five, proposed to adopt as a rule of life. (He didn't, as a matter of fact, observe it very successfully: his contempt for his fellow-men oozed, if I may put it like that, from every pore, and my young years were assailed by many terrible words!) So, though I may have a marked predilection for politeness, I realize today just what it amounts to.

Nobody had more charming manners than Paul Bourget, no one was ever more gracious than he, or more welcoming to strangers. Yet this same Bourget was guilty of making a disgraceful scene on the 29th May, 1899, when he happened to meet Paléologue in the rue Francois-Ier. 'This fellow Delcassé,' he shouted, 'is the lowest kind of swine! Oh, I know what you're going to say – justice! Well, I don't care a damn for justice!'

Not to care a damn for justice must mean that one is convinced that men in general are contemptible, and that justice cannot be applied to them. That is why our view of human nature determines our position on the Right or the Left. But it is not as simple as all that. Contempt for the individual goes hand in hand, in most revolutionaries, with the cult of mankind in general, with the result that the religion of humanity has been responsible for as many victims as has authoritarian government.

It seems to me that it is just here where a Christian can shed a little light. Barrès at thirty-five thought religion an old wives' tale for half-wits. But later he changed his attitude, and, as he grew older, his outlook on humanity was much modified. The re-reading of his *Cahiers* has made one thing obvious to me. From a certain moment of his life (the death of his nephew, Charles Demange) Barrès continually increased in stature.

X

WHEN I first poked my nose into Trotsky's autobiography, it was not, I confess, in a wholly detached frame of mind. The present state of affairs in the U.S.S.R., and the 'debunking' of Stalin made me curious, and I can now say that this extraordinary political novel (for never was history more like fiction) has led me to the discovery of a great writer, and, I believe, of a masterpiece.

The very size of the volume (more than six hundred closely-printed pages) was daunting. I brought it with me to the country, two years ago, and it greeted me from its place on my table, each time that I returned.

Getting back to Malagar means breasting a flood of printed matter, but, with so much leisure on my hands, there is just a chance that each book will get a reading. Not that I really have more time here than in town. Since each day is indistinguishable from its fellows, this sameness has the effect of telescoping the weeks. In the country, the days are long but time is short. The schoolboy who was once myself, played in this garden, and plays there still, with my children, who have not been children for a very long while, and, actually it is a grand-daughter who, at this moment, is circling round my chair. It is difficult to find any striking difference between my stay here twenty years ago, ten years ago, or last year. Nothing has budged for half a century, except the dead, and it is not true to say that they quickly disappear. They do not have to come back. Each room is inhabited by one of them. I have no feeling of speed because I have nothing by which to measure the passage of time. I know, but I do not feel, that I am being rushed onwards.

What, in the country, gives to the books I have brought with me, their chance of being read, is that, sooner or later, I shall be

driven back on all of them, like a drowning man who clings to the
first life-buoy that comes within his reach. My mother used to say
(I can almost hear her voice): 'You always feel depressed in the
country.' ... Yes, depression jumps out on me when I least expect
it, gets me by the throat without a word of warning before I can
summon up enough energy to look for some consoling volume on
my shelves, the book, for instance, of some moralist who might
produce irrefutable arguments for not being more depressed in the
country than in town. A book picked up at random is the best for
my purpose, because it makes me lose my bearings, and has nothing
to do with my gloom if I really do feel gloomy.

But it was not depression, thank heavens, which in the muted
light of this late spring, sent me to Trotsky's fat biography. The
'debunking' of Stalin has, to some extent, torn the muffling veils
from the condemned statue of his most illustrious victim. Once
Trotsky had been struck down, the way lay open for that bureau-
cratic system of which Stalin was the incarnation: and by bureau-
cratic I mean the form of government which is Eternal Russia.

I am convinced that, from the point of view of a liberal Europe,
the substitution of the Stalinian terror for the fascinating apostle
(in socialist eyes) of 'permanent revolution', was a godsend. Russia
has grown powerful, but revolution (in Europe) has been rendered
powerless.

For in Trotsky there really is something fascinating. First and
foremost, the bourgeois reader is astonished to find that a revolutionary can have some resemblance to the general run of humanity.
I was gripped from the very first pages, as I used to be gripped by
Tolstoy and Gorki. If Trotsky had not been a militant Marxist, he
would have taken his place beside those masters. The people among
whom he lived become vivid and real to us. But it is he, above all,
the solemn and observant child, gazing with a curious fixity upon
the world he has just entered, who chiefly holds the attention. His
universe was that of a small farming community in which there
was little social injustice, and where the differences between em-
ployer and employed were not great.

What was going on in the mind of this Jewish boy who was

brought up without any religion? Was it because he had no religion that justice became a ruling passion with him? A born writer, he did not, as he grew older, turn into one of those young Rastignacs with whom we have all of us, at times, been familiar. He showed no disposition to carve out a career for himself in the revolution or by the revolution. All he wanted was, quite simply, to change the world.

What mysterious hand was it that cut, one by one, all the roots of personal interest in this gifted young creature who was top of his form in every subject, which finally detached him from anything approaching a normal future, and plunged him into a destiny which was almost continuously tragic, with prisons, deportations and escapes as recurring intervals in an otherwise interminable exile?

As the story proceeds and childhood is left behind, his purely personal life becomes, to some extent, diluted and absorbed into the adventure of a revolution on the march, though without the hero ever losing the sense of his own identity, or of what he and Lenin together were alone capable of achieving. He would have shrugged his shoulders could he have heard Moscow's present leaders denouncing the cult of personality. What horrified him in Stalin was not that he might become a dominating personality, but that anyone so base and so cruel should occupy that position, and not somebody else. During the battle round Kazan, in 1918, Trotsky denounced 'the pusillanimity of an historic fatalism which, in all questions, whether concrete or private, passively seeks a solution in general laws, and leaves out of account the mainspring of all human decisions – the living and acting individual.'

This living and acting Trotsky seems to me far less inhuman than his bloody-minded adversary. But that, after all, is perhaps because, thanks to his autobiography, we know what he was like as a child, and can follow the progress of that child and recognize his presence in the ruthless man who would not hesitate to strike down the revolutionary socialists when he judged it necessary to do so.

He puts the problem fairly and squarely, takes into account the quantity of blood spilled, and gives the reasons (some of which seem valid) for his ruthlessness. 'Revolution is revolution' – he writes – 'because it brings all the contradictions involved in its development to a choice between two alternatives; life or death.' True enough, but we must not forget that Stalin, in striking down Trotsky, made precisely the same choice. That is what served as a pretext for all the slaughter, for the self-accusations of so many innocent persons and their acquiescence in the attitude of their executioners.

Trotsky denies, *a priori*, that there is any validity in our bourgeois indignations. 'In what I have said, I am making no attempt to justify the revolutionary Terror. To do so would imply a recognition of the justness of our accusers. But who are they? The organizers and exploiters of a world-wide butchery. The profiteers who burn the incense of their after-dinner cigars to the honour of the Unknown Soldier. The pacifists who set their faces against war, though only so long as it has not broken out. . . .' The rest should be read in its entirety: every arrow goes home and quivers in the target.

A hard man, this Trotsky, whose deliberate hardness, however, does not destroy his basic humanity. From the beginning of his struggle against Stalin it is abundantly clear that the issue was not so much a conflict of interests, but an almost physical opposition of two completely different natures. During Lenin's lifetime, Stalin was for ever sniffing round Trotsky, seeking him out, making an effort to get on familiar terms with him. 'But,' says Trotsky, 'the very characteristics of the man which later won him power, were repugnant to me: a narrow outlook, an empirical approach, a crude form of psychology and the peculiar cynicism of a provincial whom Marxism had emancipated from most of his prejudices, though without putting anything else in their place. . . .'

Stalin devoured Trotsky. The real shark, the authentic shark, got the better of the man who still had a trace of humanity beneath his scales. Trotsky gave himself away at more than one of the crises in his life: by his affection, for instance, for Markine, a sailor from the Baltic whom he had taken as his personal bodyguard and that of his wife and children. They adored Markine and it was a terrible grief for them when their father told them that Markine had been killed. 'A portrait of him, wearing his round sailor's cap with flowing ribbons, stood on their bedside table. . . . My boys, Markine has been killed. . . .' A picture rises up before my eyes of two pale little faces taut and twisted under the impact of that sudden grief. 'Markine had been on terms of complete equality with our children. To them he confided his plans and his secrets. He told our little Serioja all about the woman he had loved long and devotedly, who had left him. Serioja, with tears in her eyes had passed on the news to her mother. . . .' The whole of the story must be read. Trotsky, the savage revolutionary, ends it with the following words: 'When the fatal message reached us, two little bodies lay for a long while shivering under the blankets. Only their mother heard their heartbroken sobbing.'

The more I think of it, the more clearly do I see that a victorious Trotsky would have had a tremendous influence on the socialist masses of a liberal Europe, and would have attracted to himself all that Stalinism has repelled. Stalin was, quite literally, 'repulsive'. But the reasons for that repulsiveness made him the stronger of the two. What in Trotsky makes me feel that he was almost a brother, was precisely that which weakened him and led to his downfall.

*　　*　　*　　*　　*

'Tell me what you read, and I will tell you the manner of man you are.' . . . There is truth in that, but I should know you even better if you told me what you *re-read*. It sometimes occurs to me that these stray memories and thoughts of mine, might, perhaps, find a clue in the books I have read all my life-long, and have always taken up again, sometimes after considerable intervals of time. I occasionally wonder what it is that sends me back to one of them, and not to others, and almost always the answer I make to that question casts a bright light on what interests me, or preoccupies me, at the moment, even though I have not always been aware of it.

Why, for instance, on this Palm Sunday, on the eve of my departure, did I take down Newman's *Apologia pro vita sua*? Though my knowledge of his writings is very imperfect I have always had a great affection for Newman and my religious sensibility is very much in harmony with his. Besides, the fact that this is Holy Week would be enough in itself to turn me from any of the profane authors. Still, we in France suffer from no lack of sacred writers. Why, then, this Englishman? I know precisely why. My choice fell on the *Apologia* because of its title, and because at certain moments the idea has come to me – as it must have come to many writers involved in political, religious or other controversies, who, being bellicose, often find themselves up against strong opposition – to defend the position I have taken up on this or that occasion, as Newman did in this book of his, by making a detailed analysis which should leave nothing unexplained. Newman, when he became a catholic priest and was accused of lying, replied by giving a scrupulous description of the way in which his mind had worked in his passage from the Anglican to the Roman church.

What turns and twists! Scarcely have I followed him into the story than I realize what a mad idea it is to try to imitate him, so wide is the gap between the spiritual battle which he was waging, and the political battle in which I am involved. When Newman made that sublime and truthful statement about himself – he was lying sick of a fever in Sicily (at the age of thirty-two) and cried out in his delirium: 'I shall not die, *for I have not sinned against the light.*' After that, he could, without pride or false humility, settle down to the writing of his apology. The very nature of his struggle demanded it, for he was sacrificing everything to the search for truth – for absolute truth, and not truth in relation to those doubtful and relative positions of a political nature, some aspects of which are always to be condemned, even if, in our eyes, they are intermingled with the demands of justice, even though we, as christians, are called upon to defend them.

True though they may be, the conflict which rent the religious conscience of this young Oxford Anglican in the early days of the nineteenth century, would seem to be of very little interest, would, indeed, seem contemptible to a modern Marxist. It so happened that at the same time as I was re-reading the *Apologia,* I was also reading a small book by M. Henri Lefebvre: *Problèmes actuels du marxisme.* What meaning could there be for Marxists in the spiritual attitude of this privileged son of a pharisaical society, as hard and unjust, as unconscious of either injustice or hardness, as that of the England of his day? This attitude is expressed and summed up in a famous passage of the *Apologia* dealing with Calvin's doctrine of final perseverance. 'I believe,' wrote Newman, 'that it had some influence on my opinions, in the direction of those childish imaginations which I have already mentioned, *viz* in isolating me from the objects which surrounded me, in confirming me in my mistrust of the reality of material phenomena, and of making me rest in the thought of two, and two only, absolute and luminously self-evident beings, myself and my Creator. . . .'

            ★   ★   ★   ★   ★

A passage like that marks the line of division between two families of irreconcilable spirits, nay, more than that, inconceivable, the one by the other. For M. Henri Lefebvre, Newman merely passes from one rite to another rite, returns to an even more strongly marked fetichism – alienated, cut off from reality, an accessory in the exploitation of the human masses to the advantage of a pleasure-seeking minority, at the heart of which he plays a game of angels. He is an angel, flown with purity, with perfection, with understanding, and, though he knows it not, with pride. Perhaps. . . . But M. Henri Lefebvre must agree, even though he may not approve, that this angelic race, even if it does not always manifest itself in a sovereign spirit such as Newman's does, all the same, exist. It is numerous, it is victorious, and, though a Marxist society may largely extirpate it, the germ from which it springs cannot be destroyed. It is not true, so travellers tell me, that the Russian churches are attended only by old men and women. What remains of the mystic spirit in the world is indestructible. This craving, in certain individuals, is not a function of economics: it has nothing to do with history except in so far as history conforms to the nature of man, which is impregnated with the supernatural. The Kingdom of God is within us.

Whether this craving be mad or not, it remains true that for a Newman there is nothing to be done in this world but to obey it. His drama has nothing to do with a human species, temporarily damned, looking for salvation to the revolution, and seeking deliverance only in the class war. For him, the crucial question is not concerned with the proletariat. All he cares about is to know whether the Anglican Church, midway between the Protestant heresy and Romish idolatry, can recover the purity of primitive Christianity. At last he discovers that this primitive Christianity has always existed, that it goes by the name of catholicism, that Simon Peter has held the tiller since the beginning. The solitude in which each one of us lives and dies, that commonplace of all the literatures of the world, has an aspect which is less known, though not less tragic: the impossibility of communication between the two spiritual families. I imagine Marx reading the *Apologia*, Newman reading *Das Kapital,* and each heaving a sigh, amazed that any man should be so blind and so absurd. Do I know to which side I belong, of which family I am a member? Yes: I am looking for a *via media* between the supernaturalism of a Newman who, to be sure, had never sinned against the light, though he may, perhaps, have been a little too indifferent to the injustice of a world which the christian, too, has a mission to change – and the Marxist materialism, which has cut itself adrift from the one and only reality which, no matter how loudly it may be denied, does, all the same, exist. The race of Newman, the race of the mystics, is there to prove it. To what they have known they have borne witness: 'that which we have heard with our ears and seen with our eyes, that which we have contemplated and our hands have touched. . . .' If I were a philosopher, I might, perhaps, have been able to point out that this negation lies at the source of the Marxist crisis, this refusal to admit the validity of that secret confrontation, which every man born into this world can experience, from which he can receive the gift of Grace, which Newman has summed up in four words: 'Myself and my Creator.'

I believe that some progress has been made along this *via media*. We live in a gloomy world, and I find little enough to console me in it, except perhaps in such frustrations as the worker-priests experiment – a failure, admittedly, but which, at least, does point the way, and has laid the foundation for something that may be possible in days to come – action and contemplation, a way to change the world, but only by sanctifying it. . . . Such is the colour of my thinking in this time of grace in which the hope of humanity, tortured and crucified though it may be, has stirred into life, and looks at us with love, for it has a face and a name.

* * * * *

I have long been struck by what, in a life, Pascal calls 'diversion', meaning relaxation, what we invent so as not to have to think about ourselves and the horror of our condition. Such diversion may take many forms, from kicking a ball to hunting a hare, from enslaving whole peoples in the case of a Caesar, to taking possession of persons in that of a Don Juan.

Today, having observed many lives, either through the medium of spoken confidences and printed books, or because I have, myself, been involved in them, I have come to see more clearly that many seek diversion only as a means of laying a false scent, that, in fact they never cease from keeping their eyes steadfastly fixed on their unhappy lot, which is the lot of every human being since, even if his life has been fulfilled, he is constantly being threatened from all sides: in his body where death, long before dealing its final blow, has already stuck its flagged pins: in the fact that he belongs to a species not unlike the fishes who eat and torture one another, not because, like other species, they fight over their females, or, being carnivorous, seek to satisfy their hunger, but because man is by his very nature destined to murder and torment his brothers.

No, in general we do not let ourselves be diverted, we do not turn our eyes away, even when we pretend to be indulging in play. One moment's inattention, and the savage beast will pounce.

I know the nature of my own defences – but what about those of others, especially of the old? The young find a refuge in their own seething turbulence. Love, ambition and what goes by the name of pleasure, sets up eddies which are mutually destructive. Not that the mortal anguish is not already present: it has been so from earliest childhood, as when I lay, wide-eyed, in my darkened bedroom, convinced that I heard a stealthy footstep on the stairs, or the sound of breathing behind a door, and was overwhelmed by the same terror which I later learned to conceal, to master if not to destroy. What once was instinctive comes to be a matter of reason. We know, as we grow older, that the footsteps sounded, not on the stairs but in ourselves – and how many of those steps are heard by every one of us! They come from all directions: some from the secret places of race-memory: some from our own tormented bodies: some from a loved one. *La condition humaine* which Malraux used as the title for a book, raises the one and only question that must be answered, not from any logical necessity, but in our own defence. How do others deal with it? In what does the secret of their lives consist?

When confronted by a destiny fulfilled, all that really concerns me is to examine the nature of the ramparts built up by the invested human being, the trenches he has dug, his secret lines of communications, the water-holes known only to himself, everything, in fact, which has enabled him to face the terrifying experience of living, as Barrès puts it, 'where men throng most densely'. It is that curiosity which has set me reading, with a strange passion, the *Reliquiae* of Gerard Manley Hopkins, in a translation by Pierre Leyris. A strange passion, I say, because these poems which, in England, occupy much the same position as to those of Stéphane Mallarmé in France, seem to be unfathomable even to the majority of Anglo-Saxon readers. How, then, should a translation make them accessible to us? They are darkness, but darkness mysteriously peopled. We see nothing, but grasp everything. Even though the translator warns us in advance that we shall not catch their meaning, it seems to me that, thanks to the Ariadne's clue supplied by the same faith, the same love (Gerard Hopkins was a convert to catholicism) I can make some progress.

That strange life, more than any other, allows us to follow the movements of a spirit which felt that it was threatened from all sides, in spite of the pleasant ease of living in the Victorian Age, perhaps because of it, since the eyes of Hopkins, as a young man – like those of Simone Weil at a later period – were very early opened to the monstrous shame of the innumerable poor, to that earthly hell in which four-fifths of the human race live out their lives. It was not enough for him that he, an Anglican, should, by his conversion (under the influence of Newman) be cut adrift from the society into which he had been born. He renounced the world, took holy orders. But even to be a priest was not sufficient. He became that most scandalous of beings in the eyes of the English those days: a Jesuit. The greatest of modern English poets was a Jesuit. Thus, from impossibility to impossibility, does a human being move against the current, back to his true source. One after the other the traps slammed to behind this young Englishman who, separated from everything which, at that time, constituted the setting for a gentleman, and caught on the barbed points of the most constraining of all religious orders, found his way to Christ, offered to Christ his joy and his despair, and unburdened himself in poems which, during his lifetime, were read only by two friends and by Coventry Patmore. What fame has ever been more posthumous than his?

Gerard Hopkins (it has suddenly occurred to me that the excellent translator of my books is also called Gerard Hopkins: if he belongs to the same family, then I have a personal link with the poet).[1] Gerard Manley Hopkins found himself threatened by whom? by what? The fragments of a *Journal* and a few letters, show him to us as a young man who was certainly not unaware of the seductions of this world – 'His face was fascinating me last term: I generally have one fascination or another on. Sometimes I dislike the faces which fascinate me, but sometimes much the reverse' – which reminds me of something which one of the characters in one of my novels says: 'All faces wound me.' Even after his conversion, and his entry into holy orders, his *Journal* is filled, again and again, with descriptions of objects as detailed and as carefully observed as those

[1] M. Mauriac will be pleased to know that his translator is the poet's nephew.

of some of our young contemporaries. The drawings, too, reproduced in this volume of *Reliquiae*, seem almost to have been exe-
cuted with the aid of a magnifying-glass. It is as though, drawn
onwards and upwards to the heights, cut off from his own people,
uprooted from everything typically British, he embraced all that
remained to him of the outside world with an eye which let no
detail of vegetable or mineral escape – but of that world only. The
other world, that of human beings, terrified him. The judgement
passed by this inspired young man on the powerful England of the
century's end, expresses sheer horror: '. . . My Liverpool and
Glasgow experience laid upon my mind a conviction, a truly
crushing conviction, of the misery of town life to the poor and
more than to the poor . . . of the degradation even of our race, of
the hollowness of this century's civilization: it made even life a
burden to me to have daily thrust upon me the things I saw.'

This despair, expressed by the poet in words, is the despair felt,
and taken upon himself, by a young Jesuit priest. To be sure, a
tendency to hopefulness is not hope. For the christian, a certain
type of despair is not necessarily at odds with hope: it is the rending
indictment of Saint Teresa who wept 'because love is not loved'; it
is Pascal gazing upon Christ 'in agony until the end of the world'.
Gerard Manley Hopkins remains for us an enclosed arena in which
a battle is fought between a poet's creative urgency and a vocation
of self-abasement. He published nothing in his lifetime. With the
exception of two friends, who understood him very imperfectly,
nobody knew his poetry, and he had no reason to think, until his
death, that it would not remain for ever unknown. The drama was
played out at a level to which the eye cannot reach – at least, not
the eye of so ignorant a reader as I am, incapable of getting a real
grasp of these poems. It is only too true that I cannot dig deep into
them . . . but on their surface I can see a trail of blood. In the depths
there is a settling of accounts. Between whom and whom?

> But ah, but O thou terrible, why wouldst thou rude on me
> Thy wring-world right foot rock?

It is less than the truth to say that Hopkins sought no diversion.

He did not even defend himself against the object of his anguish, but looked it in the face, confronted it and took it to his arms. Such is the vocation of a christian – the very opposite of flight, of escape – a battle hand-to-hand, or rather, spirit-to-spirit. Conversion, as this young Englishman understood it, was an agonizing tearing up of roots. But that is nothing: Jacob, unarmed and naked, pitted himself against the angel. The poems of Hopkins, his comments on the struggle, are obscure because they must be. Our probing eyes cannot reach to that secret point of junction where a soul and a spirit meet, nor see into that fold of the flesh where the splinter lies concealed.

★ ★ ★ ★ ★

I have put back Newman and Hopkins side by side upon the shelf: they will talk together when I have gone. Adieu, Malagar!

The shutters of the northward-facing windows have not been opened this morning. The house already has its eyes half-shut: this is the moment of my departure, and when I have left it, the house will turn back to sleep. The summer storms which circle round, will not awaken it. I shall be far away. I am, already. The only thing left for me to do, is to go on to the terrace, to lean upon the balustrade, and, as one might look for the wrinkles in a mother's face, gather into one last gaze (for a last there must be, and this, perhaps, is it) 'the long distance of this silent land.'

But our separation will not be sharp and sudden, as it would were I travelling by train. Driving away by car does not loosen the embrace at once. Nothing is so much shared by everyone as roads, yet those which link this country house with Paris are private to myself, for the route they trace has meaning only for me. From Saint-Cloud where the motor-way begins, it is already the road to Malagar, the lonely road of Entre-deux-Mers, which the car will soon be taking. I am, perhaps, the only person here who sees it as the main highway to Paris. For I am not going by Bordeaux. After running through Benauge, and crossing the Dordogne and the Isle, just before reaching Barbezieux, we shall turn on to one of the greater arteries of an older France, the one which today bears the number 10. The narrow highway of Benauge on which we started out, little known though it may be, serves a stretch of country which has its place in the history of French painting. The modest château whose ancient tower I know is hidden (though I cannot see it) in a cluster of dead trees, is called Malromé. There died a man accursed, if it be a curse for genius to be housed in a crippled body: Henri de Toulouse-Lautrec. Behind one of those windows the dying man watched his father catching flies upon the sheet. The Baroness, his mother, long outlived him. A neighbour of ours once asked her whether her son had left any drawings or paintings at Malromé. The old lady answered that the house had once been filled with them, but that she had had them destroyed because they were 'improper'.

I do not remember anyone ever mentioning Toulouse-Lautrec when I was living at Malagar. He spent the summers at Taussat, near Arcachon, with which several of our friends were familiar. It was only later I discovered that the dwarf painter who enjoyed no prestige locally, the subject of the comic stories which I heard in the family circle, was one of the leading artists of the modern French school.

Malromé is already far behind, and Sauveterre-de-Guyenne, with its delicious name and hideous concrete bell-tower. We reach the Dordogne at Saint-Jean-de-Blignac, where the ruined bridge, which I loved, has been replaced. But old bridges are irreplaceable. The exodus was fatal to them, and no one mourns their passing. The 'ancient parapets' of France, on which have leaned so many poets, so many frenzied and despairing lovers, no longer exist. We skirt Saint-Emilion with its famous vineyards, and cross the Isle at Guitres, the last parish of the Gironde, and plunge into the wild Charente where, when I was a child, the wolves still howled (the wolf of *La Mort du loup* was a native of Charente).

The real break, the real sense of separation comes when, just before reaching Barbezieux, we join the great Paris highway. Farewell, a long farewell to my Guyenne. This is no longer my own, my native land, but Chardonne's. Everything here is delicate and silvered, like his style, and that of Fromentin. But already

Chardonne is dropping out of sight. Once Barbezieux is left behind, two ghostly figures show suddenly at the roadside, more full of life than if they had really lived. To approach Angoulême is to draw near to Lucien de Rubempré. Beyond Angoulême we shall very soon reach the spot where Trompe-la-Mort, now Carlos Herrera, suddenly saw the young man, holding in his hand a bunch of the yellow flowers called 'stonecrop'.

Here is the very highest spot of the geography of fiction in France, for, in my opinion, the central mountain-mass of Balzac's work reaches its culminating point in three great peaks: *Le Père Goriot, Les Illusions perdues* and *Splendeur et misère des courtisanes.* This steep climb, after leaving Angoulême, witnessed, I like to think, the meeting of the ex-convict who became the secret ambassador of the Spanish king, and the young creature who had made up his mind to die like Ophelia, but who was to be restored by a mighty hand to life – and to crime.

The car runs smoothly on, but at each successive hill finds once again the bulky form of the false priest trudging for evermore beside the young dandy, while the postilions put the horses into a walk. I can hear, within myself, the whole horrible dialogue. I witness, in imagination, the corruption of a young heart. It proceeds, under my very eyes, with an almost supernatural malignity, in an atmosphere of dream and disordered passions, pierced by those glittering shafts of poetry of which only the novel is capable, as, for example, when, just before reaching Ruffec, Lucien points out to his tempter the château from which Eugène de Rastignac started on his conquest of Paris, that same Rastignac whom, as readers of *Père Goriot* will remember, the ex-convict tried to seduce, but who recoiled from the pact with crime and death which Lucien de Rubempré is on the point of signing. 'The priest told the coachman to pull up. He wanted, out of curiosity, to walk on foot up the short avenue which led from the road to the house. . . .'

Two recurring themes in French fiction here combine at a high degree of tension: the craving of the young provincial which, so he thinks, only Paris can satisfy, the conviction that only Paris will reveal him to himself and others: and, in the ageing man who can no longer be an object of love, the determination to use the desires of young, ambitious men in such a way that he will get power over them, and so squeeze some last few drops from life. The possession at which he aims is not of the body – though the flesh plays some part in this murky story – but of the spirit which will give him the power of a Creator over the creature, which is the crime of all crimes.

Not all the Rubemprés of this world finish up at the end of a rope fastened to the bars of a prison, as did the wretched Lucien. But, all the same, the uninterrupted flow of young provincials to Paris passes upon the roads of France the invisible procession of those who are moving in the opposite direction, the army of the defeated who have left Paris behind them. And so I play with the thought that the carriage in which the sham canon asked Lucien to sit beside him, may, in a joint eternity, meet, at some point upon the road, that other, carrying back from stage to stage, Maurice de Guérin, bound for Cayla to die there. For Maurice, too, is the hero of a novel – though one that was not born in the imagination of any author. His beauty was not, like Lucien's, the outcome of a dream. No human brain went to his making. Meditation and brooding touched that dark countenance with the muted radiance of a light which never shows on the hard faces of those who dwell in Balzac's world. I seek for witnesses upon the road. This ancient wall, that church-porch dating from two hundred years ago, watched the passing of the young poet on his way to death.

How strange it is that a creature who was once a living reality, should merge for me into the characters of fiction! Ruffec once left behind, we bid farewell to that monstrous pair, young Rubempré and Trompe-la-Mort. I turn for one last look at the frail dandy moving in the enormous shadow of the gaol-bird in his priestly dress. A hillside hides them from my view.

We do not see them again, but they form the subject of our talk. My wife, who is the official map-reader, expresses surprise that Lucien, intent on drowning himself in the Charente, should have met Carlos Herrera on the road which, after Angoulême, diverges from the river. But it was at Marsac that Lucien had made up his mind to die in a mill-race. Where is Marsac? We look for it on the map. It is at some considerable distance from the road. The problem occupies us for a while. Guyenne and Angoulême have disappeared behind us, devoured less by space than by time. From here on, everything is bleak and dreary. Until we reach Paris we shall encounter no more characters of fiction.

All the same, the road passes by Ligugé, where Huysmans lived. But it is impossible to imagine in this setting that stiff collar and black alpaca coat. He was not the sort of man who would have walked the dusty highway in his button-boots. After Châteaudun, Notre-Dame de Chartres comes into view, and, once past that marvel, might not Péguy show himself? But there is no general agreement about the precise itinerary of his pilgrimage. It is a long time since Péguy, weighed down under a load of innumerable commentaries, and protected by his frowning hagiographers (they quarrel still about his message, each claiming it for himself) walked the roads as a pilgrim.

How far away is Guyenne now! The immense stalk of the road to which the car clings like one of the foolish insects in the drawing-room at Malagar, now given over to the night, where they mingle with the last lilacs which I picked, and die behind closed shutters. Paris is closing in on us, and I can no longer pretend that there is any link between me and the ancient countryside.

Paris has no charm for me except as it appealed to those young provincials of an earlier day. It is little more now than an immense and gloomy garage, and bears little resemblance to the place of heart's desire which it was once for them, and for me. But it is still what the modern young want. I feel, among them, like a character who has wandered out of a quite different play, the protagonists of which have long since left the stage on which even the scenery no longer stands.

XI

I HAD met with Balzac on the road from Angoulême. It was Pascal whom I found again in Paris, where I had to be for an anniversary celebration. But why do I say 'again', seeing that I am never parted from him, especially not from the Pascal of the *Provinciales,* who has been my master ever since I began crossing swords in *l'Express?*

On the 23rd January, 1656, the Jesuits were struck straight between the eyes by *La Lettre écrite à un provincial par un de ses amis sur le sujet des disputes présentes de la Sorbonne.* The title was too long for posterity to remember. It was, in fact, the first of eighteen *Provinciales,* of those 'little letters' with which the world still echoes.

How strange! Nothing could seem more dead than the subject of which they treat. Nothing could be more meaningless to modern ears than arguments about Grace, unless, perhaps, exercises in casuistry. Yet nowhere does life course with a hotter blood than in these letters. So forceful are they that it is scarcely possible today for a writer, when the Religious pick a quarrel with him, to hit back vigorously without feeling the wings sprout upon his shoulders. The mere form of address, 'My Father' or 'My Fathers', is enough to make him feel borne aloft by the sheer vigour of the *Provinciales* and set dancing on the crest of their phrases, as though supported on the pinions of that eternal mockery.

But I have never believed, as has been said over and over again in the course of the last three hundred years, that it was Pascal who put weapons into the hands of the enemies of religion, nor that the impiety of the eighteenth century and the unbelief of our own times largely derive from him. His scoffing is terrible only because it is inspired by love. There is no hint in it of Voltaire's 'hideous grin'.

There is no reason for astonishment in the fact that this Jansenist, though he trembled before God, did not tremble at being the author of the *Provinciales*. Shortly before his death, so far from repenting, he actually gloried in what he had done. 'If I had to write them again now, I should make them even stronger.' He knew, however, since it is one of his *Pensées,* that, in matters of Grace, 'the least little action is of importance because of the effect it may have on others.' He foresaw, clearly enough, that Mère Angélique and M. Singlin would be deeply troubled.

But he himself had his own reasons for not being troubled. The first of them was that he, so weak and so strong at the same time, was defending the truth. What truth? Here we must admit that he was both right and wrong: that is blindingly clear: wrong in the immediate and the contingent, right in the absolute – by which I mean, not from the point of view of worldly wisdom, but on the level of apologetics and religion, which was all that mattered to him.

He was wrong in his argument about Grace – which is the subject of the first two letters, and only half right in his attack on the casuists, whom he began to make to look ridiculous from the fourth onwards, which opens with his famous remark: 'Trust a Jesuit to. . . .'

Had Saint Augustine, toughened by Jansenius and Saint-Cyran, carried the day within the Church, she would have succumbed to a form of spiritual Terror: out of theology despair would have been born. What of Jansenism remained in the Gallican Church (our country districts were impregnated with it, as was my own childhood) has been largely responsible for that indifference in religious matters which very soon becomes apparent and which began to triumph during the lifetime of Louis XIV. *Tartuffe* and *Don Juan,* contemporaries of M. Arnaud, voiced the protest of the Gallic spirit fighting on frozen peaks surrounded by chasms into which the christian was liable to tumble at any moment, with no possibility of helping himself. The Jesuits were right in their campaign against Pascal, and it is a blessing that they won.

That the ridiculous excesses of their casuists went beyond all imaginable limits, and that they were a prey totally unworthy of so illustrious a mocker, must not blind us to the fact that he showed up less well than may at first sight appear. Casuistry is the outcome of an examination of the conscience. What, here, was excessive and absurd about it, was the claim it made to be able to foresee every possible case, no matter how preposterous, and to think that it could be the equal of the divine omniscience. If the casuists were odious when they indulged in a game of hide-and-seek with the Infinite Being, the Jansenists were no less so when, on their own authority, they assigned limits to God's love for His creatures, and obliged Him to damn four-fifths of the human race in the name of Saint Augustine.

Pascal was wrong in the attitude which inspired the *Provinciales*. What, then, do I mean when I say that he was also right, and, let me add, more right than wrong?

My answer is that the object of his attack was not merely the Jesuits, but political Christianity as such, the turning of religious truth into a weapon which would enable it to dominate men's minds. The casuists made themselves the masters of consciences; the consciences of kings and of those in high places. They knew very well what they were doing when they put soft cushions under the elbows and the knees of their penitents, who were, all of them, and in varying degrees, the masters of the world.

Pascal attacked political Christianity in the name of a spiritual rigour which we cannot but regard as the distinguishing mark of the genuine christian. In Pascal I revere the believer who will stand no shilly-shallying, but knows that what he has been taught is true. It would be the height of folly to think that belief of this type is a commonplace in the Church. Those who belong to the same intellectual family as Pascal are often made to feel that they are being rather silly. . . . This particular battle has not, even now, been fought out, but is still going on.

There is one great difference between Pascal's times and our own. The Jansenist applied his doctrine of rigour to purity in morals and to an inner perfection. He saw as something absolute this inhuman quest which cut him off from a world which, in his eyes, was condemned, and resigned himself to that condemnation. Today, Pascal would not have accepted that attitude of resignation. His demands would have been influenced by a sense of justice. He would have been struck by the fact that the number of the elect in this world was very small, and would have discovered that the responsibility lay with him, and with all his caste, and that he and they would be called to account. He would not be so certain of what it is that damns a man, and of what it is that saves him. He would wish to share with all men that drop of blood which had been shed, so he believed, for himself alone.

That does not alter the fact that the spiritual struggle inaugurated by Port-Royal is identical with that still being waged by certain christians – the clash between those in the Church who believe 'it is true' and those who hold that 'it is useful'.

I have always admired Cardinal de Richelieu for understanding that M. de Saint-Cyran, the humble priest stripped of all wordly goods, was more to be feared than an army, and for sending him to the Bastille for no better reason than that he was frightened of a man who was resolved to serve the cause of truth without compounding with the temporal power. Nor was Louis XIV deceived, who dreaded even the relics of the saints of Port-Royal, and could not feel wholly comfortable until he had violated their graves, and thrown what remained of them to the dogs.

'Eternel ennemi des suprêmes puissances' – that cry flung by Athalie in the face of Joad, is the cry of Caesar to any man, no matter how defenceless he may be, who believes that the truth is a living truth, and that there is nothing which should not be sacrificed to it – not even the king, not even the nation, not even the Party.

Caesar has never given up searching for the secret of that power which, over so many centuries, has braved him to his face. And now, at last, he has succeeded. He has found the means of reaching down into a man's very soul, of penetrating to the last stronghold within which M. de Saint-Cyran stood his ground against Richelieu. In 1956, even he would make, not an examination of conscience, but an autocriticism and confession according to the methods imposed by the Party on its victims.

I, personally, never cease to learn from the *Provinciales,* those letters, written under an absolute monarchy, by that exemplary christian to whom Christ had spoken during the 'night of tears' about the freedom enjoyed by the children of God, against which nothing can prevail. It is that freedom which gives the destiny of man its value. It is what we must all of us preserve in our own lives, in the nation, in the Church – if we belong to it – and we must restore it to the peoples who have lost it and forgotten its flavour. Try to imagine a man who, in Moscow or Pekin, should one day write on a blank page: 'Trust the communists to . . .' and *not* see a policeman appear to right and left of him. When that happens, the world will be saved again.

* * * * *

If we are scrupulous about not cheating at the game of anniversaries, then it is only the last two of the *Provinciales* which deserve, this year, to be detached from the others, because the seventeenth – bearing the date, 23rd January 1657, appeared on the 18th February, and the eighteenth, also addressed to Father Annat, on the 24th March. There is also the beginning of a nineteenth 'little letter' of which only a fragment exists. In it the Pascal of the *Provinciales* throws his last firebrand.

Though there was no time for any flame to burst from it this final shot has always meant more to me than the famous invective of its completed predecessors. I have always had a particular fondness for this cry uttered by Pascal – no longer victorious, but wounded – in the opening lines of the letter he was never to write to the end: 'If I have caused you some displeasure by my other letters, in manifesting the innocence of those whom you were concerned to blacken, I shall give you joy in this one by revealing the pain that you have caused them. Take comfort, Father: those you hate are now afflicted.' Here is language in its ultimate perfection, newly minted. Not a word has yet been altered. The water has scarcely bubbled from the earth, and nothing has so far had a chance to soil it. Re-reading this short passage aloud (like others, of Bossuet or Molière), I reflect that the 'music' of Racine is not,

149

perhaps, essentially poetic, is not the outcome of deliberate study, but belongs to the very being of language at the exquisite moment of its maturing.

Pascal choked back his nineteenth *Lettre Provinciale*. The two last, the seventeenth and the eighteenth, written exactly three hundred years ago, show, it seems to me, a falling-off, compared with the one immediately preceding them, in which Pascal all of a sudden turned his back on mockery and displayed his triumphant hatred naked and unadorned. The reason was that Heaven had spoken to him, Blaise Pascal, that the miracle of the Sacred Thorn had left him with no doubt of what the Infinite Being thought of Port-Royal and of its Knight Errant. The gathering storm which, in this sixteenth letter, Pascal set rumbling over the heads of the cruel and cowardly persecutors 'who calumniate those who have neither ears to hear them, nor mouths to answer', reminds me always of that moment in Mozart's score where the laughter is frozen on Don Juan's lips: 'Today is heard that terrible and sacred voice. . . .'

But the moment of joy is brief. It very soon becomes clear that the Commander is about to appear on behalf of the Jesuits, that it is upon Port-Royal the lightning will strike. In his seventeenth letter, Pascal had his reasons for speaking less loudly. On the 23rd December an order promulgated by the Châtelet, and aimed at the unknown author (which is what he was) forbade him, henceforward, to print and publish without revealing his name, and without a grant of privilege. This meant that the two last *Provinciales* would constitute an act of illegal publication. In the interval between them, the Jesuits struck their first blow at Port-Royal which in course of time was to prove mortal. For half a century the war continued, save for a few short intervals of truce, with scarcely a pause, until the dead had been dragged from their graves, their ashes scattered, and their bones thrown to the dogs. But, on the very morrow of the seventeenth *Provinciale,* their enemy was wounded: the death-rattle had sounded, and they knew it. A Bull of Condemnation was promulgated in Rome: every cleric, every nun was required to sign a formulary. And so it came about that the last *Provinciale* but one had to skate warily round a *'distinguo'* which would have enabled the Jansenists to escape had they been dealing with a different adversary from the one who had the ear of the Pope in Rome and that of the King of France in Paris.

★   ★   ★   ★   ★

But even when it is Pascal writing one grows tired of hearing, endlessly repeated, that it is one thing to believe that the Five Propositions are heretical, to which the Jansenists subscribed without hesitation, but quite another, and not a matter of faith, to swear that they are actually to be found in the teaching of Jansenius, which according to his disciples, they are not. I find myself saying that all this is infinitely boring. But even this *Provinciale,* which I never re-read, contains, if only a few lines, some revelation of that mind, in reality so little secret, which shows itself almost unconsciously, so that even a single fragment of its thinking sheds a blinding light.

My expectation is fulfilled. Not that I claim to have discovered anything new in a text which is everywhere available in print. But, since this seventeenth *Provinciale* is rarely, if ever, read, it is well worth while, I think, to consider attentively what I here pick out and isolate from the whole. For in it Pascal shows something of himself that is extremely characteristic: that spiritual pride and will to power which is strengthened by the slow and secret accumulations of a sacramental life. Let me begin by quoting the relevant passages. 'You feel that you have been struck by an invisible hand which makes your errors obvious to all men, and you are trying, in vain, to attack me in the persons of those with whom you think I am united. . . . Such credit as you may gain is useless to you, so far as I am concerned. I hope for nothing in this world, I fear nothing, I wish for nothing. By God's grace I stand in no need of the good will or the powerful support of any man. Thus, my dear Father, do I escape from your clutches. . . . Maybe you have never had to deal with one who is so completely out of your reach, and so well suited to combat your errors, seeing that I am free, uncommitted, unattached, uninvolved, unconcerned, sufficiently versed in your maxims and resolute to push my attack against them

151

so long as I think that God wills me to do so. No purely human considerations will stop or slow me in carrying through this intention.'

At first sight this seems to be a restatement of what Pascal writes in the *Pensées* to the effect that he can neither be harmed nor helped by any man – but the spirit which animates this passage in the seventeenth *Provinciale* is different. We are not here concerned with the renunciation of a saint who has freed himself from all earthly bonds, and from everything that might separate him from God, but with a fighter who has got rid of all that might encumber and burden him, and is taking the offensive against a heavily armed opponent. Released from everything that might hold him back, he enjoys the quasi-divine privilege of invisibility. Ariel is baiting a Caliban blind drunk with rage, who does not know whence come the arrows which he cannot avoid.

He triumphs, but not as a saint would triumph. The movement of his own words intoxicates him. That power possessed by superior minds which he extolled when he dedicated his calculating machine to the Queen of Sweden, blazes out in these words of his, but in accents so little christian that it proclaims him to be what Richelieu had already suspected in Saint-Cyran – the eternal enemy of the Great Powers of this world. Pascal triumphs in being invisible and invulnerable. The one thing he forgets is that those for whom he has fought are surrendered, defenceless, into the hands of their enemies. Each blow that Pascal strikes at the Jesuits, his friends will pay for with their honour, since, in the long run, they will sign the formulary – and, some of them with their lives, because it was from having signed that Jacqueline, Blaise's sister, died, and Port-Royal, for all his fighting, was destroyed.

To have renounced everything means nothing, if we have not, first of all, renounced ourselves. It is a strange power indeed that enables a christian, in a battle which is wholly human, to make use of that increase in strength which he owes to his purified life, when, like Pascal, he no longer has a taste for anything in the world except the opinion he has formed about the way in which nature and Grace are related, and is animated by one passion only – the hatred, wholly virtuous in his eyes, which the casuists inspire in him. Once we have begun to see Pascal in this light, we touch in him – in the man who fought so ceaselessly in defence of the faith, and, to a very great extent, and quite unaided, preserved what remained of it for us after the offensive of the Encyclopaedists – that germ of mockery of which Voltaire was the beneficiary.

★   ★   ★   ★   ★

The Voltairian venom is already present in the last of the *Provinciales,* even though Pascal did dip only one, and that a very respectful, arrow in it. For he is no longer concerned only with the Jesuits. I am shocked, for the first time, in that letter, by a sort of sly irreverence, which he employs in his references to the Pope. In the first place, how extraordinary a piece of tactlessness! Is it to be wondered at that Mère Angélique and M. Singlin should have been overwhelmed and scandalized by a champion who proved to be infinitely less dangerous to his enemies than to his friends?

The eighteenth letter moves, in part, within the narrow limits of Papal Infallibility. On that subject he says nothing that is not true. But what was at issue was the safety of Port-Royal, and he should have remembered that his demonstration was precisely what would do him ill service in Rome. He made matters worse by not restraining his malice from making an allusion to Galileo. He pretended to be not quite sure that the earth really does turn, and then adds that, if it is found to do so, a mere pronouncement by the Holy See will be quite powerless to stop it. At that point, our mocker abandons all restraint: indeed, he goes further than he had ever gone before: 'Do not for a moment imagine that the letter of excommunication against saint Virgil for having announced it as his opinion that the antipodes exist, had the effect of demolishing the New World, or that the King of Spain, though he declared that view to be a dangerous error, was not readier to believe Christopher Columbus, who had just returned from it, than the judgement of a Pope who had not been there.'

★   ★   ★   ★   ★

This irreverence might not, in itself, have brought irremediable disaster upon Port-Royal, but it is crystal-clear that Rome very soon saw in it a mortal peril for religion, and, indeed, what christian bred, in a narrow provincial society, has not felt the presence of that poison in his veins? In so far as they touch upon the civil power, the two last *Provinciales,* perhaps to an even greater extent than the more famous ones in which Pascal had exhibited more violence, make it abundantly clear that what they were really attacking was the plan meditated and pursued by Louis XIV to overthrow a heresy which threatened not only the King of Heaven but also'the most powerful of all earthly monarchs.

In 1657, Mazarin was still living, and Louis's whole attention was being given to affairs of love. Nevertheless, he only just managed to emerge safely from the Fronde, the spirit of which is still active in those pious clowns who are so complacent in their knowledge and, because of it, boast that they are free from all constraint, even that exercised by the State. But for Pascal and the *Provinciales* the Jesuits would have been less furious and the Prince less prejudiced. In short, from the point of view of orthodox catholicism, Blaise Pascal did double service in the cause of truth: by writing the *Provinciales* which directed the lightning on to the Jansenist heresy, and were one of the determining causes of its destruction, and in his authorship of the *Pensées* which, in themselves alone, have, perhaps, done more for Christ in this land of France than the forty volumes of Bossuet's collected works.

* * * * *

Discussion still rages round Pascal. Discussion still rages round Racine: this much redounds to the honour of France, and is a sign that his genius is still a living force.

I have been following, in the *Figaro Littéraire,* the reawakened controversy which has been raging round Racine. But I am determined not to become involved. No argument, whether of friend or enemy, will have the slightest effect on me. That old 'wisecrack', for instance, about there being twenty-seven fine lines in Racine, and not so much as one more, makes me want to answer that there are no fine lines in Racine, meaning by that, none which can be detached from their context. He leaves to others lines 'sharp-stamped like an antique coin.' In this game of 'Racine's twenty-seven fine lines', most people wouldn't be able to quote one from memory, and we who love him would be very unlikely to choose the same: *'La fille de Minos et de Pasiphaé'* leaves me cold, and what answer can I make when somebody protests that my adored *'J'aimais, Seigneur, j'aimais, je voulais être aimée'* which he puts into the mouth of Bérénice, is the merest platitude?

What is Racine's own is a rigorous continuity, not of dissertation, as in Corneille, but of passion brooded on, expressed, clarified and sharply delineated by means of a small number of perfectly ordinary words which, together, compose a piece of music; music without either dissonances or studied harmonies – suggestive, certainly, but antipathetic to mere dreaming, being closely linked with a reality which, more often than not, is excruciating. There is no escaping from it, not a moment's respite, as there is in Shakespeare, during which we can look at the stars, turn from present horror, and think calmly about the destiny of others. We are locked in a cage, held captive behind the rigid lines of verse, all of them alike, face to face with naked passions turning their eyes in upon themselves, describing themselves, telling us about themselves with a lucidity which their fury neither limits nor debases.

Nothing could well be less pleasing to us French. I deny that Racine is the essential poet of my countrymen, or that in him they see themselves. Montherlant's ironic mockery belongs to an unbroken tradition. Racine has bored generations of schoolboys who find their revenge in Paul Reboux's parodies. A dead queen is always held in execration by her living successor. A certain type of romanticism – the commonest thing in the world – has always blasphemed and always will blaspheme the true and simple beauty which this one man, the pupil of Euripides and Saint-Cyran, achieved, and after whom it disappeared for ever. Racine's silence after *Phèdre* is not the silence of a single author: it is the death of a particular manner. Racine still lives, but the form of tragedy which he invented has died. His crime lies in having given birth to generations of impotent copyists. His crime is Campistron pullulating for a hundred years upon a corpse.

Racine lives, but he is something of an embarrassment, because there are no longer any players capable of interpreting him, nor any audiences able to listen to him. Mounet-Sully was our last tragedian, and the type is now as dead as the Dodo. The Conservatoire no longer breeds such monsters (or is it that the cinema destroys them at birth?). I like to think of Racine thus left lonely and deserted, for, in my opinion, he was the greatest of all those who have depicted human loneliness, not the loneliness of love but of desire. When he describes love, he does not take us far. In Bérénice and Titus, in Britannicus and Junie, in Monime we have only the 'tender' Racine of the school manuals, the courtier titillated by the loves of the princes whose servant he is. His true Kingdom was Desire. Phèdre no more *loves* Hippolyte than Roxane *loves* Bajazet or Hermione Pyrrhus. The motive power in them is hunger demanding food, and seeking through crime its satisfaction. Yet how can crime avail against the object of desire who is not consenting? Hence the recourse to charms and evil spells Racine's century which was also that of Brinvilliers. Nietzsche said of the seventeenth century, 'There is something savage in it', and saw that as its reason for seeking refuge in God.

It is certain that tragedy, in the form given to it by Racine, cries aloud for the Incarnation: the horror of it demands a Redeemer. I do not know whether Racine was concerned about the fate of a world – the one he describes – which belonged to a time before the Incarnation, in which what was lost could not be saved. It is this mystery of the relationship between Christ and Time of which Jean Guitton treats in a small but closely-packed book which I have recently been reading: *Actualité de saint Augustin*. Racine's conversion is not a phenomenon wholly foreign to Racine's tragedy, both what he wrote and what he lived.

★   ★   ★   ★   ★

Every Frenchman has his own way of understanding Racine and the battle of *Phèdre* will never end. If I am to believe one of my

friends (I take no responsibility for what he says) future histories of
the stage will record that during the first few days of 1958 Jean
Racine was the victim of a conspiracy. On the boards of our most
famous theatres outrage followed outrage. My friend assures me
that people came all the way from Marseilles to join in the
massacre.

Not having been present myself, I will not blame the players,
who were probably doing their best. May I, however, make a confession? I occasionally dream of some beneficent tyrant who would
forbid anyone to lay a finger on the author of *Bérénice,* and make it
a crime in law so much as to mention Racine's name in his hearing.
Phèdre and Roxane, Andromaque and Hermione, Athalie and
Agrippine should be regarded as great divinities sleeping in the
secret recesses of some forgotten body of work until such time as
the kiss of a fairy should waken them – the fairy being a second
Rachel, a second Sarah Bernhardt, or, on a slightly lower level, a
Bartet, someone, that is, who should know what it means to follow
a long and agonizing dramatic thought through a strictly disciplined and harmonious 'vocal line', and that this double thread
should never, at any moment, be allowed to snap. We may have
to wait a hundred years for the coming of this third Rachel, this
Sarah, this unknown and inspired monster. . . . But what a thing
to ask! Have I any right to be so hard, and, perhaps unfair in my
attitude to our living interpreters of Racine? Why is it that I find
the tone of certain critical remarks so insufferable? I speak as though
I were the only person who really knows the nature of that stage
character whose name changes, though the heart is the same, who
moves from one tragedy to another, from the Palace of Buthrotum
in Epirus where Pyrrhus reigns, to that of Theseus at Troezen which
looks out upon the sea and the relentless sky.

When arguments about the way in which a work should be
presented affect us so strongly, it is a sign that, in some way or
other, it is involved with our own story, so that any blow aimed
at it strikes at us. We believe that we know, intuitively, how this or
that line should be spoken, with what inward searching glance,
when it wings its way upward to the inexorable Father who judges

lack-lustre mortals according to the law taught by Augustine and Jansenius to M. de Saint-Cyran.

At the performance of a Racine tragedy, I feel like a musician hearing a Symphony of some dearly loved master being played in the wrong key. His sufferings could be no greater than mine when I have gone with a friend to witness these executions – quite literally executions, according to him – at which Roxane, Atalide and Phèdre, seem to him to be scarcely better treated, so he assures me, than la Voisin and la Brinvilliers.

How does an actor or an actress study the part to which he, or she, is to give life? I know nothing whatever about that mysterious travail of the spirit – which is, in some sort, an outrage against the performer's own self for the benefit of another who must possess him entirely, and take complete charge. Nevertheless, I am convinced that, with Racine, possession must precede any direct study of the role. We must feel the presence in ourselves of those great tormented figures, and be conscious that they have spoken familiarly with us since our schooldays. In my own case, they have lived within me from a time long before I had the least experience of the nature of their torment. I have been dominated by them ever since I was a youngster. We learned *Esther* by heart in the fifth form, *Athalie* in the fourth, and the other great tragedies in the second, that is to say, at fifteen.

Thus, when I was the same age as Eliacin, and, like him, had been brought up in the Temple – '*in hymnis et canticis*', as wholly protected as he was, and no less ignorant of everything to do with sex, about which children today learn at a very early age (their understanding is made more thorough through the medium of charts and drawings) – there entered into my innocence a terrible creature, one single creature whose name changes from play to play. When she is called Phèdre, it is Hermione who passes before the eyes of the infinite Being. She is caught in a beam which, narrow though it is, is projected from the source of all Light, and judges, even while it reveals, us. And it reveals us only that it may more surely pronounce our condemnation. I wonder how it came to pass that the child of whom I am thinking succeeded in resisting

the Jansenist poison hidden in the veins of Phèdre, and in spite of
the prestige of Port-Royal to which Pascal had already introduced
him. How grateful I am to the Wisdom of the Church, and to the
virtue of the sacramental life instilled into us at school, for having,
when I was still so young, provided me with the antidote. Not
that I escaped entirely. But, at least, my eye had learned, even then,
to distinguish clearly the heresy of which Phèdre is the embodi-
ment. She is the Racinean heroine at the moment of her total guilt,
yet also of her total innocence.

Neither Hermione nor Roxane do violence to nature. They go
to perdition in accordance with generally accepted rules. They do
not think of themselves as monsters. It is in *Phèdre* that this creature
becomes conscious of her irremediable strangeness, and of the sin
which she is powerless not to commit, and which she commits
without wishing to do so – '*malgre soi pefide, incestueuse*' – daughter
of Minos and Pasaphaé, of the bull, the swan and Leda. . . .

To extend the posterity of Phèdre is perhaps to be guilty of
excess. Hermione and Roxane are, in any case, not monsters,
though, in their period of rut, they are nothing but 'animals'. So
much for the 'tender Racine'. He, more powerfully than anyone
before or after him, stressed the mystery which links the soul, which
is the daughter of God, of whom the best, like Jacqueline Pascal,
claim that there can be no bounds to the pursuit of purity and perfection – and confounds it with that flesh which is subject to instinct
as in every other beast.

That is saying too little. The soul in Hermione, in Roxane, in
Phèdre, far from restraining this instinct, gives to its wild frenzy
just that degree of intelligence and power needed to make it
criminal and to justify the withholding of grace. No matter what
some critics have said, Roxane is no less a princess than Phèdre,
than Atalide, than Hermione, and these are no less savage than the
ferocious Sultana. All of them throw light on that same mystery
defined by Bossuet when he expresses astonishment at 'this deep
wound in nature', at this lusting 'which binds the soul to the body
with links at once so tender and so violent.' The Redeemer, of
course, had not yet come, and no drop of blood had been spilled

for Phèdre. . . . . How far we are today from that implacability which, in the seventeenth century, lay heavy on the Gallican Church, in spite of Saint Francis of Sales! How receptive have men's souls become to the knowledge of what Bernanos has called 'the sweet mercy of God'.

There is no element of mercy in Racine's theatre. True, it contains not only these furies who devour their males, but also princesses of a different kind. It brings before us, too, the young and virtuous mother consumed with passion only for her husband, Andromache, who remains faithful to Hector, though at little cost to herself, since an innate quality of coldness ensures both her fortune and her fame. As to Queen Bérénice, surpassed by none in passion, she renounces only what escapes her grasp without hope of recovery. With Titus gone, all that remains for Bérénice is to reign: and reign she does.

Versailles must have been peopled by just such amorous women. Bérénice? – perhaps a future Agrippine. If, so be it, Hermione, Roxane, Atalide or Phèdre escape from the clutches of Venus, and pass through their Hell of love without dying of it, that is because they find refuge in a different form of passion: 'Libido dominandi', the lust to govern. 'It is a fine life which begins with love and ends in ambition.' Agrippine and Athalie have to desire human beings before desiring an Empire. But as Phèdre differs from Hermione, so does Athalie differ from Agrippine in this, that, caught in the beam of the uncreated Light, which is Jahve, she struggles. Athalie and Phèdre are delivered into the hands of one who holds them tight, and then agrees to let them go for a short while – and he is not their Father, 'Our Father', but someone who is seeking to destroy them.

In this extremity, faced by which the daughter of Minos and Pasaphaé falls to her knees and begs for mercy, the daughter of Ahab and Jezebel stands firm, faces her enemy, braves the God of the Jews, even when the knife is at her throat – and wins, because she knows in advance that Eliacim, transformed into Joas, will choose the way of crime, and that she will be avenged, has already been avenged, by the unspeakably horrible man who exists potentially within the child: *'Qu'il règne donc, ce fils, ton soin et ton ouvrage!'*

What likelihood is there that any interpretation will ever coincide with so personal an idea of Racine's heroines? So, how can I help being disappointed, each time I see a performance, not to say annoyed and exasperated? I was eighteen when I saw Sarah Bernhardt playing Phèdre in the Grand Theatre at Bordeaux, not as a woman escaped from a mental home, an ideal subject for investigation by Dr Charcot, but as a creature on whom the hand of God and of Jansenius lay heavy – that hand which Baudelaire called dreadful – crushed indeed, but set firmly on her feet again in a wild moment of recovered hope. How strongly, at certain moments, did the tide of life flow in this woman at the very brink of death! Since then, there has been only one Phèdre (Marie Bell apart, who, in my opinion, is predominantly a Bérénice, and was an unforgettable Atalide) only one, who did not seem to me unworthy of that great memory – Marguerite Jamois, just as Gaston Baty was the only stage designer who realized that he must contrive a breach in the palace wall at Troezen so as to reveal the blue of the sky, 'that motionless and sleeping blue', against which Phèdre's desire surges and breaks in a powerless confusion of spent spray.

But what does all that matter! What alone should count is what Racine wanted to say. I cannot ask that stage-designers and interpreters should breathe new life into the statues lying drowned in me since childhood under the sediment of my own destiny. I hope, therefore, that they will not take in bad part this dream of mine, now ended – a dream like those which visit us a little while before the oncoming of sleep, when the inner eye can no longer distinguish between what is and what is imagined, and we ourselves, the creatures of our making, and those of the masters, are all confusedly intermingled for a moment before being swallowed up and lost in the approaching night.

★　　★　　★　　★　　★

There is an actual witness of that world which lives again in Racine's heroines, Saint-Simon. He gives back to us the drama of Versailles the Italianate *décor* of which still rises in our midst. We also have at our disposal those stage characters, kept intact after two centuries, as though locked away in drawers, thanks to the eleven portfolios in flaking calfskin, stamped with the arms of the duc de Saint-Simon.

So great is the power of a style which imposes itself upon us with such high authority. It is difficult to parody other authors, but the difficulty here is to avoid slipping down the slope of imitation. The greatest work of fiction to appear in our time, Marcel Proust's novel, sounds the very tone of Saint-Simon in all that touches on the Guermantes' world, and it would be fascinating to study how Proust made Saint Simon's style 'a part and parcel of himself' and, having done so, developed one of his own. It should be remembered that Proust took from Saint-Simon not only the style but some part of the method. Like the Duke, he was tireless in his questioning, and conducted his voyage of discovery in the world of servants no less than in that of their masters. But other writers, too, have owed much to the *Mémoires*. The novels of Henri de Régnier, which have now fallen into ill-deserved oblivion, as well as certain features of Abel Hermant's books, derived from them – to mention only the dead.

But which of us has not fallen a victim to this obsession? Saint-Simon is a witness who does not wait till he is called to give his evidence. He speaks, or, rather, it would be truer to say, he shouts at the top of his voice, and we needs must listen. Louis XIV paid but little attention to this petty duke, one of the most recent creations, though very far from being one of the most fashionable. What were the reasons for his partial disgrace? He had resigned his commission in the army and he talked too much. It never occurred to the King that the duc de Saint-Simon was more to be feared than anybody else at Court, a man on whom he had no hold, but who had a hold on him; or that, because of this insignificant Duke, he, the Great King, would himself become, in turn, a subject, not only while he sat upon the throne, but for all time.

A witness for the prosecution? Yes and no. All things considered the King could have afforded to forgive him. No one could well have been more biased or more prejudiced than Saint-Simon, yet, where the King was concerned, antipathy was balanced by admiration. The Duke saw his master as he was, missed nothing of what was horrible in him, but, nevertheless, he could not escape from the charm he radiated. In this he is unique. He spares us nothing of what was atrocious in the man, but, like all his contemporaries, recognized the grandeur of the total composition. It flares out from under that furious pen the more vividly because the writer did not attempt to conceal the monarch's absurdities, his shameful acts, and what we cannot avoid calling his crimes.

It is, above all, in relation to what has made of Louis the most odious of despots, and has left the ugliest of stains upon his memory, that Saint-Simon appears, turn and turn about as virulent accuser and witness for the defence : – I refer to the Revocation of the Edict of Nantes and the persecution of Port-Royal – the combined effect of which was to strike a blow at religion, the mark of which is still visible. He was one of the first, and most violent, to denounce the abomination for which the royal policy was responsible, and to point out its incredible stupidity. All readers of the *Mémoires* will remember the striking passage in which Saint-Simon refers to 'the atrocious conspiracy which depopulated a quarter of the Kingdom, ruined its trade and generally weakened it; which long exposed it to organized pillage and merciless oppression; which authorized tortures and executions as a result of which innocent persons of either sex perished in their thousands. . . .' And so it goes on without a pause until it reaches the final and worst horror of all, which – 'filled every province with the perjured and the impious, with pretended abjurations by which men were forced to adore what they did not believe. . . .' But I must not cut into fragments what is all of a piece, and has no equal in the literature of the seventeenth century, except the interminable and relentless denunciation flung by Bossuet at the dying Molière.

Saint-Simon pleads on the King's behalf his ignorance in matters of religion, for which he was not responsible, and of which he was fully aware, and his habit of entrusting them to those whom he had appointed to be his spiritual directors. And here we touch the sore spot in all catholic monarchies which, in my opinion, so far from marking the great moments in the history of religion, have reduced it to its lowest ebb, as must always happen when political Christianity is in the ascendant, in other words, when revealed truth is made to serve human ends.

We know only too well what has happened when the power exercised by a confessor on a devout monarch who is also absolute master has been exploited, and the price paid for it by religion and by the country. Louis XIV died with his conscience at rest. He believed that he had been the defender of the faith, and was assured that this was so by Father Tellier and Mme de Maintenon.

About Port-Royal and the Revocation his conscience was more than clear. He had no doubt at all that, in the eyes of God, they constituted his strongest claim to favourable consideration, and that by forced abjurations and the violation of graves he would obtain forgiveness for his adulteries, his wars and his 'cleansing' of the Palatinate by methods of which the recipe has not, even now, been lost.

True Christianity is wholly innocent of these impostures, which are what men have made of the Truth committed to them in trust. This is what men have done in the past, and continue to do in other ways. But great is the Truth and shall prevail. Port-Royal, of which not one stone remains upon another, raises its voice for ever against Versailles. The religious policy of Louis XIV was the fruit of a double offence against revealed truth. One was committed by an ignorant penitent who shifted on to other shoulders, in matters of religion, what it was his public duty to decide for himself, and for which he alone was responsible before God: the other, by those ministers of religion who used their spiritual authority in favour of a Party, and allowed Grace to be exploited in the interest of their masters, and of their own will to power.

The little duke saw this as clearly as he saw everything else: the abysm of ignorance at the bottom of which the Very Christian King found himself bound hand and foot all through his interminable reign. Prejudiced though he was, this witness who stood midway between the detractors on one hand, and the panegyrists on the other, provided ammunition for both Michelet and Bainville. And this contradiction remains the sign of his truthfulness.

XII

WHAT WE read is not a matter of chance. All my living springs
communicate: Pascal, Racine, Gide. The centuries have nothing to
do with it. Deep down, the sheet of subterranean water is the same.
I come back to Gide. It is because of Madeleine, his wife, that I
have made this return. She has become a centre of attention: she,
who suffered so much from the printed word, is now a subject for
books.

The wife of André Gide had a passion for self-effacement. Her
last wish was that she should disappear entirely – should be a mere
nothing in the world's eyes. She wanted to escape for ever from
that wretched story in which the pure and the unclean were so
strangely intermingled, in which the angel never ceased from playing the beast, or the beast the angel: the story of André Gide.

Gide dead has committed the one action which could make
my friendship for him turn, for a moment, to disgust. He has
dragged that great and secret spirit into the glare of a publicity
which, of all things, filled her with horror. He took advantage of
the fact that the dead are defenceless, are given into our hands. He
seized the opportunity to tear from the night which covered her
this child of God who asked only to be forgotten.

But, since the act has been committed, we can draw some profit
from it. Jean Schlumberger, who knew and loved Madeleine Gide,
has understood that only by making sure that the light now beating
down on her is total, can we make reparation for that cruel wrong.
Nothing must be left in obscurity. It is for us to see that Madeleine
Gide – now that Gide has thrown her to the lions – is presented as
she was, and not as Gide wanted us to think she was.

This book: *Madeleine et André Gide* – a masterpiece of spiritual
biography – tells the story of a soul fast bound to a satanic creature.

Eloa responded to the love of the dark angel, but he did not bring her to perdition. Whether she accomplished his salvation, or whether she suffered in vain, is a secret known only to God. But, at least, she remained unsullied and incorruptible. That exquisite diamond lit with its fires the darkness of a destiny which, in the spiritual order, is terrifying to contemplate.

But it is no longer because of Gide that she holds our attention. It is for her alone that we shall read those passages, only too few in number, which Jean Schlumberger has made available to us. We have nothing more to learn about the ageing Narcissus who, for so long, went on describing his own reflection in the stream. But of her – so secret, so withdrawn – we hope . . . what is it that we hope? What is it we expect?

I did not know her, but I have met others of her race. Nothing is more useless than to indulge in argument about the comparative merits of men and women. But I do believe that there is a degree of perfection to which a great feminine soul can reach which is not attainable by us men. My personal experience leads me to think that such souls are often to be found at the meeting-point of Protestantism and Catholicism – as in the case of Madeleine Gide, or of Stoicism and Catholicism – (of this, Simone Weil is an example), or of Catholicism and a heart given over entirely to the passions of the heart. Here I can give no name, but of such lovers, I can think of more than one who ended by grappling to themselves not a single individual, but Love incarnate.

What Madeleine Gide owed to her Protestant upbringing was spiritual sincerity. Though, for a long time, she remained in ignorance of Gide's peculiarities, which were of a kind that she was too pure even to suspect, she had learned from the days of her girlhood to bring a lucid and inflexible judgement to bear upon the man she loved, no matter how subtle, how indirect, how impenetrable, how clever he might be in concealing what he did not want her to know.

Many years before she married Gide, she recorded her diagnosis so clearly that there seems to be nothing more to be said about him. 'A moment came' – she wrote – 'when I had a very sad, but quite definite feeling that, so far as the end to be achieved was concerned, you and I would, from then on, each of us follow a separate road ... God grant that that may not be so. ... I was saddened and frightened by my awareness that you, André, were more than ever an end unto yourself, that nothing else interested you, that no other love was possible for you! ...'

That passage comes from a secret diary which Madeleine kept in 1891 and 1892: and when, twenty-six years later, moved by an impulse of clear-sighted despair, she burned Gide's letters, and, in a state of frozen misery witnessed the fury of the literary man shouting that they had been 'the finest ever written', his utter misery served to confirm the summing up which she had made as a young girl. Those letters had been addressed, through her, to his future public, and constituted the finishing touch to that self-portrait, the painting of which was the sole end which André Gide had set before himself, his sole concern, his sole interest (as it is, perhaps, of each one of us whose trade it is to spend our lives in writing, and in putting ourselves on view).

The commonplace that there can be no love without respect, was certainly true for Madeleine. She could not help loving the strange being who had been dear to her from childhood, and was, in so many ways, deserving both of love and admiration, and she could not help being filled with a sense of horror, not because of what he was – only God could know that – but of what he did and of what he inspired others to do. Over and above any question of frustration there was the evil which was slowly eating into the soul which lived so far withdrawn from the world, and I cannot share Schlumberger's optimistic view that, by and large, the life of this couple was a happy one, and that Gide was to blame for having, in some sort, misrepresented and slandered that happiness.

* * * * *

That he yielded to the temptation of dramatizing himself and stressing the black strain in his character; that he arranged the facts to fit this dramatization, does not in any way alter the underlying truth in the destiny of a saintly creature who, from childhood, had been exposed to an evil made incarnate in those who were closest to her, and had passed from the hands of a mother who was a guilty wife and a cause of scandal, to those of the young man called André Gide.

Since I did not know her, I can but accept the statements of so unimpeachable a witness as Jean Schlumberger. All the same, I cannot help feeling that he has underrated the significance of the deliberate withdrawal and effacement of a woman who scarcely ever lived with her husband, except at Cuverville – though that, in itself, is of no great importance. What should be noted, however, is that though she never ceased to have a high regard for him as a writer (she even went so far as to think of him as the French Goethe!), in later years she refused to read anything he wrote (save for a few fragmentary scraps in one issue of the magazine which was serializing *Les Faux Monnayeurs*).

Nothing shows more clearly the horror, the sense of shame, perhaps even the fear of a public scandal, which kept her, as his wife, in a constant atmosphere of gloom and misery. Here, it seems to me, Schlumberger has shut his eyes to what must be regarded as little less than a martyrdom, the worse for having neither a beginning nor an end and inseparably bound up with every minute of her life.

Her nostalgia for the Catholic Mass was bred of a craving for something that Protestantism could not give her: faith in the redeeming power of suffering. She believed that acts were of no avail, that André could derive no spiritual benefit from what she was enduring, that she was prevented from redeeming a soul so deep sunk in evil. This rejection of the whole doctrine of the Communion of Saints was part and parcel of her Protestant faith, yet something told her that she would not suffer in vain.

What inclines me to believe that this was so is the peace which marked the end of her life. Schlumberger sees in it a proof that husband and wife had recovered the harmony which had once marked their union. But could she really have been ignorant of what so many books and periodicals were hinting, of what Gide had become in old age, and gloried in being? If she were not, then how could she have recovered any sort of peace?

Is it too rash an assumption that she found the peace in which she died on that frontier of which I have already spoken, where, loyal Protestant though she was, she had compounded the honey of which she stood in need, by bringing back from behind a blurred dividing line the principles of a truth in which she had not been instructed, but had discovered for herself?

There may, too, have contributed to the indulgence which she showed towards the sinner, at the end, a less simple view of sin than that taught by the churches. The books she read, the intellectual climate of Cuverville, prepared her mind to conceive that a crime, the causes of which were so largely pathological, might perhaps not seem to the Eternal Justice so horrible a thing as it did to the theologians. There had been a time when, according to Gide's own statement, she had seen her husband as a criminal and a madman. But already, in that early condemnation there is something that calls for, that demands, the attenuating circumstance.

⋆　　⋆　　⋆　　⋆　　⋆

I can easily imagine how the group in which her husband played the part of 'enchanter' must have appeared to one whose compass-bearings were so firmly set on God. I know it from having myself been attentive to, and having played a small part in, that spiritual struggle, that war of religion, which was unloosed by the return to the Catholic Church of Dupouey, Jammes, Ghéon, Copeau and Du Bos, of which, for believers, the salvation of André Gide was, in some degree, the stake.

This war showed at its most violent round the deathbed of Jacques Rivière, and when Du Bos flung in Gide's face the bomb of his *Labyrinthe à claire-voie*.

There can be little doubt that, in the course of this struggle, the catholics must, more than once, have shocked and irritated Madeleine Gide, perhaps even frightened her away, and that at a time when she was so near to finding the road to Rome. An admirably dignified letter which she wrote to Claudel is proof of this.

Gide was only too glad to have an occasion for accusing his friends. Their pharisaism, and what he called 'their *apologétique à coup d'ostensoir* had, he said, fortunately disgusted him with the Church. The truth of the matter is that he would never have yielded to anything or anyone, and he knew it. I believe in God's infinite respect for the liberty of the individual soul: Gide's *no* had been spoken, that *no* which only by a miracle could have been withdrawn at the last second, in the last breath, because 'with God all things are possible'.

Perhaps, on the other hand, it was the assumption of prophetic powers by those catholics who so lightly sent their brother to damnation, that drove Madeleine Gide away. But though she stood firmly shoulder to shoulder with her husband whenever he was attacked, she must have abhorred the group of which he was the hero, and the dramas to which it gave rise. The strangest of these was the overlapping of two loves: it is as though we were watching one of Shakespeare's equivocal comedies, at the end of which the princess turns out to be a prince.

When two beings are so closely bound together as were these, we must be careful not to crush one under the virtue of the other. Madeleine, who was the elder, who had not agreed to marriage until she was twenty-five, and then after a long series of refusals, may not have known the actual nature of the thorn in Gide's flesh, but she knew that there was *a* thorn, and had accepted that knowledge in advance. She would not have wished any other destiny for herself, or, to put it more precisely, any other vocation, for she can never have doubted that 'the faithful wife sanctifies the faithless husband.' Entrenched within her faith, as Gide was in his, no less unshakeable than he was, no less obstinate, she remained upon the bank from which the prodigal had pulled away, not so much despairing as pensive: '*Toujours je la connus pensive et sérieuse*' ... I am glad that Jean Delay in his book, on Gide's early years, quoted that line from Sainte-Beuve, and applied it to Madeleine.

So defenceless and so frail in the eddies of passion, in the jumble of intrigues tied and untied by the Spirit of the Bizarre, she was, to all appearances, defeated, and the book which her husband wrote about her after her death looked like an act of vengeance, not directed by him at her, but by the demon who possessed him against the sweetness and compassion of her saintly soul. Yet I remember the last word spoken by Gide on his deathbed, in which there sounded, I shall always believe, the cry of a soul on the very brink of darkness, hearing itself called by its name: and the voice that uttered it was both that of a woman and a child, of Emmanuèle, of Alissa, of Madeleine.

I recall that sinister stretch of marshland in the heath which, at the time of our summer holidays long ago, we called *'le grand marais'*. We loved to go there to pick the gentians, blue as summer skies. The wife of André Gide makes me think of those unsullied flowers waving above the pestilential swamp and in fancy I lay upon her grave one of the blue bunches which, as a child, I clutched so tightly in my hand.

*　　*　　*　　*　　*

After having lived for several days in the spiritual presence of Madeleine André-Gide, I have been moved by curiosity to look again at what I wrote about Gide at the time of his death. The various items seem to me now to sound a rather priggish note, to be a bit stiff and affected, but, then, I never could be wholly natural with him. Such as they are, I give them:

If, as M. Singlin said to Pascal, 'the greatest charity we can show towards the dead is to do what they would have wished us to do while they were still alive' – then, we should spare a great writer who has just entered into eternal life the conventional flatteries of a funeral oration. One of his greatest claims to fame is that never, in the whole course of his career, did he once stop trying to be absolutely honest about himself. I shall not daub this dead man's face with paint. Imperfect christian though I am, it is as a christian – and it is what he would have wished of me, and expected from me, that I now meditate beside his grave. I do not pretend to have mis-understood the deadly lesson of *l'Immoraliste* – deadly for him, but also for us, in so far as we hearkened to it. If what christians believe is true, then Gide knows now what all of us will know before long. What is it that he knows? What is it that he sees? When Lamennais lay dead, his brother wandered round La Chesnaie, sobbing out: 'Féli, Féli where art thou?'

For Gide was very different from the picture most people had of him. He was the very reverse of an aesthete, and, as a writer, had nothing in common with the doctrine of art for art's sake. He was a man deeply involved in a specific struggle, a specific fight, who never wrote a line which he did not think was of service to the cause he had at heart.

What was that cause? It was firmly established on two levels. The most obvious, and in the eyes of the world, the most scandalous thing about it was that he had set himself not only to excuse, to legitimize, but even to recommend a certain way of love. But this was not the worst. Gide convinced only those who already shared his tendency. I do not believe that there was ever yet a hunchback who became one by persuasion. But this teaching of his was nothing but the application to his own particular case of a far graver determination, dating from his youth, which was to break with the moral law in its Christian form as taught by the churches.

The extremely important part played by Gide in my own life derived from this choice which he had made, without any attempt at concealment, at one definite moment, a choice no less spectacular, if I may say so, than Pascal's famous 'wager'. No one can ever have laid a bet against Christianity more calmly, more rationally, in spite of his moments of prudence, of his flashes of repentance, of his brief relapses. Such cases are far less frequent than one might think. Most men choose not to choose. Very few are prepared to take the hazard of deciding that evil is good, and good evil, to venture, as Bossuet says, 'to overturn that tribunal of the conscience which has condemned all crimes'. But that is precisely what Gide did, with a calmness, serenity and joy which makes the heart quail.

This was why his catholic friends saw him as the apostle of Lucifer. Was it by mere chance that he lived at the centre of a furious spiritual battle? The conversion of Jammes and of Dupouey which led to Henri Ghéon's return to God, followed by that of Jean de Menasce, of Jacques Copeau, of Charles Du Bos, the exchange of letters with Claudel. . . . There can be no doubt about it, Gide lived in a whirlpool of Grace accepted, Grace repulsed. There were moments when even he seemed to yield, as when he wrote the ardent pages of *Numquid et tu*. But it was never long before he pulled himself together, and went off, striding down his own especial road, wrapped in his great cloak, with a terrible look of happiness on his face, valuing his joy above all else, that joy which he soon ceased to distinguish from pleasure.

A constant concern in matters of culture and of outward appearance, a perpetual effort, marvellously rewarded, to ennoble his particular type, his easy, distinguished, aristocratic carriage, preserved him from having to play the role of helot, which he left to other, lesser writers who came after him. We must have been living in a strangely unobservant age, ignorant of, or incurious about, contemporary trends, for the award to André Gide of the Nobel Prize not to have provoked a movement of amazement, even of terror throughout the world.

Gide's destiny has always seemed to me to have been shot through with the supernatural . . . like that of other men, you will say, but that I deny. For the most part, other men are just sinners, 'poor sinners'. Gide was not a poor sinner but a strange pilot, towering above a generation dedicated to 'curious and gloomy errors', and holding the wheel in a powerful grasp.

What of his work? It is among the most significant of our time. This is not the place to study the influence of his critical thinking, which was embodied in *La Nouvelle Revue Française,* and the establishment of the true values which it set up. For me, *Les Nourritures terrestres, L'Immoraliste, Amyntas* can never wholly lose the charm with which the fervour of my twentieth year endowed them. But Gide, like Jean-Jacques and Chateaubriand, was one of those writers whose lives are a great deal more interesting than their works. They are at the very opposite pole from Shakespeare and Racine who vanish from sight in the radiance of their created characters. Like Rousseau's *Confessions* and Chateaubriand's *Mémoires d'outre-tombe,* and for the same reason, it seems to me that Gide's *Si le grain ne meurt* and his *Journal* will long keep active that ferment

in the dough of humanity which it was their mission to provoke.
. . . For evil or for good? On that point I will not commit myself:
'All is Grace.'

It is not for us to judge what God expects of a human being, of
a human life. How is it possible to believe that a Nietzsche or a
Gide were not intended to be what, in fact, they were? What
happens in that moment of the gathering dusk, when the soul, on
the very point of parting from the body, ceases to hear or see anything belonging to this world? During his last lucid moments,
Gide may, perhaps, have remembered the words he wrote, not so
long ago, in that short book which he dedicated to Charles Du
Bos: *Numquid et tu*. 'O Lord, as a child I come to you, as the child
you willed that I should become, the child who gives himself into
your hands. I resign all that was my pride, and, in your eyes, will
be my shame. I listen, and to you I commend my heart.' The man
who was inspired to write that prayer, perhaps remembered it in
the silence of his final hours.

★ ★ ★ ★ ★

'His most discriminating literary admirers like to forget that on
five or six of the most important points in human thought, he was
as positive and as clear-cut as any mind with a reputation for vigour
and brutality.' Those words were written by Barrès about Renan.
What a revealing light they cast on André Gide!

That mind which wanted to be unbiased, did its best to be so, and
believed that it was, about essentials, was nothing if not positive.
It was this contrast which gave to it so great a charm. How readily
did Gide bow to your arguments! With what feigned detachment
did he leave you with the last word! But, left to himself, with his
open note-book in front of him, he re-occupied in strength all the
positions he seemed to have surrendered, passed over to the offensive, armed himself with all the concessions you had thought it
good tactics to make, and turned them, with a sort of blunted
fierceness against you, which did not matter, but above all against
the truth you thought you had established. The *Journal* is filled with
little else but those solitary and cruel reprisals at the expense of some

interlocutor who had been so foolish as to think for a moment that he could get the better of an argument with André Gide.

He was charming, supple, sinuous, 'kindly and gracious', ever ready to lapse into a softened mood, capable of being demonstrative, ready, on the slightest excuse, to be moved to tears, exquisite in conversation: these characteristics one cannot stress too often, because I can think of no other man with so keen an intelligence, who could combine it with what I can only call a quivering openness and sensitivity. But under all that grace and charm, there was a tautness of will, a clenched jaw, a state of constant alertness to detect and resist any external influence which might threaten his independence. A state of alertness? That is putting it mildly: beneath each word he wrote, he was carrying on sapping operations against the enemy city where a daily fight was going on against natural instincts, where the satisfaction of the passions was given the name of evil, where an especial curse was laid on pleasure, or what Gide regarded as pleasure.

Yet, this enemy city was still his city, the one where André Gide, the Calvinist, had been born into slavery, where, from youth up, he had suffered, and, with him, those many million human beings on whom the laws of the Christian City laid the same interdict. .

There was a Spartacus in Gide. He was the leader of a slave-revolt at the very centre of the Roman order. Spartacus was defeated after a short two years of rebellion, but André Gide, after half a century of constant victories, flung *Corydon* in the faces of bourgeois, priests and pastors, boasted in his *Journal* of a far greater number of exploits than Oscar Wilde had needed to make him acquainted with the dismal glory of hard labour, and, in return for all these provocative activities, got the Nobel Prize into the bargain!

It is by no means certain that, in his heart of hearts, André Gide did not look on all this success as in some sort a curse. He knew that the magnificence of Wilde and Verlaine had been paid for to the uttermost farthing. I have an idea that there were times when he wanted to be a martyr. I remember how, one evening, many years ago, he spoke to me with something like longing about the prison where Gustave Hervé had expiated his anti-militarist opinions. That, I think, showed Gide's greatness. It was no senile exhibitionism which led him to make the revolting confessions which are to be found in his later *Journals,* but a desire to declare publicly that he had committed those same acts for which other men are still condemned and dishonoured. Never has the relativity of the moral code been so vividly displayed than in predicaments of this kind when the making public of a bad or even horrible act is occasioned by a demand for justice.

Beyond good and evil, this Spartacus led the way into the promised land of a new morality, at his heels those gangs of slaves who thought that they were breaking their chains, though, in fact, it was only Gide who achieved freedom. For him alone did this miraculous reversal operate. The ill-starred race to which he belonged got no benefit from it. To none of his disciples did he bequeath what he had enjoyed: all the gifts of the artist, a high degree of culture, maintained and enriched up to his dying day, an art of living deliciously at odds with a society on the demands and duties of which he had declared open war though without having to give up those comforts which it bestows on its more privileged members. To realize this, we have only to take a look at the younger, and far less distinguished representatives of this monstrous buffoonery of the western world, when they reveal in public the squalid secrets of the bedchamber, and perform indefinitely the hideous and joyless music-hall parody of the married state.

Inimitable Gide! With what feints and passes he always managed to ward off his heavily armed opponents! With what ease did he overthrow them one by one, and leave them sprawling in the clang and clatter of their Maurras breastplates, their Thomist panoply, while he, so nimble, in his Mephistophelian cloak and doublet (or was he not, rather, Faust, disguised in the devil's cast-off clothing?) stepped over their prostrate bodies, and hastened to his pleasures or his reading.

Virtuoso of the limited edition, of the book that is hard to come by, carefully cultivating his seeming unsuccess the better to ensure a more solid fame, it was, from the very first, on the fewness of his readers that he staked his money. In France, a land of peasant holdings and small shopkeepers, the gift of literary reputation is in the hands of three thousand discriminating persons. We no longer have a national literature. The *Nouvelle Revue Française,* Gide's own child, was the official organ of this coterie which could dispense rewards at will. Through it, he formed the opinions of us young men between 1910 and 1914. When I think back to those days, it seems to me incredible how many authors of all ages, from Théophile Gautier to Bourget and Henri de Régnier, he made us throw overboard. But how should we not have been fascinated and enthralled? It is a rare occurrence for culture and taste to reach so high a level in one man, who, moreover was free of all ideological shackles. I have said that Gide, like Jean-Jacques and Chateaubriand, will live on only in those of his books which treat directly of himself: *Si le grain ne meurt* and the *Journal,* because it is he who interests us, and not the creatures of his invention. But I was forgetting that he remains the one and only subject of his imaginative books: *L'Immoraliste* is he: *La Porte étroite* describes the cerebral love on which he built the painful ambiguity of his life. All through *Les Faux Monnayeurs* which, taken by and large, is a failure, runs the pulsating vein of Edouard's *Journal.* His presence in everything he wrote gives a lasting quality to his work.

Gide the virtuoso of dialogue: with his friends, with his adversaries, with himself, with Christ. He was the only one of our elders who had this remarkable gift. Barrès lived withdrawn behind his defences, a monster of indifference and inattention to everything that was not himself. Claudel; A Matterhorn at which one looked lovingly from one's window, but one cannot carry on a conversation with the Matterhorn. Jammes, sparkling with intelligence, a marvel of upward-leaping and spontaneous poetry . . . but having absolutely no understanding of others. With Gide, on the other hand, *how* one could talk, or, rather, how one could have talked if the first young man who came along hadn't always, unfortunately, distracted his attention. I never enjoyed anything approaching intimacy with him except during the few days when I had him, so to speak, under lock and key at Malagar, and twice in the course of two ten-day periods at Pontigny.[1] When Gide formed an attachment he browsed on it at leisure, but it was the very devil to establish the attachment!

The old Ariel has now been dispersed to the elements, and his going was his final gift to us. It administered a faint shock to the small republic which drowsed away the time in the editorial offices of the weekly press. 'Ah! what a deal of interest will M. Renan's death arouse!' – exclaimed the young Barrès – a piece of youthful impertinence which conceals the greatest praise which an old writer can be accorded by his juniors. Gide's death has not separated him from us. Of him it cannot be said, as it was said of that same Barrès: 'Gide has wandered away. . . .'

* * * * *

It sometimes irritated Gide to feel all round him so many christians on the prowl. At the same time, he enjoyed playing up to them. But he attributed their relentless pursuit to what he held to be a marked feature in their outlook, namely, a refusal to relax their efforts until they had got the largest possible number of birds into their net. Some of them did, in fact, give him good reason to think that having the last word was all they cared about. I have known several of these specialists in conversion who kept a 'game-book', and wore round their waists the scalps of the penitents who had fallen to their gun.

But, if the christians who were hot on Gide's heels had been merely obeying the dictates of this infuriating mania, they should, logically, have carried their activities into other fields, as well. Yet, I have never heard that Giraudoux, Jules Romains, or any other libertine of letters was ever pestered by the convert-hunters.

There is no getting away from the fact that Gide's case was a

[1] Early in the twentieth century, Professor Paul Desjardins instituted, at his home, the former Abbey of Pontigny, in Burgundy, a ten-day period every year (the "Decades de Pontigny") to which intellectuals from every country came to discuss cultural, religious and other topics. These gatherings were a form of lay retreat. (Translator.)

very special one. In the first place, it was he who had set the hunt afoot, by which I mean that, having been born a christian, and a fervent one, at that, he had started an argument with what we could not help feeling was a divided mind: had broken free from all dogma, but not from the Scriptures: had become estranged from his native Calvinism, but had fallen under the influence of the catholic affirmation, and was hesitating before taking the next step, very much aware of those eddies of grace set moving all about him by the successive conversions of Claudel, Jammes, Dupouey, Ghéon, Copeau, Du Bos and many others.

The mystery of these several conversions, following hard on one another among men who were his familiars, was something, whether he liked it or not, which touched him néarly. This he did not deny, and *Numquid et tu* bears witness to the existence of a passing phase of fervour in this hero of our spiritual drama, from which he never completely withdrew till the day of his death.

Now yielding a point, now breaking off the action, he managed, almost to the end, by employing a high degree of subtlety, to maintain a firm stand against his christian friends. He himself wrote in *Si le grain ne meurt,* speaking of the first time he took ship for Africa : 'I made my farewell to Christ with so painful a sense of uprooting that I still doubt whether I have ever really left him at all.'

This sense of uprooting was, from the christian point of view, the basic cause of his essential error. Finding it as impossible to renounce Christ as to renounce himself, the only course left for him was to apply to his own case every word spoken by the Lord. It was a game at which he excelled. His *Retour de l'Enfant prodigue* is a masterpiece of evasion.

The first letter I received from him in April 1912 (dated from Florence) contained a violent protest against something I had written – I forget in what periodical – to the effect that *Le Retour de l'Enfant prodigue* had distorted the meaning of the Gospel parable. So obvious is it that this is so that I remember my astonishment when I realized that my words had deeply pained him. 'I am writing,' he said, 'to protest with all the strength at my command against your use of the word *sacrilege* in relation to my *Enfant prodigue,* and against the charge you level at me of having stripped the Gospel parable of its divine meaning. I wrote those pages in a mood of piety and respect (is it possible that you have not *really* read them, or that having read them you have failed to grasp the emotional seriousness of which they are the expression?).'

The ambiguity here is obvious: as though the very seriousness of Gide's version of *The Prodigal Son* did not reinforce the distortion! But the fact that he thought it necessary to protest was a sign that Gide the christian recognized the gravity of the charge brought against his false parable. From the point of view of faith, nothing could more resemble what we mean when we talk of the 'sin against the Holy Ghost'. It is that which explains the violence shown by some of his friends, first and foremost by Claudel who had led the attack against him armed with the plumed helmet of hope, the tomahawk of faith, and the double-edged battle-axe of charity.

Gide's case was unique. The majority of christians never get beyond the letter of the catechism. They have had no knowledge of God. It is a word which, for them, has never had any real content. They deny, yet do not deny. Christ has never been in their lives, as he was in that of André Gide, the friend of whom Lacordaire speaks, whom once we met on our road when we were young, who has loved us and been by us beloved. They have not taken the trouble to make him say what he did not say, before turning their backs on him. If we are agreed that only those will be for ever lost who have deliberately renounced God, in full knowledge of what they were doing, and as the result of a choice long weighed and considered, then I do not remember ever having come across a more glaring instance than that of Gide.

It goes without saying that in the christian view only God can judge the reasons which determined Gide's attitude, some of which were, beyond all doubt, deserving of respect.

True enough, but this is no place to mince words. The fact of the matter is that Gide's particular form of erotic satisfaction lay at the very centre of his drama. The struggle he waged was about that and about nothing else. For him the point at issue was the legitimization of a special type of desire. This, in itself, is not the attitude of a base or vicious mind. Gide's standard was a high one, in that it implied the need to be in a state of complete and perfect balance, which meant that he was to refuse nothing, to deny nothing of the contradictory aspirations of his nature at its deepest level. But nothing can alter the fact that this demand, made by himself to himself, was bound to result in that reversal of standards for which there is no forgiveness: 'evil be thou my good.' That was precisely the situation which Gide was busy formulating when he wrote *Le Retour de l'Enfant prodigue*. The adulteration of the Parable led him to undertake a basic subversion.

Here it is necessary to dwell upon the special nature of Gide's character. Christ in his teaching seems to take no account of personal tastes. It is not his concern to know the bizarre inclinations of this or that individual. His commandment – and this is true for all of us – is – that we be pure, that we renounce our lusts, *no matter what their object may be*. The world's condemnation of homosexuality operates on the social level and has nothing in common with Christ's condemnation of *all* defilements, nor with the blessing he has accorded to those who have kept themselves pure: *Beati mundo cordi quonian ipsi Deum videbunt*. Many pure hearts have strangled in themselves a tendency which Gide not only excused, but approved and glorified. What it comes to is that he was demanding special treatment for one especial vice. Remembering the words put by Pascal in the mouth of Christ: 'I love thee more fervently than thou has loved thy filth',[1] my conclusion is that Gide loved his filth above all else, but first of all denied that it was filth. And here, for the believer, there intervenes another aspect of Gide's life – the angelic.

To make it possible for agnostics to understand the interest shot through with pain which Gide's case aroused in his christian friends, I will quote, without comment, three passages (though I could find many more of the same kind). The first two are from Gide's own writings. One occurs at the beginning of the second part of *Si le grain ne meurt,* where he says: 'Though I have recently come to think that an important actor, the Devil, played a part in the

[1] H. F. Stewart's translation.

drama, yet I shall relate that drama without, in its early stages, referring to the intervention of one whom I identified only much later.' The other is an extract from the *Journal des Faux Monnayeurs:* 'There are days when I feel in myself so massive an invasion of evil, that it seems as though the Prince of Darkness were already establishing hell within me.'

The last I take from Julien Green. Describing, in a quite recent publication, Gide's behaviour to him, he says: 'After my return to France in 1945, I never met Gide without his trying, in one way or another, to attack my faith.'

Don't misunderstand me: from the catholic point of view there is nothing in those passages which should make us despair of the salvation of a friend whose reasons were never base and often dictated by concern about the less obvious points of moral teaching, and when one would least have expected it of him. Thus, for instance, certain admissions in the last volume of his *Journal,* are introduced for the sole purpose of showing that the very same acts committed by him, dishonour other men, and that he had been privileged not to share their fate: he demands his share of disgrace. Never was there a case which called upon us, with such good reason, to remember the precept: 'Judge not!' and Saint John's words, when he says that the Lord came among men not to judge but to save.

I have tried, here, to do no more than try to cast some light on the reasons for that sort of blundering busy-bodying of which André Gide's catholic friends were guilty during his life. Not that I regard myself as being less of a sinner than he was. Far from it! Gide was never a 'poor sinner': he stood erect and triumphant, the very image of defiance.

XIII

CRITICS CAN sometimes be very frivolous. Chance and the leisure of a country existence have recently given me an opportunity to read some of their comments on the *Carnets* of M. de Montherlant. 'Fancy a writer of his eminence bothering to give us the scrapings of the barrel!' That seems to be the prevailing attitude. But what they call scrapings would be negligible only if the writer were negligible. Even if they were devoid of all interest, that very fact would give them a certain importance, at least in my eyes. The fact that the author has published them during his lifetime, at the most brilliant, the most productive stage of his career, is, in itself, significant, or should be, for the critics. An author's attitude to his work, his manner of presenting it in such a way as openly and shamelessly to get the most out of it, his determination, especially, to leave a self-portrait in the public mind by handing over his most intimate jottings to the kind of people whom he has never ceased to lash with a contempt which has rarely been equalled, all this, surely, should set us trying to discover the man behind a body of work which is no more than an ill-adjusted mask.

But that is not my present intention. When we authors have rounded a certain cape in our life's journey, we no longer devour each other, any more than we bandy compliments. We each of us occupy, or like to think that we occupy, a little niche of our own. We don't indulge in mutual challenges. If one of us suddenly started baying the whole pack would soon be in full cry – and what an uproar that would produce! Still, there is no getting away from the fact that authors know infinitely more about one another than does the most unbridled critic. There is nothing to equal the judgement which flows through ourselves and empties itself on the heads of our professional neighbours. That is the criticism of creators – but the law of the jungle forbids us to make use of it.

I can speak less calmly of this particular confrère than I can of any other. I confess that it was not without a certain feeling of bitterness that I read, in these recently published *Carnets,* the letter I wrote to the then young author of *La Relève du matin.* Montherlant and Malraux! How I revelled in the first rays of your literary dawn! Of another dawn as well. I have a vision of myself reading, when you were scarcely more than children, the Preface to *Sesame and Lilies* by a man called Proust, of whom I knew nothing. From that moment I went about hungrily questioning all those who knew him personally, and I well remember one old lady talking to me about 'little Proust'.

But to go back to the *Carnets* of M. de Montherlant. I had a pretty shrewd idea of what I should find in them, even if I found nothing else – something which none of the critics so much as mentions (evidently they despise it): and find it I did: a style which, if it be true that 'style is the man himself', plumps us down fairly and squarely at the centre of the problem presented by Montherlant's work and his life. For it at once becomes obvious that there is a contradiction between the figure which has occupied the centre of the literary stage for the last thirty-five years, and the manner of writing, which springs straight across three centuries from the deep deposits of the classic age without the slightest hint of pastiche. It is the easiest, the most casual, the least self-conscious style imaginable, poles apart from the studied, 'composed' manner of a Gide or a Valéry, or from an instrument tuned to a highly personal pitch, like Proust's. In its naturalness his way of writing can be compared only to that of Colette, with this difference, that Colette kept her nose so close to the ground that it is an understatement to say that she never moved so much as a single step from nature. Montherlant, for his part, has never moved a step from his school books, has never ceased playing the Roman, and this puts him in constant peril of becoming turgid, though certainly not in these *Carnets.*

Here is the man, some of whose attitudes I can scarcely approve, showing himself to us as he was, from day to day, over a period of years, and here is the admirable style which is himself and not himself. Never was it more true that 'the I is another'. In the continual action which we bring against him (I must admit, with reference to at least a couple of his books: *Les Jeunes Filles* and *Solstice de juin*, with indignation and fury) in this action, when he is not speaking through a fictitious character, as in these *Carnets*, Montherlant shows as the most implacable of witnesses against himself – the most ingratiating and the most venomous (as when, for instance, he says: 'The secrecy which others observe where we are concerned, keeps us walking over the thin crust of an abyss. We live at the mercy of their silence.')

But against this witness for the prosecution there stands another, for the defence, who puts up a stubborn resistance to the Manfred which is so obstinately imposed upon us. That witness is the style, which has never varied since he first began to write: a certain tone, at once familiar and noble, a voice which is now that of a youth, now that of a mature man. I can hear it sounding in these *Carnets*, and even when it says what is horrible in my ears, I recognize it as one of the alternating pair of the *Dialogue avec Gérard*. I have never re-read that last chapter of *La Relève du matin*, but nor have I ever forgotten it. 'I believe in the seriousness of life.' That is the last rejoinder. It still runs through the outbursts of this Don Juan who has never finished killing the Commander, for the Commander is himself. I have often said of Montherlant, in my moments of anger: 'There's nothing genuine about him but his style.' That was tantamount to falsifying the indictment I was bringing against him, for style authenticates a work, and, through the work, a life.

What went wrong? So much good fortune and so much fame imply some obscure form of shipwreck, and not in the sense that every life, no matter how successful, is a game lost before it is begun. How can I explain what it is I feel about his books? A great artist who can never say anything that is not, in the matter of style, inimitable, tells us something quite different from what he set out to tell – which showed quite clearly in the books preceding *Les Jeunes Filles*. To be sure he has never been anything but himself from the beginning. From the moment of his setting out, he had made his choice – never to say no to any desire. But in every desire he discerned an infinite exigence. 'Our desire admits of no remedy.' He used those words of Saint Teresa as the epigraph to one of his books. I have come on some of his sayings in my notes; would he, I wonder, acknowledge them today? For example: 'It is the soul, rather than the body, that desires bodies'; and this: 'To wake in the night tightly pressed in the arms of somebody, and to realize, having forgotten it in sleep, that she, though capable of catering to our pleasure, is not worthy of our tenderness, and then to clasp her with groans.'

For a long time I thought that Montherlant and Gide (who, I have reason to believe, could not abide one another) had one characteristic in common, much to be dreaded by those who think as christians, that of having deliberately, at one moment of their lives, laid a wager against God – which is not so frequent an occurrence as one might think, since the majority of men have never known the God whom they think they have renounced. But I was wrong. Gide, as a fervent little Huguenot, had been really of Christ, and, in order to gratify his passion, had had to wrench himself free from Him. So far as it is possible to judge from outside, it does not seem likely that Montherlant had ever been the young man at whom the Lord had looked in such a way as to lead the evangelist to say 'And he loved him.' He might, perhaps, protest against this verdict, and if I am wrong, I ask his pardon. I am basing it upon something he wrote about the days when he was still playing at football in the yard of a catholic school. He speaks somewhere of his *catholicisme à l'Italienne,* and I very much doubt whether he ever got beyond that stage. When he says Rome, for him the Vatican is jumbled with the Palatine. I remember being scandalized by something he says – I think, at the beginning of *Le Songe* – when looking at the crucifix hanging above his work-table. And, indeed, how could a young man so entranced as he was by the beauty of the flesh, ever have been expected to love a God of whom Pascal said that he so loved suffering bodies that he chose for his own incarnation one more racked with suffering than any other in the whole history of the world.

Montherlant's choice was made within the frontiers of paganism. The alternation which has ruled his life operates for him only between two poles which are not under the dominance of the cross. He had listened to the lesson of the great men of the ancient world, but others, too, who were less great, had found the way to his heart. There is, at his finest moments, something of the stoic in him, but I am inclined to think that what he finds really attractive are those lower depths of human nature through which Suetonius drags us, of which Tacitus writes in such cold horror. To say that even Nero did not seem to him to be repulsive, is to say too little. He makes a bad business of defending his liking for a man who, having attained to a position of power which enabled him to satisfy desire in its most extreme form, fled it and died in a latrine with only one young slave who had remained faithful to him, at his side.

The danger in alternation is that it ends by becoming no more than a balance between satiety and hunger until such time as death takes a hand, even though it be an ignominious death.

This writer, in whom contempt is like a passion which he never tires of satisfying, is filled with a feeling of reverence for what goes beyond contempt. The fact that, never for a moment, does he turn against himself his gift of expressing contempt with magnificence, is sufficient proof that he was never a christian except 'à l'Italienne' (the expression is his, not mine). 'We must needs come not short of horror when we know ourselves.' Those words addressed by Bossuet to the Maréchal de Bellefonds do not apply to M. de Montherlant, who comes not short of horror only in his knowledge of others.

Perhaps at one moment of his life he did manage to establish himself in that ideal Rome where only Caesar wore the tiara. Perhaps he succeeded in maintaining a balance between the frugal requirements of a noble nature and the satisfaction of desire. To be reassured of this, one need only re-read *Les Olympiques* and *Le Paradis à l'ombre des épées*. But it was for no more than a moment. What is the worth of a moral code like that of the stadium, which is valid only to the young? Montherlant is beginning to discover what I have good reason to know better than he can, that life is not short; and if that truth exists which Plato would have us strive to reach with all our heart and with all our soul, it could not be that of one brief stage of a lifetime. If it is indeed the Truth, then we should find it, ever faithful, beside us when all others have deserted us.

We are what we do: only our actions can define us: that is the teaching of today. But we are also what we might have been, and what we may be able to become. This assurance enables the christian to reach a better understanding, or so it seems to me, of the man called Henri de Montherlant, whose chosen part it was always to be driving the world to exasperation and imposing himself upon it. There are a certain number of things which a writer is come among us to say, which he must say, even if he has decided to sacrifice everything to what he desires. Whatever part he elects to play, if he has a mission to give utterance to noble things, then, no matter what the cost, he will unburden himself of them, and with the voice given to him for that purpose and for none other: but there is a flaw in the metal.

Here I must break off, as I do not wish to pronounce on merely literary matters. I began with the intention of pointing out that the *Carnets* of M. de Montherlant deserve more attention than the critics in general have devoted to them. And now, in spite of myself, I have aired some of my thoughts about this writer who has been so greatly praised and so greatly disparaged, who is, at once, so triumphant and so little understood, who is now approaching his declining years, who once wrote this semi-blasphemy (does he, I wonder, remember it?) 'Little though he represents of hope, let us not undervalue God.'

*　　*　　*　　*　　*

By way of a marginal note to what I have said about Montherlant's *Carnets,* I would refer here to two very harsh judgements made by Bernanos and quoted by André Rousseaux recently in his regular gossip-column. The first of these was about Montherlant, and it need not long detain us – those two men could never have understood one another. The other is concerned with Henri

Massis, and here the finger of criticism touches one of those wounds that never heal. For Massis was one of Bernanos' first companions when he started on his career as a writer and, with Robert Vallery-Radot, helped to draw the attention of the public to *Sous le Soleil de Satan*. It is for Massis himself to tell us, should he think it necessary to do so, what it was that separated the two friends, and led Bernanos to utter the cruel words to which André Rousseaux refers.

This calling up of the ghost of Bernanos, now that he is no longer with us in the flesh, is a matter of concern to all of us, to those, especially, who are still involved in the confused hurly-burly where, though we have not taken his place, we have, at least, survived him. There can be very few among his masters and his comrades on whom, from time to time, Bernanos did not turn with a sort of inspired fury. Whom did he not, in turn, first adore, then burn? Maurras, Daudet, Claudel, Maritain, and many others, myself included. . . . God knows with what sarcasms he flattened out the more obscure!

Why should we care what he said about us, now that we are treading the road to death and silence, to an unbroken accompaniment of praise and insults? Have we not already grown indifferent? No, or not at least, to what came from Bernanos. The author of *Dialogues des Carmélites* did not, after his death, survive as, say, Valéry and Proust have survived. From that life of suffering, from that murky, lightning-torn body of work, comes a cry for help, addressed to us, his brothers in the Faith; a cry provoked by neither literature nor politics, but rising to the surface from far greater depths than the residue of the quarrels of a generation, three-quarters of which has been already swallowed up.

Not one of those who were victims of Bernanos' outrageous treatment (among the christians, at least) has harboured a grudge against him. It is as though each was the only one who knew the very secret links that bound them together. I do not believe that a single one of them will deny the validity of the reason which I venture to put forward, namely that our relations with Bernanos were in the nature of intercession.

If, then, we feel justified in invoking his judgement against one of his brethren (and, spiritually speaking, that is a serious matter) we must, first of all, be quite sure that what is at issue is a critical thought calmly expressed, and not the product of one of those bitter rages which sometimes swept over him. And our mistrust will be redoubled when we lean over and watch the undertow of Bernanos' thought eddying round Maurras and the *Action française* – the undertow of a passion divided against itself.

As to the outburst against Massis, which André Rousseaux is pleased to consider as 'a piece of masterly criticism', though I, personally, can find nothing in it which really seems to fit the author of *La Défense de l'Occident,* whom I know well, in the sense of knowing a lifelong adversary – an adversary rather than an enemy – and with whom, over a period of thirty years, I have found myself crossing swords. Henri Massis, according to Bernanos, when scarcely more than a child, got himself fixed up 'in the name of Pascal, or, at least, of some notable nonentity of Port-Royal, much as M. de Montherlant, at the same age, became closely involved with an anarchistic and woman-hating nobleman who, maybe, had borrowed the appearance and the manners of his first Jesuit confessor. It is I who am crazy to think of these bizarre couples as being in any way unique, crazy to raise the cry of imposture against these unfortunate creatures who, having been from birth more or less deprived of any deep-rooted sincerity, have worked hard for twenty years to achieve it through the medium of a purely imaginary character.'

If it be the truth (a superficial truth at best, which is certainly not sufficient to give us the key to the secret places of the man and the writer) that Montherlant set himself to ennoble his type, to model it on the pattern of certain Roman or Spanish figures, it is certainly not true that Henri Massis, a writer concerned with ideas, ever showed any similar preoccupation, or that if he did, it was not the dominant characteristic of this catholic *à la* Maurras who was engaged in an intellectual battle which became a conflict of friendships.

Maurras, Maritain, Bernanos all lent themselves to certain doctrines. It was a very different impulsion which drove Bernanos to go beyond the political realism of the *Action française* to fight, as this catholic did, all his life long, at the very centre of the Maurras movement, in an effort to integrate his faith with it, and to take his stand in its support, even when Rome fulminated.

So long as the struggle lasted, I, God knows, remained in the camp opposed to that of Massis. But now that those dark years are behind us, and the battle-ground has shifted, I still see Massis motionless in precisely the same spot on the field, now almost deserted, in the gathering shadows, upright beside the grave of his defeated master.

Fidelity is, today, the word I should choose for him, if I were compelled to retain only one. It can, admittedly, be understood in different ways. It was because of fidelity to Christ that Bernanos took a firm stand against the Christ-less catholicism of his first master. Yet, if what Maurras is supposed to have said on his death-bed is true – and it was quoted by the duc de Lévis Mirepoix in the speech he made at his reception into the French Academy, if he really and truly said that, it is the finest utterance ever inspired by the approach of eternity in a man whose ears had been closed from childhood. I quote from memory . . . 'For the first time I hear somebody coming . . .' if it be true that those were among the last words spoken by the master of the Action française, then Henri Massis, who had mounted guard faithfully till the end, had found his justification.

The cruellist invectives of Bernanos remain in touch with that subterranean layer of charity which gave warmth to his whole life. We must, therefore, be on our guard against isolating them, separating them from their secret context. He never did, nor on this point was he ever embarrassed by contradictions. Take my own case: when, precisely I cannot remember, but at some time in the thirties, he wrote something pretty scathing about my work, comparing it to a cellar, the walls of which are sweating with moral anguish. Nevertheless, all through that period I was regularly receiving from him handsome copies of his books, all of them inscribed, often in words which went far beyond the requirements of professional comradeship, as, for instance, this, on the fly-leaf of *Les Grands Cimetières sous la lune:* 'This book can make its way only by advancing through the breach which you so bravely and so nobly opened. May you not find it too unworthy of you. With all my admiration and all my love.'

The many hard blows he gave me were all made up for, on his return from Brazil, by this testimony which I wish to record here, since it expresses, I feel sure, his last thoughts about me, if it be true, as an eye-witness assures me, that, during his last days, he spoke my name in that same spirit of friendship: '. . . I believe that many matters between us could have been clarified had we known one another better. But I also think that, in spite of all the things which should have brought us together, we had, in our youth, now long past, been so differently orientated to life, that any real mutual understanding was impossible, even though we were in agreement on fundamentals. Yet, I know from experience how often your great name is linked with mine by many friends across the seas who, perhaps, know better than we do, what we have meant to one another. It is in their hearts that we find ourselves at last united, in the expectation of being so in the sweet mercy of God as in an eternal morning.'

I deny that vanity plays any part, no matter how small, in the impulse which has led me to quote these words. But, though freedom of criticism should never be questioned, it is the bounden duty of all men of letters, when their lives are drawing to a close, to make clear the spirit of brotherhood which unites them in 'the sweet mercy of God' – no matter what they may have written or spoken about one another.

The literary comedy, the participants in which arouse feelings of pity in André Rousseaux, has a reverse side which is far from comic. From Gide, taking his secret with him into death, to Maurras suddenly catching the sound of God's approaching footstep: from the bed on which Bernanos entered into the mystery of the blessed agony, to that where Claudel – on whom he had poured out so much praise and so much insult – begged that he might be left to die in peace – there ceaselessly circulates the invisible

grace uniting all of us who, to the best of our poor abilities, have
set up our work in the eye of heaven, and not in words alone.
Others may laugh, but we know that what we are making is a
burnt-offering. Bernanos knew it, too; his groans were often
audible when the agonizing task of tearing a story from his heart
had left him drained and exhausted. I doubt, very much, whether
he would ever have spoken with contempt of Montherlant's
twenty-eight volumes even if, like André Rousseaux – who has
an acute sense of hearing – he had caught the sound of 'falling
rubble', for nothing can collapse which has not first existed, and
only nothingness is sheltered from destruction.

All human work is menaced, none of it can remain intact, and
all of it, sooner or later, will perish. I have seen, at Olympia, the
great columns lying in the grass, but they still sing to the glory of
the unknown builder who twenty-seven centuries ago raised them
in honour of the gods.

* * * * *

No, Georges Bernanos would never have spoken slightingly of
a man's work, though he cared little what he said about the man.
He knew what the writing of a single book costs its author. But
let me make this clear that not one book, nor several books, necessarily add up to a 'body of work', that talent alone is not the decisive
factor. By what then shall we recognize its authenticity? Perhaps
by the effort, which is the same for all novelists no matter how
different, to disentangle, through their fictions, a very secret skein
in themselves for which most men care little, and of which they
are barely conscious. 'My strange heart' – said Maurice de Guérin.
But what heart is not strange? The heart of Bernanos most certainly was. The priest in him who was like no priest in real life, the
quality of priesthood which he could make manifest only in
fiction, and, quite literally, had dreamed. . . .

What does it cost a man to be a writer? I expect that such a
question, at this time of day, will provoke a smile. It is true enough
that the romantics made all that business about the poet-pelican
feeding his ungrateful young upon his heart's blood, pretty

ridiculous. In this matter, the romantic movement put society in the dock. Today we no longer hold that society is called upon to worry about the poet *qua* poet (or the novelist, if it comes to that: I have never succeeded in drawing a clear line of division between them). The fate of the poet concerns himself alone, and no help can come to him from outside.

The novelist, unlike the critic, does not have the work of others as his starting-point. In the tapestry he weaves, the thread is drawn from the most secret part of his being, even though none of the figures who take shape in the pattern in the least resembles him. To this inner and deep-delving labour of the spirit, to this mysterious process of metamorphosis, there is a corresponding agony which varies in different authors. In Bernanos it reached a remarkable degree of virulence. What that man suffered! – as a writer, I mean: the act of writing was a torment to him.

About this we are better informed today, thanks to the labours of the late Albert Béguin. Not long ago he added a long note to the only authoritative edition of Bernanos' last book, *Monsieur Ouine* (*Club des Libraires de France*), in which he gave the curious story of its making. It is, in its way, a moral tale, for it seems that the sinister M. Ouine laid what one might almost call a curse which was never for a moment lifted, on the manuscript to which he owed his existence. Other writers will not find anything strange in the torment and misery which went to the making of *Monsieur Ouine*. Albert Béguin shows us Bernanos in the grip of an almost physical torment which is only too familiar to his fellow practitioners. How well I recognize the cry which sounds in one of his letters! – '*Mon vieux,* I have been trying for the last two weeks to make up for lost time, and have been working away at my new book from morning till night. But I am writing in a sort of dense darkness: less than ever do I feel capable of judging the value of what I am doing at the cost of so much pain!' . . . and again: '. . . I simmer away for hours on end in the recesses of gloomy cafés, chosen because they *are* so gloomy that only by having something to do can one avoid dying of boredom. But when I've got through with my scrapping, tearing-up, recopying, and feeling as though I'm writing on emery-paper, I reckon that my average rate of progress is about a page-and-a-half a day....'

That's roughly a picture of all of us, though particular habits and manias differ with different temperaments. Every writer is heavy with child and chooses the place where he will drop his young. With Bernanos it was an inn-parlour or a fly-blown café, though how anyone can write in a café is beyond my comprehension. I should have to have been deprived of every other alternative before even trying! Still, it was in a café that Bernanos managed to produce the number of pages for which his publisher was waiting – for he was paid by the page – always giving.

But, no matter where the act of parturition takes place, the business of writing involves difficulties, a special variant of suffering all its own, which, in my own case, has not grown less after fifty years of authorship. I have reached a point at which I can never bring myself to settle down at my writing table except when it is a question of giving pleasure to a photographer. I usually work on my knees at my allotted task which, unlike that of the sculptor or the painter, does not demand the handling and shaping of materials, and leaves no trace of his craft on the man who lives by his pen. There is nothing to protect him against the dream he drags from within himself, against the monsters who will never have an existence beyond himself unless a reader offers them hospitality and by his attentiveness bestows upon them the gift of life.

What reader? To be read and judged is undoubtedly an ordeal, but not of the kind imagined by the public. Listen to this further heart's-cry uttered by Bernanos, for it echoes the doubts and agonies felt by most writers: 'I no longer believe in myself: I have lost faith in myself, just as one quite simply loses one's faith. I am heart and soul in agreement with any fool, provided he thinks or writes ill of me.' Our critics, even when they are our enemies, have no better readers than us, and none more easily convinced. They have no idea of the harm they do us, nor, for the matter of that, of the good when, in spite of themselves, admiration flashes through the clouds of their abuse.

All the same, the pain which authorship caused Georges Bernanos had its origins at a far deeper level, and had nothing to do with the mere difficulty of writing. No doubt the hard conditions of his life, the work he had to do which was at variance with the natural leanings of his character, had some hand in it. A Bernanos acts as a lightning-conductor. But we must dig deeper than that. His torment was born of what he discovered, of what his work made him conscious. The man who overflowed with an infinite hope, seems, at the end of his life, to have lost all hope, for hopefulness is not hope. *Monsieur Ouine* makes this abundantly clear.

I am one of those who found the novel disappointing. But that is because I had the misfortune of first reading it in its unrevised form. Now that I have been able to *get inside* this great and sombre book, it certainly is not, for me, what it is for Albert Béguin, its author's masterpiece. Nevertheless, more than any other of Bernanos' novels, it casts a revealing light on the spiritual adventure in which the act of writing involved him. It was of this that he was thinking when he said: 'All adventures of the spirit are calvaries.' There is always the danger that they may end fatally. Georges Bernanos did not come alive out of his.

In one of his letters he defines the novelist as a man who 'lives his dreams, or re-lives them, without being aware of it.' According to Albert Béguin, Balzac was just such a dreamer. Perhaps: but a novel never amounts to anything, never becomes a masterpiece, unless the fiction is so transmuted into reality that it compels us to forget the dream from which it was born. In *Monsieur Ouine* we are struggling, from beginning to end, inside a nightmare. Never, for a moment, do we feel (or, at least, I do not) that we are at grips with creatures of flesh and blood. All the same, so overwhelming is its power, that we are made privy to the unendurable vision which Bernanos the christian had of the world at the very moment when there was nothing left for him but to pass into eternal life.

Monsieur Ouine was first called *La Paroisse morte*. Did Georges Bernanos, in his darkest hour, really see France as an agglomeration of 'dead parishes'? I have often wondered how Péguy, who gave his life when the French revival was at its height, would have reacted to what Bernanos witnessed, the headlong decadence of the period between the wars, and that dismal descent which, since the Liberation, has not been checked for a single day.

Monsieur Ouine is the expression of an agony which extends far beyond the drama of France. In a world where the power to discriminate between good and evil seems to have been almost lost, Georges Bernanos went further than any of us in the knowledge of the exact nature of evil – not sin, but evil. 'The Son of Man came among us to seek out, and to save, what had been lost. . . .' But what if what has been lost shall remain lost for ever? What if the creature who is free to choose damnation shall prevail over the eternal love? Bernanos in *Monsieur Ouine* ventured to the extreme point where the dark wave of despair beats and breaks. He could do so without weakening, because he was borne up by the hope of all the saints. But perhaps it was because he had seen M. Ouine face to face that he died.

XIV

DURING THE Occupation, Jean Paulhan managed to persuade me that a prose-poem (by M. Francis Ponge, I think) called *Le Cageot* was a really admirable production. It would never have occurred to me that so absolutely characterless an object could, through the power of words, succeed in acquiring so intense a life as did that *cage* in its crude reality. I cannot help wondering whether it is not from this cage that M. Robbe-Grillet, a sworn enemy of the psychological novel, has developed his idea of the novel of the future in which objects will establish themselves as objects before they are anything else, where things will lose their 'romantic heart', and the universe its false profundity, where there will be nothing left for the novelist but the surface level at which the visual and descriptive adjective will replace all the false beauties of an older style.

He may be right: I am prepared to agree with everything he says. Still, I cannot resist an impulse to kick. The point at issue particularly concerns the writers of my generation. I do not, for a moment, think that my young colleague wants to see all of us dead, but he does look forward to the death of the psychological novel, and of everything to do with it.

There is no vice in him. He has never tried to settle accounts with anybody, as did Jean-Paul Sartre with me, on the eve of the war, with a degree of violence which I have never resented. For I happen to be one of those on whom, when they are at death's door, extreme unction has a revivifying effect. To his youthful aggressiveness I owe it that I gave more attention than usual to the novel at which I was then working. Of all my books, *La Pharisienne* shows the fewest signs of haste. Since, too, it was best understood by Protestants and, oddly enough, in Sweden, I am, perhaps, to some extent indebted for my Nobel Prize to the author of *La Putain respectueuse.*

Consequently, I will do my best to forget that I am, more or less, personally involved in this rough-and-tumble. I will try to find out what it is in me, other than an instinctive conservatism, that makes me set my face against M. Robbe-Grillet's arguments. I shall keep my ear cocked, without any hostile intention, when this young colleague of mine resumes his series of articles on the Craft of Fiction which he began in the last issue of the *Nouvelle Revue Française.*

On that occasion, it is true, I had done barely more than read the first few words when I began to feel my hackles rise. M. Robbe-Grillet had coolly and calmly headed his article with a sentence from Nathalie Sarraute: 'The mere fact that the novel clings to out-worn techniques classes it among the minor arts. . . .' Heavens above! – can there really be anyone so half-witted as to believe that a literary form which can boast Cervantes, Tolstoy, Dostoievsky, Dickens, Balzac and Proust, is a 'minor art'? I am conscious of a horrid doubt. Can it be that my young colleague's contempt for old-fashioned techniques extends to the works of these writers to whom the whole Western world is in debt? Is it conceivable that there should be a novelist who would refuse to admit the reality of Natasha Rostov, Lucien de Rubempré or David Copperfield on the ground that they were born of a living mind and heart, created in their author's image, and that it was *his* mind, *his* imagination which gave to them a life which is all their own, and presented them in settings which are merely 'states of mind'?

But 'the cage' is also a state of mind, and so are Cézanne's apples and the kitchen-chairs painted by Van Gogh in his shabby room, with his pair of old 'beetle-crushers' standing under it. In every work of art there is always someone speaking to someone through the medium of sounds, colours or words – somebody talking about himself to somebody else.

I take up the cudgels for no specific technique. To some extent I am an enemy to all of them. In the non-plastic arts, all techniques, as soon as they are clearly defined and imitated, consciously or unconsciously, become false. Of such a kind is the mystery of technique in novel-writing. It is essentially the secret of its inventor, and can be used only once. I must doubt whether any one of the masters who worked before we were born, was ever aware that he had a particular manner or a particular method. The one he used, and others may have used before him, becomes his own because it enters into the creation of a style which, so soon as it is established, is unique, irreplaceable.

Can M. Robbe-Grillet imagine what the equivalent of *A la recherche du temps perdu* would be like, written by a man full of theories about the Craft of Fiction, surrounded by all the 'no-thoroughfare' signs, the psychological and metaphysical prohibitions set up by the technique of the cage? The genius of novel-writing consists in the novelist's discovery of a world to which he holds a key which he alone has the right to use. The imitator, the disciple, who thinks that he can steal his master's secret, or has inherited it from him (has M. Robbe-Grillet any disciples?) may, for a short time, delight his readers, but it will very soon be obvious that his gold is but gilt.

M. Robbe-Grillet's antipathy to the dismal 'musts' which swarm over the corpse of the psychological novel, is, therefore, not only justified, but healthy. I must admit, however, that I find great difficulty in seeing any enrichment of the form in his technique of the surface and in his hatred of going deep. The really great novelists do not, as he appears to think they do, dig down in the hope of finding some buried truth: on the contrary, it is the most secret part of their being that rises to the surface and becomes incarnate in their imagined characters. I feel pretty sure that no good novel is ever written by submitting to any clearly-defined body of rules. The unknown Proust – if such there be – now in the course of writing his book, is, at this very moment, inventing a language, developing a style and making masterly use of all the freedoms of width, height and depth of which the great novelists never have deprived themselves, nor ever will.

* * * * *

When Alphonse Daudet wrote *Jack* and *Le Petit Chose* he thought of himself as the French Dickens. *Jack* and *Le Petit Chose* do not prove that Dickens' manner was a bad manner, but only that it suited Dickens and nobody else. His method becomes 'method' only when others make use of it.

An ageing writer, once he begins to imitate himself, drops to the level of his imitators, no matter how great he may once have been. I am inclined to think that no true greatness has ever known this particular fall from grace, and that if a novelist is so afflicted, it is a sign that he never really belonged to the race of the gods.

It is not that I take exception to M. Robbe-Grillet's ideas, or not, at least, before I have undertaken to examine and discuss them. No, what worries me, and makes me think that his procedure is open to criticism, is that it starts from the definition of a technique, and then goes on to apply that technique strictly, whereas all the great peaks of fiction are crowned by books, no one of which possesses the same features as any others, for the simple reason that no identical method has been applied to all of them. If, some day, M. Robbe-Grillet comes to write great books it will not be due to the fact that he has laid down certain laws, but only because he has been able to forget them.

✱   ✱   ✱   ✱   ✱

'Dichtung und Wahrheit' – Poetry and Truth – are the two terms of the title which Goethe gave to his Memoirs. We must be careful not to see them as opposites, for, in fact, they intermingle. Not that Poetry is Truth in any absolute sense. 'What is Truth?' This is not the place to attempt an answer to Pilate's question. All I would say here is that no work of art can be said to exist except in so far as it pierces through appearances and reaches – I won't say, the Truth, but something that is true. You may say that that is a truism. I agree: it is, and my only excuse for insulting you with it is that it serves as a starting-point for thought. But I am marking time and getting no further, I can merely repeat that nothing the author has fixed in words, or the painter on canvas, can hope to endure unless it manages to express something that really *is*. When everything else has been consumed and destroyed, at the bottom of the crucible this hard stone remains unaffected – the true work, the masterpiece.

Poet or novelist, musician or painter, each of the great ones bores in the little field of his own individual destiny, and what leaps out like spouting water, is what will never perish, or, rather – for all that is written or painted perishes sooner or later – what has a chance of survival because 'it is true'. *Phèdre* is true: Van Gogh's chair and the heavy country shoes beneath it are true. Three bars of Mozart are true, beyond the power of the human heart to bear. And always it is the same truth: the truth of which our age has lost the secret. That, at least, is how I see our age: not that it is a particularly debased age, but because it makes an ostentatious show of nothingness, and is, in some sort, an upstart of nothingness.

'What today is beautiful in literature is its truth' – Claude Mauriac wrote recently in the *Figaro,* when reviewing Andrè Gorz's *Le Traître.* That word 'today' did, I confess, surprise me. Evidence that the beautiful has always been the truth, that it is, in a certain manner the 'splendour of truth', comes to us, serried and sparkling, from the past, whether close or distant, and not from today. To be sure, we must be cautious in dealing with our young contemporaries, and not deliver against them a verdict of which the appearance of some great work, today, perhaps tomorrow, may well make nonsense. Perhaps I have undervalued what they have already produced. I have no desire to be a blind *laudator temporis acti:* but, after all, the past is all that we, who live in it, have left. I deny that, at any moment in our history, art has been a lie. It could not be, for either it is authentic or it is not – unless, of course, we have decided that the processes of art, the technical methods and the rules accepted and obeyed in any given period were untruthful in themselves, and so the conveyors of untruth. My own view is that, on the contrary, they have been the very condition of a deepening exploration of the human spirit which has never been surpassed or even equalled.

I do not, however, reject that – 'what, today, is beautiful in literature is its truth' – completely. A point in favour of the new generation is its determination to have done with the lies of second-rate art, of that sort of half-way-house of art which was cock-of-the-walk not so long ago. The authors who were making an honourable career in literature when I was a young man, would not have gone far in 1958 – perhaps not even the best of them. . . . I spent part of the holidays re-reading Barrès' *L'Ennemi des lois* (perhaps the pleasure I derived last year from exhuming *Un Homme libre* had put me in the right, receptive mood) but, oh! how frivolous I found it! Who, nowadays, would dream of handling Fourier or Saint-Simon so perfunctorily! How self-sufficient the tone of that book is, how inadequate! Nothing is left of what I found so impressive when it first appeared. A great deal more, I agree, is demanded by the modern reader. The time has gone by when a man could set up as a writer, and enjoy a popular success, who had no genuine understanding of anything, as was the case in the early years of the century. The reign of the philosophers has compelled even us, the old hands, to do a little hard thinking. I feel rather pleased with myself for finding it so easy to come to terms with André Gorz's *Le Traître* which, once, I should have given up as a bad job after the first few pages. How wrong I should have been! Increasing age makes us more serious-minded.

That, however, does not alter the fact that horror of the unauthentic, a deliberate contempt for style and for its blank windows, all this *plus* rigorous self-discipline, a determination to deal only with what can be seen and touched and felt in the immediate present, will never be sufficient to reach to the level of truth from which alone masterpieces are born, and, so far, it has not been. Claude Mauriac is fully aware of this. What he finds deserving of praise in André Gorz is 'the need he feels to carry further and further the investigation he is making into the precise nature of his thoughts and emotions,' '*to push his exploratory method to a point at which its very success becomes self-defeating*'. I wish to point out, however, that this aesthetic of defeat does not, in my opinion, apply to *Le Traître,* which is the story, in the form of a journal, of a young, half-Jewish existentialist, expatriated and hunted down, whose mind is outraged by the excruciating conditions of the life he is compelled to lead. He is a reincarnated Kafka who has returned to the very world he foretold and described. As Isaiah saw, across the centuries, the passion of the Son of Man, so did Kafka see that of the young Gorz who, at the time when he was writing, had not yet been born. But we must beware of judging *Le Traître* as a work detached from the man in whose brain it was conceived. Somebody is there, busy 'killing' by the sheer force of his intelligence, and we listen to him (we cannot help ourselves) no matter how long he goes on talking, since, while he does so he remains undefeated. We shall go on listening for so long as he lives – he, and those others who talk about themselves, describe themselves, as though seeing themselves with eyes infinitely more piercing than our own, or, rather, differently constituted from ours, adapted to a different kind of vision.

*   *   *   *   *

There is no resisting them (at least, not for us whose habit and profession it is to be readers). But in the worlds of the theatre, of the novel, and, more especially, of poetry – what are the works which the men of this generation – convinced that they are the first who ever identified beauty with truth – are presuming to compare, and compare favourably, with those of the past? What justification exists for their superiority-complex? The mere fact that the younger writers are preoccupied with 'self-defeat' is evidence enough that they have run aground where the great masters triumphed.

And here I suggest that the work ends in self-defeat only because the man is self-defeated. Perhaps no other literature is possible from now on than the type of destructive analysis practised by Michel Leiris and André Gorz. If this is so, then there is nothing left, outside such confessions, but the opaque world of objects, and, so far as novels are concerned, we can count on nothing but a succession of 'robbegrilleteries'.

Actually, I don't believe anything of the sort. Man will assert himself, once more, in art, and, in it, find himself again. It is too soon for us to return to dust while we are still alive. A day will come, perhaps it is already here, when human personality will become re-established in works of art planned and composed, when the work will again find its fulfilment in a face, in a look, in what that face and that look expresses of a truth which we can never re-discover unless we take it as our point of departure, and already possess it.

* * * * *

'Ending in silence with Rimbaud, in a blank page with Mallarmé, in an inarticulate cry with Artaud, *allitérature en allitérations* ends by melting away with Joyce.[1] . . . For Beckett, on the other hand all words say the same thing. If we follow this line of argument to its logical conclusion, it becomes apparent that only by writing *just anything* can this author give expression to what he wants to say. . . . Like Beckett, Michaux has come to see in *paralysis* the one unimpeachable reality. . . . If they are not mad, like Artaud, or, in a certain sense, like Kafka, the majority of our young writers ape madness, like Beckett and Bataille, or, like Michaux, seek a substitute for it in drugs. . . .'

To these characteristics pin-pointed by Claude Mauriac in *l'Allitérature contemporaine* should be added the special form of impotence which shows itself in eroticism – that blindest of blind alleys in which nearly all of them meet.

I am prepared to be told that this is what real literature is. It is not for me to judge. It is not my intention to raise a laugh: besides, I have always numbered some *allitérateurs* among my gods. But there is one question I should rather shyly like to ask: is it by chance that drug-taking, feeble-mindedness, madness – real or feigned – eroticism, and, finally, impotence have afflicted these fortunate-damned! May it not be that, even before they had begun to write, they had committed violence upon the person?

At this point, somebody will break in: 'You are a christian, I know what you're going to say before you say it, and let me point

[1] *Allitérature* is a word invented by Claude Mauriac. Its English equivalent would be 'anti-literature'. I have kept the French form for the sake of the play on words in the above quotation. (Translator.)

out that, for an agnostic, it is completely valueless, and, indeed, is without meaning.' It is true that for me the soul is something real: I would go further, and say that it is the essence of reality. But, just because that is what I believe, I do not want to bring it into the argument, but to rely, rather, on my own personal experience, the experience of an old-hand at writing who has been accustomed, ever since his brain began to work, to question others, as well as himself, and not only his contemporaries. Books communicate certain confidences which, in the case of an author whom we love, are for our ears alone. Benjamin Constant says things to me which a hostile critic would never hear.

It is not because I am a christian that I denounce, in these *allitérateurs* a basic error in their view of man. How significant is their hatred of anything smacking of psychology! What they are out to attack is not a science, not a method, but its object. Their determination to stick only to the most elementary, the most deeply buried part of the human complex is, in itself, a denial of the *person* as experience – or, at least, my experience, shows it to be.

In order to limit themselves to this elementary and stagnant part of the individual, this magma, or sludge, they have had to do violence to nature as we know it – upon which christianity sheds its own light. But outside the circle of that light, man remains what he is. What name, for instance, are we to give to that force in, say the atheist Sartre, which makes him indifferent to the career of dramatist in which, as in many other fields of activity, he could have reigned supreme, and has flung him into that doubtful battle where he fights alone, not recognized by the party to which he cannot belong though he will not consent to be its enemy. It is the eternal 'neither with, nor without you can I live . . .' which is not merely a matter for the heart to decide, but which determines our relation with God and, in the political struggle, with men.

I am not a philosopher, and I suffer a good deal from that fact at a time when, more than at any other, the battle has been joined on ground chosen and marked out by philosophers. But no matter how negligible I may be as a 'thinker', I find that the closer I come to my end, the more do certain pieces of evidence emerge into the light, and refuse to be ignored. First of all, so far as I, personally, am concerned, what distinguishes the weak from the strong periods in any given destiny is its being at odds, or at peace, with itself. Does this mean that man should have a certain requirement of man? Yes, certainly it does, and quite apart from any question of christianity. Every human being, though he may be ignorant of metaphysics, has a vocation. What I find so distasteful about the *allitérateurs* – even though, in a sense, they do attract and fascinate me – is their stubborn determination not to know what they want, not even to want to know, their refusal to try to find out, their desperate eagerness to have nothing to do with 'wanting' in any form (more than usually striking in a man like Bataille), or, rather, their denial there is any such thing as willing or wanting. What difficulties they make for themselves by fighting so hard not to be aware of, or to forget, it! Anything that might serve to show that they are 'somebody' is deliberately pushed out of sight, for they have rejected the 'somebody' as they have rejected the literature which is the expression of that somebody.

I agree that the object of literature *may* not be the somebody whom you regard as an arbitrary projection of the human mind, without any roots in the real, and that its proper habitat is that confused, indeterminate, obscure and swarming region where being, taken at its source, has not yet undergone any deterioration. That is a matter of choice. But what I deny is that we ought no longer to take into account what Pascal (and many others before and after him) revealed in so blinding a light when he compressed it into the five words from which he would never be parted: *Greatness of the human spirit:* that we ought to be ashamed of our inheritance and pitch it overboard. So extreme is my indignation that all I can do is to summon to my aid that celebrated allitérateur, *Ubu,* and to borrow from him the key-word which he was the first to be inspired to write in six letters.

*   *   *   *   *

But what if man, in process of making himself, of becoming, cannot, *without falsehood,* be immobilized in his primitive condition of swarm? That is the essential problem, and you evade it. No doubt, what man becomes is, in your eyes, what he is not: the christian, in particular, the penitent who seeks to recreate himself in the image of a divine model, which he can do only through sanctity – and that, for you, is tantamount to destroying himself. I leave you the last word, for there is no point in countering one statement with another statement. But answer me this: is there not, at the very basis of what you call *allitérature,* a law violated, a sin committed, though not in the very mysterious sense given to that phrase in the Gospel? I am referring to a sin against the spirit of man as he is, and as you do not want him to be, a sin sanctioned, from now on, by impotence and madness.

To say that I agree with the author of *L'Allitérature contemporaine,* that there is no work of art worthy of the name which is not, by and large, tinged with madness, is already to give a reply to that question, and, in some sort, to 'give you best'. Each man's especial madness nourishes what is born of him. That is what Flaubert's *Madame Bovary, c'est moi* means, and André Gide's statement that no work of art can be fully achieved without the collaboration of the demon – the artist's own demon. There is no less of madness in *Bajazet* or *Phèdre* than there is in *Hamlet* or *Macbeth.* The poetic framework, no matter how rigid it may be, changes nothing. The really great writers are allitérateurs who have got the better of, and conquered allitérature. So outstanding an allitérateur as Marcel Proust was prouder of having constructed a planned work in which design was paramount than he was of anything else. He told me so himself, in a letter. When Francis Jammes suggested that he would do well to excise from *Swann* a word (I forget what word) which had affronted the ears of the old faun turned pious, Proust begged me to get him to understand that one single stone removed from his Cathedral would bring the whole edifice crashing to the ground, and that on the word to which Jammes had objected rested a flying-buttress which was absolutely necessary to the stability of the crowning pinnacle of *Le Temps retrouvé.*

Those allitérateurs who fail to dominate their madness, and tame the beast, are ultimately devoured by it. Many of them have pretended that they were devoured as the result of a deliberate act of choice, or actually believe it. What is certain is that they have been believed, and that their defeat, in which they glory as in something consciously willed, has come to be regarded as a victory by this generation – the most conformist of all the generations which I have been in a position to observe over a period of fifty years, during which I have watched the river of ink to which I have contributed flow by.

Their hatred of style is hatred of the man they refuse to be. Not that there doesn't exist a way of writing well which is the worst of all, or that a really good style is one of which we are not forced to be conscious. All the same, when one of these new reformers declares, as I have actually heard with my own ears – that Claudel is a half-wit, and that Colette wrote bad French, I hurry home, open my La Fontaine and once more read *Le Renard ayant la queue coupée:*

> *Que faisons nous, dit il, de ce poids inutile*
> *Et qui va balayant tous les sentiers fangueux?*
> *Que nous sert cette queue? Il faut qu'on se la coupe.*
> *Si l'on me croit, chacun s'y résoudra.*

La Fontaine is the man to go to for advice in these days of allitérature, for he is madder and more free than any of you, breaking up his lines and playing so gracefully with the pieces in his madness, that nobody notices it. Ah! I can fight no longer. I who have been more deeply involved than most of my juniors in the catastrophic story of our modern world, will put no compulsion of myself to love it. Nothing can alter the fact that, my age is what it is, and that for the last twenty-six years I have been a mere survival. I ought, by rights, to have died in 1932. I find nothing now to please me in this lunatic and bloody-minded age with its ubuesque techniques, its torture-chambers and its adults so debased by the cinema that *Tintin* is their chosen favourite, and that their daily paper can avoid bankruptcy only by teaching them history and literature by means of infantile strip-drawings. It is an age which can see no difference between the silence of a Rimbaud, a Mallarmé, a M. Teste and the inarticulate mutterings of imbeciles. (It is this last point, I think, that the author of *L'Allitérature contemporaine* should have stressed. He should have made more of the fact that there are two different forms of allitérature, and have pointed out what it is that separates them.)

All this was proclaimed by a mere boy in 1873. 'Calamity has been my god: I have lain in the mud and dried myself in the air of crime. I have played tricks with madness, and the Spring has brought me the hideous laughter of the lunatic.' Yes, Rimbaud knew that the laughter of the lunatic is hideous. He could bear it no longer. He had reached a point where he could no longer laugh nor speak. This thought had been given to him: 'I have dreamed of finding a key to the festive merriment of an older world.' And then, suddenly, this cry bursts from him (oh! for the brief space of a lightning-flash before the shadows close down upon him): '*That key is charity.*' Yes, and ever since those words were written, and Rimbaud chose silence, his wretched posterity has been fumbling for that lost key.

XV

THANKS TO those *familiar quotations* stored up and collected by Mondor, I can hear again the very voice of Valéry, and that little mumble at the end of his sentences in which something wonderful was lost for ever. I can see again those nimble fingers of his, occupied in that most useless of all accomplishments – since there are tobacconists at every street corner – the rolling of cigarettes in which there was always too much paper and too little tobacco, which came unstuck, and ultimately killed him. Valéry who consigned me to outer darkness (by never reading anything I wrote) – which didn't matter because he treated others in the same way, and only Gide took it amiss: Valéry who stopped dead where, for me, real history begins. One of his last utterances was: 'I look at nothing but the wall.' Mondor reminds us that he had written elsewhere: 'I have no eyes for the world. I have turned my face to the wall. There is nothing on the surface of that *wall* that I don't know.'

But he would never have written *La Jeune Parque* if that wall had been nothing but a wall. What we must allow in the matter of his refusal to yield to Pascal, and to take a bet about what the wall conceals, is that it came less from a fault or a vice – the pride denounced by all preachers of sermons – than from a virtue, the scrupulousness of an intelligence in love with its own rigorous discipline.

Since it happens that, not from choice, but because the same tide landed them on my table, I am reading, almost simultaneously, Mondor's two books about Valéry, and Michel Butor's novel, *La Modification*. It occurs to me that this vigorous discipline of Valéry – which he got from Mallarmé – has done a great deal to nurture the supercilious art (if I may make so bold) of my austere juniors. Even though Butor may not set much store by *La Jeune Parque* (I don't know whether he does or not) the fact remains that this obsession about seeing nothing but the wall – not the wall of Plato's cave, but any old wall – shows clearly in the novels of the new school. I doubt whether they would have greatly appealed to Valéry (what novel ever did appeal to him?). But it is certainly true that what he most insisted on is now being practised in a form of writing which he ranked very low in his scale of values – not that that has anything to do with it. At the age of twenty, Valéry proudly declared: 'I accept nothing I cannot see.'

* * * * *

Yet, it is true that Valéry had a horror of the 'naturalists', and on this point was at one with Claudel. I feel pretty sure that he would have found little to interest him in the objects displayed by our new authors with so implacable an attention to detail. (I open *La Modification* at random, and read: 'on the electrically heated rug, a scrap of biscuit is lying aimlessly in the middle of one of the diamond-shaped units of the pattern, between the shoes of the lady in black' etc). Actually, this sort of thing is at the very opposite pole from naturalism, which was a variant of romanticism. Zola contrived his effects, distorted and blackened, played tricks with the real. The novelists of today see only what they see. If the real has any meaning, it will emerge of itself – that belongs to the unforeseeable in art, and Valéry, no doubt would have rejected it, since he would have refused to admit that there is anything in poetry which works independently of the planned and the deliberate. To say that he mistrusted inspiration would be an understatement. Nothing could well be more planned and arranged than the work of our modern technicians of fiction, for the very simple reason that technique is their ruling passion. Their determination never to go beyond the object, and to represent it exactly as it is, demands a strictly limited vocabulary and the driest of dry styles – a Jansenism of expression which led their leader to say (it was to me, of all people, that this talk was addressed!): 'Colette writes badly.'

What we have here to study with the closest attention is the astonishing interlacing of several journeys from Paris to Rome and from Rome to Paris, made by Michel Butor's hero. There is no confusion. Each journey remains distinct from every other, and the whole pattern is a perfect example of the art of counterpoint applied to the novel. Yes, indeed: but, to be quite honest, it is not much fun for the reader.

There must be no indulgence in 'fine writing' on the pretext of 'suggesting', but only a firmly controlled display of what *is*. That is the lesson of these 'moderns' – to suggest nothing, but to focus the eye on what occupies the field of vision at a given moment, and in a given place, with the result that the thoughts and passions of the hero of *La Modification* which do not arise from what he is actually seeing or touching, are treated in as arbitrary a fashion, and with as heavy a hand as in a novel by Bourget. I would point out to Michel Butor that Bourget, too, had a passion for Rome, and that the Eternal City occupies no less space in *Cosmopolis* than it does in *La Modification*. He would be well advised to buy the book on the occasion of his next journey, and to read it in the 8.10 Paris–Syracuse Express (it is time these young men's arrogance was taken down a peg!). It remains for me to say that Butor's remarkable novel marks a stage on the passage from laboratory to public – it is a Robbe-Grillet product made digestible – though that, I suppose, in the eyes of the apostles of the pure milk of the word, implies a fall from grace.

★　　★　　★　　★　　★

But to go back to Valéry. What, I think, that poet, now long at rest, and these very much alive prose-writers have in common is a certain rigour of mind. This was, with him, undoubtedly a virtue and goes far to explain how, when the poet's pious wife was faced with the spectacle of a wise man turning his face to the wall, and not praying, she found comfort in the words: 'he was *such* a hard worker!' That is indeed true, for he spurned all facility and sought only perfection. 'Be ye perfect as your Father in Heaven is perfect.' There is no blasphemy in extending Christ's demand to cover the work of a human artist, when dealing with Valéry.

Still, the fact remains that this rigour of mind was a limit beyond which he did not go, and that I, personally, prefer a man who jumps into the sea, like Simon Peter, to join his God, the brave man who is ready to face risks, to take someone at his word and to place infinite trust in that word because it comes from someone he loves, and not from someone who can offer proofs to show how right he is. Similarly, I prefer authors who are ready to jump headlong into their writing without thinking of their safety. True, they will not bring up from the depths such marvels of chiselled and incorruptible beauty as *La Jeune Parque* or *Le Cimetière marin,* but they will make other discoveries. Over this essential difference between men's minds one can brood for ever. To understand or to love? Not that those words are necessarily contradictory: but love does carry knowledge beyond the point at which Valéry stopped. It can pass through walls like the risen Lord – and through that particular wall against which Valéry butted his head. He wished to know nothing else, and leaned his face against it when he died – that face, so noble and so spiritual in the absolute sense of the word, which Mondor shows us, which I can see looking unsmilingly at me from the already yellowing photograph in my library, on which he wrote: 'To his friend F.M.':

> *Que si j'étais placé devant cette effigie*
> *Inconnu de moi-même, ignorant de mes traits,*
> *A tant de plis affreux d'angoisse et d'énergie,*
> *Je lirais mes tourments et me reconnaitrais!*

* * * * *

We live in an age when it is not necessary to see a man constantly to know all about him. I don't suppose that I ever exchanged more than a dozen words or so with Paul Léautaud, but his *Journal,* his personal confessions on the radio and occasional glimpses of him at the theatre, told me more about him than I should ever have got from the casual chatter of an acquaintance or the confidences of an intimate friend. A man so fundamentally simple, who wanted nothing about himself to be concealed, had little difficulty in unburdening himself. In this he differed from Gide, who, up till the day of his death, and after it, has never ceased from surprising and shocking us. I am thinking, in particular, of that last, extremely intimate note-book in which he deals with his married life. By comparison with it the worst of his confessions seem almost mild.

There are hypocritical church-goers who, by dint of making the gestures of devotion end by actually experiencing it. In just such a way did Léautaud become a genuine cynic. The very minor horrors which he confides to us in his *Journal* seem exceptional only because he displays them publicly (what sex-life would not seem horrible when so publicized?). They do not conceal the child-like simple-mindedness of the man-of-letters in the pure state, the man of letters who is that and nothing more.

The *Mercure* of the years round 1900 was a culture-medium in which black insects, in a pervading smell of paper and ink, rubbed their antennae, blissfully ignorant of everything that wasn't the gossip of newspaper offices, the academies and the back-stage world of the theatre, or hadn't something to do with the intrigues connected with the earliest Prix Goncourt awards.

Léautaud moved in a very small world the inhabitants of which bragged a great deal about their amorality, but, nevertheless, had several virtues to their credit. Perhaps the first of these was poverty, about which we christians make a great song and dance, though in the days of my youth it was not christians (including ecclesiastics) who most practised it, but those poorly-paid literary men whom nothing really excited but the printed word. Read, in Léautaud's *Journal,* about that darling scheme of his, long-cherished, of a trip to Rouen with Rémy de Gourmont. In order to bring it off, Léautaud had first to scrape together fifty francs – no easy matter. The whole story, the description of the train journey, of the arrival in Rouen, of the splendours of the hotel . . . the whole thing is just a small boy's adventure with precisely that thrill in it which I used to feel at the age of ten, when I set off for the summer holidays, and the sixty-mile journey by train separated me from my daily haunts more completely than would an Atlantic flight today.

Fundamentally, Léautaud never outgrew his childhood. He had, for instance, the small boy's love of dressing up, not as a cowboy or a brigand but as one of his pet authors. Stendhal, whom he tries to copy in everything, ought to have been his model, but he couldn't *look like* Stendhal. Physically, the two men had nothing in common. The nephew of Rameau, on the other hand, was a character who allowed him a free hand. Paul Léautaud, grubby-looking, with a greasy collar and a dirty shirt was, all the same, a bit of a dandy. He modelled himself on his idea of what a down-at-heel wit of the eighteenth century would have been like, with the addition of a few details borrowed from the 'bohemians' of the romantic period. There was something of the actor about this son of the prompter at the Comédie-Française. He went through life in 'make-up'.

This worship of appearances, this need he felt to express in externals the 'character' of the man-of-letters, makes me more and more conscious, as I read Léautaud's *Journal,* of the incredible emptiness behind the mask. What *can* the literary life be without the work which alone is its excuse and justification? Only an ambition to write 'something', even though it be a failure, can exonerate a man-of-letters like Léautaud, who was completely indifferent to social obligations, and wholly detached from that human drama which goes by the name of politics. Proust is a good example of what I mean. For him, the prime duty of getting his book written took precedence of everything else. All that might distract his mind from it, was evil in his eyes. That was Proust's essential *truth,* but can it ever be that of those who, though men-of-letters, have nothing in them which remotely resembles *A la recherche du temps perdu?*

* * * * *

Speaking of this *duty* to his book, which he held to be paramount, Proust said: 'What task won't people take on, just so as to have an excuse for not doing just *that* duty! Every sort of public occurrence, whether it be the Dreyfus Affair or war has been made to provide writers with the necessary pretext: – they want to see justice done – they want to help in bolstering the national morale – they haven't got time to think about literature. . . . But pretexts are valueless in matters of art. Intention is not enough. At every moment it is the duty of the artist to follow his instinct, which is why art is more real than anything else, the most austere school of life, the true Last Judgment.'

But Léautaud carried no unborn work within him. For a long time he had nothing to say, beyond giving expression to what he observed in himself. And what was it he observed? What was he? What was there left in a man who was devoid of all faith and all hope, whether metaphysical or worldly, who had no real interest in ideas, who knew nothing, seemingly, of the passions of the heart, and gave the name of love to the furtive fumblings of sensuality? Nothing. But that nothing is the very bedrock of the man-of-letters who is *only* that and nothing more. And here, I would make a gloss on Pascal and say that it is more difficult to attain to Nothingness than to the All. As a portrayal of Nothingness Léautaud's *Journal* is not without a certain value, may, indeed, be a work of considerable importance. It certainly has a better chance of survival than the ambitious *roman-fleuve* to which he did not dedicate his life, and which would certainly have foundered like all such armadas of fiction. For in literature mere bulk cannot save a man from nothingness. Léautaud's instinct did not deceive him. His laziness did not deceive him. He will continue to exist only because he refused to have any existence.

What strikes me in Léautaud, in the boy-who-never-grew-up but assumed the trappings of Rameau's nephew and tried to frighten us – is a suppressed, an almost imbecile sensibility which found an outlet in cats and dogs and monkeys. One can enjoy stroking a cat all day long. At any age one may like the warm presence of an animal against one's chest or on one's knees (they never keep *me* warm!). Animals do not know that we are old and have grown ugly, nor can they console us for that unpleasant fact – or so it seems to me. Was this Léautaud really a man with a sensitive heart? Listening to his 'feature', one evening on the radio, I caught him in the very act of putting on a tender act. He was speaking of Jammes, and of the poem in praise of Jammes written by a poet now long forgotten, Charles Guérin:

O Jammes, ta maison ressemble à ton visage . . .

I, too, had loved the piece and, like André Lafon and Jean de la Ville, had got it by heart. As Léautaud proceeded with his reading using the same inflexions which we had used long since, his voice gave him away. I felt absolutely certain that the tears were running down his cheeks.

And so it came about that one evening, though he did not know it, I mingled my tears with his. Was it not to this cynic Léautaud that almost all the young men of my generation owed their introduction to modern poetry? His *Anthologie* taught me all about it, straight off, when I was eighteen.

The poor chap lived in the contemplation and terror of death. Poverty and thinking about death are two of the roads which lead to God, and have, I believe, given comfort to many. Léautaud tender-hearted? How he interrogated the corpses of those whom he had known, with what a maniacal concentration! When the object was his own father, that icy curiosity makes one shudder. Yet, strange to say, we turn from the corpse and we do not yield to Léautaud's obsession, the obsession of an old, pig-headed Narcissus, who bent over everybody's mortal remains and greedily sought in them the image of his own decomposition.

* * * * *

A country neighbour whose presence here coincides with my holiday, is a great lover of books, and talks of them to me with the eagerness and avidity of a starving man who, for once in a way, has been given the opportunity to eat his fill. It is a joy for me to happen on so faithful a friend, but I cannot help feeling how far I am removed from those reasoning processes which, now in him, are precisely what they were in me when I first began to read for pleasure, that is to say, when I was seven. For at that age, my brothers and I were always arguing about the comparative merits of the Comtesse de Ségur and Zenaïde Fleuriot as passionately as we did about Corneille and Racine, and, later still, about Bourget and Barrès, until, at last I reached the point, beyond which I have never gone, at which Baudelaire, Rimbaud, Mallarmé and Proust inspired me with considerations, constantly renewed, and endowed those mortals whom they initiated into their music with an inexhaustible intelligence.

We authors instinctively go in dread of oblivion. But this fear owes much to lack of thought. I am pretty sure that an André Gide, a Marcel Proust would stand to gain a great deal from an interval of silence in which neither their works nor their lives would be mentioned. I should be only too happy if people would stop talking about them, and so give us a breathing space in which to forget them, and increase the pleasure of re-discovery. We should know very much better what death has made of them if only the literary commentators would give them a rest. Gide and Proust provide them with a rare hunting-ground. Drieu la Rochelle once wrote a novel called *L'Homme couvert de femmes*. There is too, a person whom one might describe as an author covered with critics, a book smothered under a burden of appraisals.

This, I think, applies with especial force to Gide, whose work is, in itself, a commentary, and amounts, at its best, to an account of himself by himself: a variant of that deliberately planned sincerity, of which Jean-Jacques was already a past master, but planned in his case by about the most uninhibited and cunning intelligence there has ever been, so that it leaves us nothing to add, each reader being free to project his own particular beam of light whether borrowed from the Gospels, Freud, Nietzsche or anybody else; whereas our pocket-torch changes nothing in the human landscape etched in *Si le grain ne meurt*. We may all have our own views about the part played by heredity or upbringing in Gide's sexual behaviour, but they contribute practically nothing to what we know of his life and his writings, now that both have reached their term. But we could reflect upon them at leisure if only the busybodies of criticism would be silent. 'That is quite enough about the lump on Anthime's head!' – I quote this piece of pertness straight from Gide's own *Caves du Vatican*. How wonderful if some critic could bring himself to say at last: 'That is quite enough about Gide's sex-life!'

But Proust, at least, did not write his confessions. The field is free. True, but that does not alter the fact that, for the last forty years, far too many people have had a finger in the Proustian pie. Back in 1914, I could still breathe freely. I had spent a long time splashing about in the book, and fondly thought that I had views of my own concerning it. At the dawn of Proust's fame, round about 1922 or '23, I remember sitting at a dinner-party next to a very old and very dignified lady who did me the honour to explain that she had been careful to have something to eat before coming, so as to be able to listen at leisure while I discoursed to her on Proust. She put her gloves in her glass, and turned on me the small, terrible face of a blood-sucker. I used to enjoy my food in those days with the double greed of a man of Bordeaux and Les Landes. I cursed inwardly – Why can't you let me eat my dinner, you old Carabosse! – however, in my most honeyed tones, I said: 'Proust, Madame, attacks the human personality and leaves it in shreds....' 'In shreds!' repeated the blood-sucker with an air of deep concentration.

What should I tell her today? Every inch of the ground on the Guermantes' Way and Swann's, has been overrun and trampled. Proust, I admit, did not expose himself through the medium of direct confession, so that more than one interpretation of *A la recherche du temps perdu* is possible. But had he 'anatomized' himself, we should still, each of us, have added our own grain of salt. See, for instance, what is happening to Michel Leiris who has carried auto-investigation further, one would have thought, than is possible, or tolerable. All the same, round Michel Leiris, who says all there is to say about himself and should be a hopeless subject for a commentator, the commentators are already swarming.

*   *   *   *   *

All literature oscillates between these confessions of a being turned in upon himself and upon the deep mud in which the person he might have become is diluted, and the so-called classical works, detached from their creator, composed according to an inviolable body of rules, and imitating the great models. The same waffles come endlessly from the same moulds. We recast the novels of Balzac, as Voltaire and his successors recast the tragedies of Racine.

. . . That is an over-simplified generalization for the use of simple souls. But what matters here is not so much what I write, as the feeling that makes me write, the attitude of detachment, I would almost say, of disgust with what was once the great business of my life. For what have I done, like my comrades, but concentrate my attention on the destinies of characters now frozen within the covers of many books? We men of letters belong to a curious species of Peeping Toms. To be a writer is not so much to be a creator of characters, or a teller of stories, as to track down an elusive truth through what others have told us about themselves, and to confront it with what we think we know about *ourselves*.

If I am now disgusted with that occupation, my disgust, my detachment is, perhaps, a sign that the last and final detachment is at hand. I withdraw from books which are foreign to my own, no less than from those I have, myself, secreted. But from what, in spirit, do I not withdraw? I no longer believe in what I read, or, rather, I have become a stranger to it, as I have to the ritual gestures of my social self.

I seemed withdrawn and inattentive to a lady, at the last Academy reception, at which, so she wrote to me, Gaxotte and I gave her the impression of two schoolboys chattering away to their hearts' content, because they knew that there was no master in the world who could 'keep them in'. Well, on that occasion I confess that the public facing me was no more than a painted canvas, and that the important folk crowded together on the steps of the arena were no more real to me than the fair-ground pictures of my childhood. The charming 'great' in their embroidered coats, exchanging flatteries and compliments in the front row, belonged to a child's world. They had come from a rather dusty toy-box, as though this old nation of ours in its dotage, even at its last gasp, was still intent at playing with lead soldiers or dolls. If ever it has to give up the ghost, which God forbid, it will expire with an Academician on one side and a Marshal on the other.

Please forgive me! Politics are more than a little responsible, more than I can explain here, for this outburst of bitterness. But, politics apart, a *taedium vitae* takes us by the throat at certain critical moments in our lives. An immense ebb-tide leaves us on a muddy shore among dead jelly-fish. But the Creator is not drawn into this breakdown of creation. In this bath of gall, faith is called upon to prove itself. It stands untouched and turns this bitterness, at last, to sweetness. For this collapse of appearances is the collapse of something that has separated us from the eternal love. That love they reveal, as they crash to the ground.

XVI

IT IS very rarely, now, that I deliberately take down a book for re-reading. It is as the result of some chance meeting that I renew acquaintance with an old friend. I mooch about among my shelves, and then, suddenly: 'Why, if that isn't Moll Flanders!' – just as if I had unexpectedly run across the old filcher of watches in the street. But what is it that prompts me to wave to her, to take her along to my room, and to hear all over again the story of her life, which I haven't, really, had time to forget? I met with Daniel Defoe's masterpiece relatively late in life. It was Edouard Bourdet, I think, who, one day at Tamaris, lent me Marcel Schwob's translation.

What has sent me back to the book is the recent appearance of a new and more complete version by M. Denis Marion, equipped with notes which are not confined to the special case of Moll Flanders, but contain matter of the greatest interest to all of us whose job it is to tell stories. It is M. Marion's contention that Moll Flanders *is* Daniel Defoe, in the same way as Flaubert meant when he said *Madame Bovary, c'est moi*. According to his latest translator, Defoe enriched his heroine with many characteristics and qualities taken from his own personal tragedy.

He may be right: but what most strikes me in reading this very conscientious translation, is the really miraculous fact that in this book we have a woman speaking who never, once, reacts as a man would do, and never says anything that only a man would have said. Nowhere else in the whole history of the novel is there an instance of a male author merging himself so completely with a female character.

But here I must ask a question which nobody ever does ask, for fear, I suppose, of being thought stupid: what does '*Madame*

Bovary, c'est moi' mean? The answer is by no means self-evident – though the journalists who always have it ready to hand in their lists of familiar quotations seem to think it is. Incidentally, did Flaubert ever put it down in black and white, and, if so, where? I suppose I knew that once, but I don't now. It would be worth taking a good deal of trouble to trace it back to its context, if context there is. I am inclined to think that it was just a sudden 'mot' dropped casually in the course of a conversation.

However that may be, I am prepared to take my oath that when Flaubert thought about Madame Bovary and himself, he did not really believe that there existed a 'mystic parallel between their two destinies' – as M. Marion asserts. All Flaubert meant was that Madame Bovary was born of his own flesh and blood, and made, like an unhappy Eve, from one of his own ribs. It hasn't needed the coming of Freud to teach novelists about repressions and how they frequently release potentialities in themselves through their characters. It is perfectly obvious, from a study of Flaubert's earliest writings, that he was Emma's young brother. She is the caricature of all he had once believed in, and thought that life would give him: the incarnation in fiction of a tremendous and frustrated hope.

*　　*　　*　　*　　*

It does not seem to me that there was any similar relationship between Daniel Defoe and his woman pickpocket. Perhaps, in his case, the transposition was deliberate. He had certainly known the inside of Newgate, but as a man mixed up with affairs of state, employed by the king and used as a secret agent by the Prime Minister. There seems to be little doubt that, towards the end of his life, he was playing a remarkably squalid double game, that he had betrayed his friends, and had as much to be ashamed of in his life as Moll had in hers. In any case, even if the novel was the outcome of a perfectly conscious and planned transposition, such a transposition has remained so completely concealed that it seems far more likely that Defoe got hold of the confession of an authentic adventuress, thief and prostitute, or had had an affair with some such woman who had confided in him. So perfect is his art that he can identify himself with what he is pretending to imitate.

Even when Moll Flanders preaches and beats her breast, she does so as a professional. Her whole behaviour is an illustration of that perverse law of human nature which drives the author of an act, no matter how shameful, to repeat it, no matter how horrible it may appear in his eyes or what dangers it involves.

In those early years of the eighteenth century, capital punishment was generally regarded as the most legitimate and most solidly established of social institutions. Anyone who had stolen even a yard of cloth would be sure to swing for it, in an atmosphere of universal satisfaction. This risk did not act as a deterrent on Moll Flanders. We see, as it were, the complicated machinery of cause and effect which drove Moll forward, taken to pieces before our eyes – not through the medium of motives but of facts. She never pleads in her defence, nor does she offer any excuses for her actions, not even that of having been born in Newgate. She does not see herself as a heroine, nor does she pose as the victim of anybody but herself. It never occurs to her to accuse society. In no way is she a forerunner of Marion Delorme or of La Dame aux camélias. She rings true, with the truth that scorns both embellishment and distortion. Even in her most perverse and vicious moments she retains a certain quality of good-breeding, which was the climate of her times and makes one think that vulgarity was the child of that falsity of feeling which came in with the Romantics.

* * * * *

But the man who wrote *Moll Flanders* also wrote *Robinson Crusoe*. M. Denis Marion would have us believe that the drama of Defoe's life was solitude, as it is of so many men and women, of almost all men and of all women, and that it was this cross that dominated the career of Moll Flanders.

I know too little about Defoe to venture on a contradiction. Here, again, the transposition, if it exists, is invisible even to the most piercing eye. There is nothing in the solitude with which Moll Flanders had to contend in any way different from that of any woman of her condition who had been born outside a respectable social class. She worked on her own from choice, and because she knew, only too well, the price she might have to pay for having accomplices. It was the solitude, too, of an old woman, for the story takes her beyond the 'change of life'. But there is no drama in that. She would have thought Michelet's 'the hideous torment of old age' merely ridiculous.

She never complains of being lonely, except in so far as it has certain immediate disadvantages: and I do not believe that she was ever capable of indulging in such a high-flown sentiment as – 'What solitudes are all these human bodies!' Perhaps, in certain turns of phrase, we catch a note of pride in the fact that she could not share her destiny with anybody, and in the crimes she had committed, some of which, like her incestuous marriage, had been involuntary. She did not drape herself in her fatalities, as in a tragic robe. The idea of going to bed with her brother quite simply disgusted her, and she escaped from the situation in which she found herself, without making a lot of fine speeches about it, or thinking of herself as a daughter of the Atrides.

Moll Flanders never trod those heights where such thoughts as 'the tragedy of solitude' exist, and I very much doubt whether any man of 1725 would have been able to do so. Where do we find any expression of that particular form of human misery before Rousseau and the romantics? In Pascal? But solitude is treated, in the *Pensées,* as only one aspect of the wretchedness which is the lot of men without God. The time had not yet come for that idea of a desert on the specifically human scale, into which the later romantic hero loved to plunge: 'sole witness of his glory and his reason'.

If the highest peak of the art of fiction consists, for the novelist, not so much in merging himself with another, but in becoming another, and the more so, being a man, to become a woman, then *Moll Flanders* is an absolute masterpiece. It was written in 1722 by a forger of confessions and memoirs, whose purpose, no doubt, did not go beyond making money. To say that he showed the contemporary novel the line that it should take, and gave to it the character which it has, ever since, retained, is to say too little. Daniel Defoe achieved in this book a degree of perfection which, in its own kind, has never been surpassed. I am acquainted with no other fictional confession which has succeeded in conveying so great a sense of authenticity, and this leads me to think, though I can produce no proof that I am right, that Defoe had been on terms of great intimacy with a female gaolbird, a high-level prostitute, from whom he had received, in the privacy of the bed, confidences which a romantic would have loaded with a heavy weight of gloom, whereas for him they were no more than a source of entertainment in a century when it was a general belief that all human beings were responsible for their actions, did not either glorify or blacken them, and did not regard themselves as victims when the time came to pay the penalty.

★   ★   ★   ★   ★

To pass from Defoe to Henry James is all part of the treat I give myself when I return to my home in the country.

The Bostonians, the most recently translated of James's novels, is an early work, which though it is extremely attractive (it is, in fact, more approachable than the books of his maturity) is not, or so it seems to me, one of those which can help us to form a true estimate of his very personal output as a whole. So far as I know Marcel Proust never tackled any of James's fictions, though his *oeuvre* does, to some extent, form an outer bastion, in the nineteenth century, to the great Proustian mountain-range.

Reading *The Bostonians* has led me, once again, to wonder whether Freud can be said to have enriched the novel as a literary form. Do the books which were written and published before the coming of the Freudian cult, and before *A la recherche du temps perdu,* really seem so sketchy and superficial compared with later productions in which sexuality reigns supreme and every variant of love can be called by its name without a blush?

But to return to *The Bostonians.* In this novel James has been at pains to introduce us to a feminist group in the Boston society of the eighties, when it was fashionable to get excited over the emancipation of women. There is nothing in it, I agree, to hold the attention of the modern reader, and, if it has aroused my interest, that is for reasons which have nothing to do with feminism.

What is *The Bostonians* 'about'? A woman of the upper middle-class, Olive Chancellor, by no means in her first youth, takes a great liking to a girl of a humbler social class, who happens to have a great gift for public speaking. Olive determines to exploit her young friend's talents in the service of the feminist cause. The novel tells the story of her jealous possessiveness. The girl, Verena, is caught in the toils of Olive who belongs to that rapacious type of female who hates men, and does all she can to keep her charming prey from falling into their clutches, those, in particular, of a broad-shouldered Southerner, who, in the long run, turns out to be the stronger of the two.

The strange thing about the book is that, never once in the whole course of the drama, is the sexual aspect of the situation dealt with, or even suggested. The question of a passionate friend-ship in itself, the manifestations of which cause no embarrassment either to the woman who feels it, or to the girl who is its object, never arises. It provides no occasion for scandal, and produces no malicious gossip either in Boston or New York. There are no un-pleasant hints about the couple: in fact, the book might have been written by somebody who had never heard of Gomorrha, of some-body, I would go so far as to say, who had lived in a world where the existence of that vice had never even been heard of. It is true that the Victorian society to which Henry James belonged, had taken quite literally – not because it was virtuous but because it was hypocritical – the advice of the Apostle: 'Let not these things be spoken of among you.'

But would not the novel have gained in depth if the question *had* been raised, if Olive Chancellor had not been virtuous, or if, while abstaining from any actually criminal behaviour, she had been aware of the abnormal nature of her leanings? Whatever the answer to that question, the fact remains that *The Bostonians,* free though it is from any hint of physiological treatment, offers the most searching study I know, of an extremely unpleasant situation, that of a man and an Amazon at daggers drawn over a young woman. It is perfectly obvious that feminism is used as an alibi, not only for the characters in the novel, but for the author, too, and for his Anglo-Saxon readers of 1886. Under cover of this fiction we are told all there is to tell about this type of conflict between two women and a man – all of them equally high-minded – not in terms of the horrible things that might have been done but only of the feelings of those concerned.

It might well be argued that the uninhibited treatment of sexual problems, so far from enriching the novel-form, has actually impoverished it, and that the invasion of fiction by sex is one of the reasons for its decadence. On the other hand, it might be maintained that this invasion has, in fact, destroyed only the psychological novel in its traditional form, the possibilities of which had already been exhausted, and has given a new lease of life to the art of fictional narrative.

This is a subject for debate. I, personally, am inclined to think that sexual obsession has over-simplified the novelist's task, and has attacked the art of fiction at its source, because it tends to destroy that barrier of prohibitions which, within and without the individual, in society and, especially, in the family has been erected against the passions, and this passion in particular.

'Speak for writers of your own age' – I shall be told by members of the younger generation: 'we have changed all that. It is meaningless to say that sexuality has invaded the novel. It occupies a prominent place only in so far as it activates the characters of our novels. That does not depend upon us, the authors; we ought not even to be conscious of it, since all we know of those characters are the gestures they make, the things they see, the words they speak. All that *The Bostonians* entitles you to say is that within the structure of a carefully composed psychological novel, in which human beings are described both from the outside and the inside, within a framework which arbitrarily determines their nature, sexual considerations are what we most easily do without. The painter arranges the model in the pose which best suits him, is free to clothe him or her as he will and to choose the light in which the sitter is to be displayed. That done, he contrives the drama into which he has decided to precipitate his victim.'

These words, which I have put into the mouth of a purely imaginary modern novelist, help to define the position occupied by Henry James on the frontier-line between two epochs. Graham Greene, writing of him, has said: 'he was mainly concerned with dramatizing . . .' – which establishes the author of *The Bostonians* in the tradition of the classical novel. But he goes on: 'he was especially careful never to intervene in his own person'. In this James shows himself to have been a forerunner of the technique which is, today, in the ascendant.

But I have wandered away from the question which I asked a while back: has obsession with sex enriched or impoverished the novelist? It would be of considerable interest to limit the problem to the work of two significant writers, very different from one another, but both situated on the edge of the same Dead Sea.

It has always seemed to me that Proust's novel, *qua* novel, achieves perfection only when (from *La Prisonnière* onwards) the sexual cancer, long suppressed, is at last brought into the open, becomes generalized, and, ends by so debasing, not to say, destroying all the characters, as to leave none of them untouched except Proust himself, who is left standing erect among the ruins of his own work, and saves it.

Now that André Gide is no longer with us, and we can take in at a single glance the man and his work as a whole, we are in a position to judge more accurately to what extent his one and only preoccupation dominates them and narrows their scope. His ambition to be the French Goethe merely accentuates and makes ridiculous an impoverishment brought about by an insurmountable and base obsession.

The more I think about it, the more convinced do I become that an aesthetic system demands, also, an ethical one: mastery. The same law holds good for the artist and the man. He will dominate his work precisely to the extent that he dominates his life.

XVII

SUCH KNOWLEDGE as I have of the Argentine writer, Jorge Luis Borges, dates only from yesterday, and even today. It is too soon for me to have anything of value to say about him. But what I have read so far has given me a very strange view of the French writers of my generation. What dull-witted bumpkins we almost all of us are! An Ariel like Borges – a rather too knowing Ariel for my taste – who has more than one trick up his sleeve, and whose erudition has an uncomfortable resemblance to the dust we keep for throwing into people's eyes – this species of Kafka who does not take his labyrinth tragically, and would be as pleased as Punch to lose himself, and us, in it – has opened my eyes to the fact that practically the whole lot of us in France have never stopped ruminating the cud of Naturalism.

*　　*　　*　　*　　*

A history of contemporary literature might not be unfairly described as being little more than a record of the various attempts which have been made to escape from that gloomy enclosure in which the descendants of Balzac, Flaubert and Zola have, for the last hundred years, been cropping away at the same grass. And not only they, but the posterity, too, of Lucien Leuwen and Adolphe. For there exists a psychologic naturalism, held prisoner of that which is more closely linked, perhaps, with what comes from observation and analysis than is that other naturalism dedicated to depicting the outward appearances of things. The race of Jean Racine, all specialists in the 'human heart', is outstandingly loyal to clear-thinking and disciplined expression, and extremely hostile to what the eighteenth century called 'enthusiasm'.

Hugo thought that by freeing art from all the conventions of pseudo-classicism, he could reach 'the truth'. In fact, the history of French romanticism is that of an attempted escape from reality which never came off. At his worst, that is to say, in his writing for the theatre, Hugo succeeded in escaping from the restrictive bonds of observation only to fall into the meretricious and the empty: while, at his best, in his lyric poetry, he never got beyond an outpouring of the most ordinary and superficial feelings. *La tristesse d'Olimpio* is the commonest and most widely shared form of emotionalism in the world.

To escape from the apparent real and by so doing to reach down to a more secret and truer reality, was the muddled aspiration of the romantic movement, which found its true fulfilment only in the adventurous exploration of a few poets, not 'damned', as some of them have been called, but marked out, to be chosen vessels, by a rare privilege, since we can count them on our fingers.

If French romanticism was, by and large, an effort to escape which came to nothing, a certain number of individual experiments did, in fact, succeed, those of Nerval, of Baudelaire – who found the key in Edgar Poe – of Mallarmé, with M. Teste in hot pursuit, of Lautreamont and Rimbaud, after whom our later surrealists have breathlessly panted. None of them took precisely the same road, but they had in common the fact that they were engaged in the same adventure of escape, and in every generation they have attracted those who belong to what is called the *avant-garde*.

The main body of our romantic writers always ends by finding its way back to the familiar pastures where things have an apparent reality, and men are what they seem. But the striving to escape is never interrupted, and, more often than not, is stimulated from outside. The foreign influences in this direction are almost always anti-naturalist: Kafka, Faulkner. It should be noted, however, that, since the coming of Freud has taught us that dreams are not prompted by fantasy, the unreal has ceased to be their field of action; the dream-key no longer opens a door into a world of marvels. On the contrary: dreams have come to be regarded as the very source of what is at once the most carnal and the most spiritual of realities.

★　　★　　★　　★　　★　　★

The nodal-point of these contradictions is, I find, situated within myself. When I question my own history, by which I mean the history of my sensibility, I notice that the poetic power of child-hood to transfigure and to dramatize, has, in my case, been carried to extremes. I have lived at the centre of a universe which was at once delicious and formidable. I was a voracious reader, but had no taste for fairy-tales. When a 'grown up' told me a story, I had first to be assured that it was 'true'. It had to be about something that had happened, or, at least, that could have happened. For me the land of marvels had to be inhabited and filled with the kind of people I met with, the kind of objects that I knew. I scorned dwarfs and giants, and was interested only in what my small and ink-stained hand could touch.

Nor can I leave religion out of account. My young years were saturated in it. It laid siege to me from all sides – from without by means of its liturgy and church-observances, by the glittering sign-posts which marked the course of the year, their splendour mingling with the candles of the Christmas crib, the spring-time smells of Easter and, later, those of Whitsun already drenched in heat. From within, by the habit, which I acquired very early, of talking to somebody whom I could not see, though he could see me, and to whom I was answerable for even the least of my thoughts. Over all this universe there hung the drama of salvation, the sound of terrible things said in low voices about the death of my grand-parents who were not church-goers; about the constant risk I ran of an eternity determined by my sins – which in so young a boy could be scarcely more than trifles, though how was I to know that?

To revert to what I was saying: I believe that the practice of religion from earliest childhood bred in me a taste for the dream which would turn out to be true, for an invisible reality. I knew that nature could be imbued with grace, for I had lived with that

233

knowledge long before I had had any idea of what 'grace' and 'nature' meant.

Much later, my horror of the kind of universe I found in Zola, came, not from what he showed, but from what he did not show. I should have found his books less repellent had the invisible been not only absent from them, but denied. I never needed to have this invisible affirmed in order to breathe freely in a fictional world. It was enough for me that it should be possible, that no door should be nailed up. What could be more purely material than Balzac's world, less pervious to Christian Grace than Proust's? But neither author denies this other side (or place) in the human story he is telling. It is just that they are unaware of it (as a rule, but not always). That is enough for a reader of my kind to imagine the extensions which they left untouched, to contrive openings through which the wind of the spirit might blow, that great wind of Pentecost without which, for the christian, there can be nothing but dead worlds. In so far as we believe that nature is shot through with grace, that 'Everything is grace', as Teresa of Lisieux said, some years before Bernanos' country priest, then indeed, it is from nature that all poetry springs. The great novels are a proof of it, for the poetry they breathe is that of humanity and is not a mere matter of language, as those know well who never grow tired of reading, in *Les Illusions perdues,* of Vautrin's meeting with Rubempré, or of going back to *Un Amour de Swann,* or of being madly in love with Natasha Rostov. One of the heroes of Jorge Luis Borges reveals an obscure truth when he interprets the meaning of the stripes on a tiger's skin. The naturalists were not deceived in their belief that this truth is visible in even the most insignificant of faces, in the humblest of gestures, or that the breeze which moves the leaves of the plane-tree under which I am writing these words knows the secret of the world. But they deny that there is a secret. I do not ask that the novelist should affirm anything. I would go so far as to agree that any positive affirmation on his part is to be shunned and runs the risk of destroying his work. All I ask is that he shall not deny what for me is spirit and life. The naturalist novel died of this denial.

*　　*　　*　　*　　*

But what sort of a figure do I, a christian and a novelist, cut in this debate?

On the 7th May, 1928, André Gide published a letter addressed to me. At first I was delighted. The occasion for it was my *Vie de Jean Racine*. 'It is a truly wonderful book,' wrote Gide, 'and I do not often use that word about the books of today.' What a floral tribute! A great deal too floral! I should have guessed that there was an asp hidden somewhere under the leaves. I was bitten even before I found it.

'What it all comes to,' went on Gide, 'that you are asking permission to be a christian without burning your books, and you see to it that they are written in such a way that, though a christian, you do not have to disavow them. To this (the reassuring compromise which allows a man to love God without losing sight of Mammon) we owe that tormented conscience which gives such an attractive expression to your face, and such an extra fillip to your writings. It must be very welcome to those who, holding sin in abhorrence would be deeply disappointed if they could no longer take an interest in it. . . .' And then, this parting shot: 'Fine sentiments make bad literature. Yours is excellent, my dear Mauriac. If I were a better christian, I should, no doubt, be less your devoted follower.'

I am, at this very moment, correcting the proofs of my reply to André Gide, which is in the form, not of a letter but of a book: *God and Mammon*. The title sums up the contents. The accent should fall on the conjunction, on the 'and' which makes it clear that I have tried not to contrast two antagonistic forms of worship, but to show them set face to face in a heart incapable of choosing.

God and Mammon first appeared in a near-de-luxe addition (*Le Capitole*) which has long been out of print. It is now being re-issued by Grasset. Nearly thirty years have passed over those forgotten pages, of which I, myself, have retained only a confused memory. I find them again as I might find a lost key, and a key is precisely what the book is. I have never written anything about myself which probes quite so deeply into my dark places as do in chapters II, III and IV of this essay. Nowhere else have I stripped myself to quite the same degree. And so it comes about that a small work, long unobtainable and almost forgotten, turns out to be the most important piece of writing that I have devoted to my own 'case'.

I admit that there is something fatuous in pretending that one's own life-story may not some day seem important to others. Still, there are very few instances of a writer, if he has confided much, revealed much, of himself during his lifetime, *not* becoming an object of interest and research to some faithful soul after his death. I had a letter the other day from a nun in New York on the subject of René Schwob. She had, she told me, translated one of his books, and was now writing a thesis about him. It gave me great happiness to know that the works of our friend, René Schwob, now scarcely ever read in his own country, should have made a landfall on a distant shore, and found a saintly woman to give them hospitality.

We are wrong to regard as comic the complete certainty felt by our fellow-writers about the lasting quality of all the paper they have blackened with ink. And so it is that *God and Mammon* has become in my hand a key, once lost, now found again, and I hope I may not be accused of vanity for thinking that after I am dead others will try to fit it to a lock.

I do not hesitate to ask myself a leading question about the little book which is still capable of blowing old ashes into flame. Was Gide's mockery enough to produce the flicker? There should be sufficient matter there for an extended and edifying demonstration. My readers would be offered the spectacle of Grace employing the most free-thinking of writers to force one of the most religiously inclined (seemingly) to exhibit his own confusion of mind and uneasiness, to remount and settle himself once more into the saddle. Yes, it would have been fun to develop that line of argument, but only half-true. It may be a fact that Gide's letter was the immediate occasion of my getting to work on the subject, but it did not, of itself, provoke the feelings which find expression in the book under discussion. Gide's challenge happened to coincide with a crisis through which, at the age of forty or so, at the midmost point of my life's journey, I was passing.

The end of youth is an anticipation of old age, and brings with it a disquiet peculiar to itself which might be attributed to the 'noonday demon' were it not wholly different from that described by Bourget which is what we usually mean when we attach that label. All the same it is true that the demands of life, the movement of nature in ourselves, are strengthened at such times by the certainty that all will soon be ended, is, in fact, ended already.

Gide appeared upon the scene just as a doubtful battle was raging. If I were to renounce my christian faith, it would have been at that moment, as is plain from an article of mine called 'Souffrances du chrétien' which had appeared some months previously in *La Nouvelle Revue Française*.

The issue of that battle appeared to be still in doubt, though actually it was nothing of the sort. If *God and Mammon* means anything, it is just that. Whereas the majority of human beings, to whom christianity is a birthright, free themselves from it on the frontier-line of youth and middle age, and desert it without a struggle, there are always a few who, no less attracted by the world and no less capable of passion, do not make good their escape, but, as the result of a more than usually severe crisis, become aware that nothing will ever happen to them except within the limits of a religion which they have not chosen of their own free-will and to which they belong only because they were born into it.

In *God and Mammon* I attribute that point of view, not only to myself, but also to Arthur Rimbaud. It offers a clue to the deciphering of Rimbaud's destiny, of finding in it a meaning which, perhaps, is as little to the purpose as are the shapes of gods and monsters which, for our own entertainment, we see in the clouds. Yet I remember that Charles Du Bos attached great importance to what I wrote about Rimbaud in this little book. Re-reading those pages now, I feel inclined to say to myself, as we did in treasure hunts, 'You were getting warm!'

God and Mammon, which stands at the centre of my work and of my life, is like a hearth heaped high with ashes from which a small flicker still leaps now and again; and the fire may take hold again later. Consequently, I have brought together under this general title, in the new Grasset edition, some other writings which were dictated by that midmost-of-life's-journey mood, and are imbued with the same sense of spiritual distress. First in order comes *Souffrances et bonheur du chretién,* followed by some explanatory notes which I contributed to an album of photographs by Jean-Marie Marcel, taken at Malagar, to which I gave the title: *Les Maisons fugitives.* Last of all comes *Hiver* which appeared with 'pieces' by Gide, Colette and Jules Romains in a New Year's gift volume constructed round the seasons.

Produced at different times over a period of some ten years, these odds and ends all echo the noises of a battle which, though it may have lost some of its violence, has never been entirely broken off. Even old age has not put an end to it, but has only made it seem less close and less urgent. From a promontory which dominates the ocean and the night, I sometimes turn my face to the plain where ghosts are locked in battle, though only in thought and in desire do I intervene in the struggle.

Only one of the component parts of this volume has no connexion with the 'noon-day crisis': *La Vie et la Mort d'un poète* (André Lafon) which belongs to a much earlier period, having been written in 1924. I have included it only because it is now out of print, and is unlikely to be given a new lease of life on its own. It has been put on board, not because it is, in any way, a key text, but as I might take with me on a journey some faded photograph, about which those who come after me, finding it in the family album by chance, might say: 'Who's that?' Perhaps, when I am no more, others will hear that beating heart and muffled voice.

To go back to *God and Mammon.* It makes it perfectly clear that I have never resigned myself to the necessity of accepting the compromise of which Gide made such fun. Even in those days, I had a strong presentiment of what I now know: that the conflict between Christ and the world admits of no coming to terms. Kierkegaard's *Journal,* which I am just now reading, tells what is, in effect, the story of my own life. 'The disadvantage of having been brought up in this religion,' he writes, 'is that one has so constantly been impressed by its gentleness, that one has almost come to treat it as mythology: – it is only at an advanced age that one discovers its rigour. . . .' Too late? No: that is the secret of Grace: it is never too late. Time does not exist, and all the love of all the saints may be contained in a sigh.

* * * * *

The closer I come to death and to God, the less do I yield to the demands of my fiction-writing daemon. That alone justifies Gide's attitude.

The ageing novelist dreams the books which he no longer writes. The characters to whom he once gave a family and a name, whose behaviour he studied in certain given situations, whom he placed at a definite point in time and space, can no longer break free from the limbo of an imagination which has lost the will to be creative. They stay within it like insects whose metamorphosis has suddenly been checked, they are grubs which will never burst upon the world as butterflies.

I do not intend to ask myself here why it is that this particular novelist has decided to write no more novels – at least not at this stage of his life, for maybe, tomorrow, the business may start all over again, and the stream begin to flow once more. If, for the time being, he has chosen silence, it is not that he has changed, not that his gifts have weakened, nor that his power has lessened over a certain family of human souls, some members of which are to be found all over the world, and have remained faithful to him. But the Age, the atmosphere of the Age, is no longer as favourable as once it was to the hatching of the germs which he carries within himself. A work of fiction cannot grow, cannot burgeon except in a generation for which it is fitted. It does not get beyond the dream-stage. Just now only one type of character haunts the novelist of whom I am speaking, a character whose story he will never write. I try to *see* this being who has, as yet, neither a body not a location. He is, if I may so describe it, in the pre-natal state. He has no face, and never will have. He seems to me to be very different from those extremely fleshly creatures who people my books. He is, as it were, riding free, unencumbered by the weight of a body. What set moving those quivers, those tremblings which the passions of the heart imposed upon the heroes of my books, and prevented them from having ears for anything else, was the muttering and murmuring of youth within myself, so long as it lasted – and God knows it lasted beyond all rhyme or reason! There is nothing of all that in the character on which I find my imagination now brooding. The same force floods him now as when he was young, but it has suddenly become 'available' because passion has ceased to control it. Never has it been so strong because, where feelings are concerned, it has never been so free. Let me sketch roughly the matter of this unwritten novel. The man in question, now totally freed from the tyranny of passion, finds that, in fact, he is more tightly bound than was Gulliver in Lilliput, by those very obligations by which he had let himself be enslaved in the course of a long life during which all that slipped from the greasy-pole dropped into his waiting hands without his having to make any other effort than to be his own charming self.

Released from the passions and tragedies of the emotional life in which he had previously been imprisoned, this man, fast bound in a net of honours, will find himself becoming involved in an entirely different type of drama, played out on a very different stage from that on which the passions of the heart had formed the plot, a drama of which conflicting interests supply the conflict. Not that I imagine him to be caught up in politics. Nothing tempts me less than a work of fiction in which two opposed conceptions of society are at odds. The clear-sightedness of this ageing man will, I feel, be enlisted in the service of a different type of struggle, of the kind on which, when we are young, we are careful not to concentrate our faculties. From then on, this imagined character of mine will be so haunted and possessed by it, that he becomes incapable of seeing anything but that monstrous conglomeration, in the lives of almost all men, of principles to which they give lip-service, and behaviour which gives the lie to them, without anyone being indignant or embarrassed by that tremendous contradiction.

My hero will break that rule of the social game which requires blindness by the mere fact of his concentration on human beings and their behaviour. He will break the rule of the game, not because he has been visited by Grace from on High, but because he will describe, precisely as he sees it, the lie which is endlessly repeated in the tangle of human relationships. The man I am imagining would not be a particularly fine character, not a redresser of wrongs, but merely somebody whom old age has made 'available' so that no desire – he no longer desires anything – will interpose between what he sees and what is, will no longer colour nor distort the evidence of his eyes.

It would give an added sharpness to the story if the man in question belonged to the world I know: if, as artist or writer, he were a member of one of those professions to which Valéry applied the term 'frantic'. 'That is what I call those occupations of which the main-spring is the opinion a man has of himself, and the raw material the opinion that others have of him. Those who pursue them, condemned to a perpetual candidature, are necessarily afflicted by a certain seeking out of honours which is shot through by a type of persecution mania which never ceases to torment them.' Paul Valéry concludes this thought by adding one more horrible characteristic: 'Each of them bases his own existence on the non-existence of others, who must be forced to recognize their own non-existence.'

Now, these damned souls of art and literature whom Valéry describes, are, for the most part, for ever talking about their attachment to principles. They are communists or nationalists, christians or atheists, or anything else you can think of. But, no matter what they profess, their lives are dominated by one consideration only: themselves and what they are pleased to call their work.

My elderly hero must be suddenly confronted by somebody who is different, somebody who has escaped from the Rule, somebody whose whole life is determined by a principle (whether religious or revolutionary does not matter). In this way, the spirit of sanctity will violently invade the book, will, in some sort, shake my elderly man to his foundations, by compelling him to concentrate upon his own contradictions the implacable eye which, so far, has been focused on those of others. He will become an object of horror to himself. It is the fact of his own existence which he will be no longer able to contemplate.

At this point death enters the story. In what form? Here I find myself hesitating: suicide or the turning of the whole man to God – God served through the suffering of His creature, and apprehended directly through prayer. Suicide or conversion: in either case a refusal any longer to endure a system of universal trickery. There are instances in which sanctity has played a part in fiction, but nothing of any value has been written about suicide, at least not about the particular form of suicide to which a man is driven, not by personal catastrophe, but by life itself when it becomes something beyond endurance. No specific incident will be necessary to activate the will to death in my imagined suicide, the choice of nothingness in preference to continued existence, because, in his case, there is already a refusal to accept the inextricable web of lies in which the human fly is caught.

So far as I know, the Dostoievsky of *The Possessed* and Georges Bernanos are the only writers, in the field of fiction, who have had the slightest inkling of the true nature of that homicidal mania which the creature turns against himself. Personally, I dread those gloomy haunts into which I am being led by an imaginary character whose story I do not know.

Had I tried to tell it, I know from experience almost certainly what would have happened. Other, more reassuring, faces would have swum into my field of vision, and an altogether different adventure would have taken shape, which would have had no discernible connexion with that of the elderly gentleman, who would have suddenly evaporated, as though he had never been conceived except as a figure, roughly sketched, in some drama other than his own. It may be that each of the novels I have published has concealed another which would have been my real book, the book which will never be written.

*   *   *   *   *

Here I break off these notes and memories. They shall have a sequel, but only if my inner life has one – for that is the only life worth telling – and if I keep my sight so that I can continue to work backwards against the stream of time with the help of what I have read in other days.

INDEX OF PERSONS

The names of fictitious characters are printed in italics